Charity'
Thanks for reading Porch
Music. Hope you enjoy it.
Kathy Mare...

Porch
Music

a novel

Kathy Maresca

TOUCHPOINT
faith

Inspirational. Positive. Encouraging.

PORCH MUSIC
By Kathy Maresca
Published by TouchPoint Faith
a TouchPoint Press imprint
Brookland, AR 72417
www.touchpointpress.com

Softcover ISBN: 978-1-956851-45-8

Editor: Kelly Esparza
Cover Design: David Ter-Avanesyan, @Ter33Design
Cover images: (Front) Blue Grass Band Instruments by sandraadamson (Adobe);
(Back) Native Seminole choir, item number PE0406 used with permission from the
Florida Library System, from the Irvin M Peithmann collection.
Interior images: Ma & Children; Ma, Mom, and Siblings; UF Museum
provided by Kathy Maresca

Visit the author's website at kathymaresca.com

First Edition

Printed in the United States of America.

For my mother
Betty Surrency

Prologue

Junior's Dance Hall

Middleburg, Florida
August 1952

Janie

Last time we came to Junior's, one of those mean-talking Pinter boys got mad when Mama wouldn't dance with him, so he up and called her a swamp Indian. It caused a ruckus that left one of his teeth smashed into the sheetrock of the dance hall. I had the front door open, one foot in and hoping to lead Mama out, when Daddy hauled me and my little brothers off the porch and made us wait for him in the car. I couldn't see nary a thing from way out there. I felt every bit of it, though, how tore up Mama's stormy Seminole heart was. She squalled all the way home and every night for two weeks. But early this evening, she started swaying and singing. She turned to me with a smile and her secret wink. "Are you ready to go dancing, Janie?"

"Yes, ma'am. I'm good and ready."

My twelve-year-old knees bounce to "Broken Carted Mule." Every time Junior's band plays this song, I wonder all over again why the man needs a mule to find a wife, but I reckon it's one of those things I'll figure out when I get older. I stick my nose up to the float glass window, so I can watch Mama swirl across the scuffed oak floor. Saturday nights mean fancy dresses for the ladies, shined cotton and calicos. The men look so plain next to them, in their pistol-leg pants and short sleeve button-down shirts. Me, I've got on my green flour sack dress, and I use the hem of it to wipe away a little cloud of fog from the window pane.

"Wheel around!" calls out Old Man Tucker.

Mama said she'd help me find a wife,

One who wouldn't cause her no strife.

My papa gave me a mule and cart,

Handed me its reins and said be smart.

"Weave the ring," Tucker yells out his next call. The dancers pick up the pace a little, and a bunch of old ladies sitting together in folding chairs and facing the floor, fan themselves. Old men stand in the corner, cigarette smoke puffing from their thin, wrinkly lips. Bare yellow light bulbs hang from ceiling cords. Whew, Junior's is one ugly joint. Maybe when grown-ups are having fun, they don't care about how things look.

With his guitar propped up against the colonial blue clapboard wall, Daddy sits with us on the porch of the dance hall. He watches while Kenny and Benny, who've been out of diapers near about a year, tussle from one spot to another. Every now and then, Daddy gives me a wink and warns me about drinking too much bellywash. That's what he calls Coca-Cola. I tip my head far back, drink the last drop of the cold, sassy liquid, and set the bottle on the floor.

When Daddy stops by the store on the way to Junior's, I like to reach in the cooler and test the icy water for the coldest spot. Then I pull out one bottle at a time until I find a Coke that looks and feels just right. Bellywash is good anytime, but it's extra good during dog days. Mama starts talking in June about hating August because that's when dog days are here. Used to, I'd wait all summer, thinking we're fixing to get a puppy, but I haven't seen one yet. Shoot, I'd settle for a full-grown mutt.

Somebody help me stop that mule.

My young heart's acting like a fool.

I found the prettiest gal in town,

But she has gone and turned me down.

To keep my mind off the sweat rolling down my neck, I peel a little paint from the outside walls. I sure wish some cans of Sherwin-Williams would sneak off a store shelf, roll over here, pop their shiny lids, and splatter fresh color on this place. A few of the boards along the front of the building sag like they are tired out from holding up a bunch of people. Like it's saying amen to the shack it's attached to, the screen in the door bulges out near the bottom of its wood frame. I've never been inside of Junior's, except for the toe of my left shoe, but I bet I'd forget about how bad things look if I could go in and dance. There's no use thinking about it, though, because I know Mama and Daddy would tear up my behind good and proper if I tried such a thing.

Mama was supposed to be dancing with her younger brother, Percy, tonight, but he showed up drunk, staggering around like somebody who's twirled around and around until he can't stand up. When the fiddlers got started, the music knocked the dizziness right out of him, and he straightened right up. Uncle Percy's been grabbing a new girl for each dance, leaving Mama to find a partner every time the song changes.

Seems like I ask Daddy the same thing one Saturday night after the other, but maybe I'll get a different answer this time. "Daddy, why don't you go inside and dance with Mama?" Like always, Daddy tells me that he'd rather be picking than dancing. He's real patient, knowing his chance to play the guitar will come before closing time.

When the music rests a couple of beats, the buzz of hungry mosquitos and the croaks of tree frogs sound a little bit like a harmony. I catch a whiff of the cornfields behind Junior's, sticky, earthy, and sweet.

"Forward up and back!" Tucker shouts louder than the music. The ladies take three steps toward their partners, curtsey, and then take three steps back.

Weren't too long till I found another girl.

How she made my young heart jump 'n whirl.

Well now she took off with my mule and cart.

Now all I got's nothing but a broken heart.

Benny starts whimpering, so I pick him up to watch Mama with me. She's coming from the far end of the long, narrow floor, her yellow flowered dress fluttering up like butterflies circling her knees. Her hair falls from the silver comb on the back of her head.

Uncle Percy, who left the dance floor and joined the band up on the stage, sweats like a rainstorm. His shirttail hangs out, and his thick black hair falls onto his forehead. Maybe he forgot his pomade. Uncle Percy has charmed a whole bunch of the ladies this evening, including Old Man Tucker's new young wife, Luella. Every time the band sings "made my young heart jump and whirl," Percy shakes his hips a little. Short but quick Luella, who sings terrible but hasn't figured that out yet, moves closer and closer to my uncle. She leans toward him, looks deep into his eyes, and kicks her right leg back when Uncle Percy does his rooster strut. Every time my uncle wiggles his tail feathers, I picture him hollering "cock-a-doodle-do."

"Promenade home! Partners to your places, like the horses to their traces," yells out Tucker. Mama and the others dance back to where they got started at the beginning of "Broken Carted Mule." My mother's chin quivers and her chest rises and falls. She's sporting a smile that makes her look happier than I've ever seen her.

Kenny plants his palms on Daddy's thigh, bounces up and down, and moves his head with the beat of the music. I hold Benny up even closer to the window and try to rub away his dirt necklace. Kissing the back of his sticky neck, I give him a chance to see the happiness on Mama's face. I crisscross my arms over his chest and squeeze him tight. He lets out a little yelp and pats my arm with his tiny hand a few times, like he's making his own music. Hope hugs my heart.

Chapter 1

Mother Nature

Starke, Florida
December 1952

Rose

Cupping one side of her head with her hand, Grace, who is a wee five-year-old, hollers at me from the foot of the bed. "Owwww! Rosie, my ear hurts. Bad!"

It ain't easy to treat your sister good, when your own ears, nose, and feet are froze like the blocks of ice used to keep milk and eggs from going bad. "I'm cold, Grace. Let me stay under these covers awhile." *Please, Gracie, please.*

Sun sifts into the bedroom, a telling on me. I should've been awake already. Something that feels like big jawbreakers is a starting to dance in my gut, and I jump out of bed, mash my arm into my stomach, and tear through the kitchen. Momma sits at the table, her coffee giving off a hefty aroma, a smell that makes me feel even sicker. She don't bother looking at me.

Mean cold air hits me hard, a whipping itself straight through my flimsy cotton nightgown. The outhouse sits, just steps away, but I ain't going to make it. I hurl. Still bent over, I wonder how in the world you can have sweat on your forehead when frost is on the ground. Yesterday morning I told myself I was sick from something I ate the night before. But that ain't it. A couple of weeks ago, I missed my woman time.

I'm in trouble.

Momma stares at me from the porch. She pushes back her shoulders, takes in a big gulp of air, and stomps over.

"Rose Monroe, what in the world is wrong with you, sick in the yard, first thing on a cold morning?"

"All those fried taters I ate last night." Momma won't put up with no answer. When she asks one question, you know she ain't going to stop till she's asked a bunch more.

"You've got yourself in a mess, huh, girl? Huh? Answer me!"

"No, ma'am." The truth can get a girl into a whole lot of trouble. Momma leans over me till we're eyeball to eyeball. She snatches my hair.

"Lying dog! No mind what I tried to do for you . . . do with you, you gone and turned out a fool, just like . . ." Her short red hair stands up on top of her head. Momma's emerald eyes squint, and her mouth turns up on one side and droops on the other.

"Momma, you're hurting me."

Quick as grease popping from a pan that's gotten way too hot, she lets go of my hair. I start to fall but catch myself and stand up straight. Her palm strikes the left side of my face. Tears scald my cheeks. *I'm scared she'll beat this baby right out of me.*

"Sixteen years old and you're already ruining this family's good name. Your papa's hard work, his honest self, it ain't going to mean a thing to anybody in this town anymore. Not a single, solitary thing. You better go get yourself married and out of this house . . . or we'll send you off. And you ain't going to like one bit where you'll find your sorry self." Momma turns her back and walks away.

"Momma! Momma!" I holler until she looks around.

"Rose, don't go flappin' your jaws! Keep 'em shut. If you don't, my other girls'll grow up thinking they can do like their big sister. I ain't going to let this family's good name rot away." She hauls up the back porch steps.

Momma's right. I'm no good. I feel shame everywhere, deep inside, up in my head, and all over my skin, everywhere I let him touch me. I should've said no when the kissing got wild. I forgot everything Momma tried to teach me. But songs like Carl Smith's "Let Old Mother Nature Have Her Way" don't help you one bit. They spill out of car radios, a coaxing girls into back seats, making them believe that blazing lips and burning hearts can overturn the laws of creation.

Mother Nature's played one good trick on me.

♪♫

Momma stands at the stove, getting dinner ready for Papa and my big brothers. They come home from the fields every day, a few minutes past noon, tuckered out from farming. I'm a wondering if it be worse than washing dishes and clothes all day long. Our wringer is wore slap out, like everything else we got around here. Crammed full of diapers, it jitterbugs across the porch. You know, that old machine's a lot like Momma. When it gets in a cranky mood, it shakes the whole house. But that washer is the onliest help I got, so I yank another diaper through the Maytag.

The smell of grease hovers in the air, grilled cheese sandwiches and French fries, getting my stomach to lurch. I got a good notion to eat a piece of the apple pie Momma baked first thing today, try to settle it down. I run my hand across my belly. It's still firm and flat.

"Rose Monroe!" Momma yells. I peek into the kitchen.

"Yes, ma'am?"

"When you get all the dinner dishes done, I got a mess of collards you need to wash afore supper. You better make sure you get them veins out good."

"Yes, ma'am."

"Last time you cooked them, they was tough. Terrible, you hear me? Your papa was good and mad, and not just because they was chewy. Remember how you left them dead things floating in the collard juice? How you didn't wash 'em good enough?"

"Yes, ma'am. I'm sorry. I'm a going to wash them perfect today."

"I ain't about to eat bugs again this evening. Or rubbery greens, for that matter. Rose, can you do even one thing right?"

"Yes, ma'am." But can I do anything right? Messing up comes so easy to me. Momma's going to holler at me all day about how I ain't taking good enough care of my brothers and sisters, them out of school for Christmas.

"Your papa's going to be madder 'n a warthog, Rose, if you ain't got that figured out already. So be watchful with supper. You hear me?"

"Momma, what if . . ."

"What if?" Momma balls up a fist. "Did you and that boyfriend of yours ever think on what if?" She cranes her neck to look out the window. "Here comes your papa and my good boys."

Papa and my older brothers make their way to the house. Homer, the oldest, looks out from under the hood of our rusty Ford sedan, closes it, and runs to catch up with Papa. No matter how hard they work, there ain't never enough money to buy a new car or move to a house big enough to hold us.

"Rose Monroe, are you listening to me? I'm going to feed them children soon as your papa and my boys get done. Stay out of my way. When I'm serving them, you talk to your father."

I ain't never seen Papa carry on mad, the way Momma says he will, but I ain't got the guts to tell him. I'd rather lie down on that cold ground, go to sleep, forget this mess I'm in. No more worrying. No more being ashamed. No more being poor. No more wondering how I'll come up with money to take care of a baby if its daddy turns and runs the other way.

The washing machine starts to make a racket, and I dart over and unplug it. Papa, Momma, and my brothers gather round the kitchen table and eat while I sit outside on an old ladderback chair. Betsy, Sally, Lonnie, Delores, Grace, Mark, and Mickey play in the yard. Now and then Grace sticks her tiny finger in her ear. The sweet oil I poured into it this morning ain't seeming to help.

The back door squeaks open, and Papa comes out to the porch. "Rosie, your Momma says you got something to tell me."

"Yes, sir." I look up into his worn, gray eyes, knowing what I got to tell him is a freight train that'll flatten the life out of him. I wrap my arms around my stomach, hang my head. Tears fill up my eyes, drip down my face, and drop onto my plaid skirt. My whole body shakes.

"I done believe I got it figured out." Papa's voice drones sad like a hurdy-gurdy fiddle. "Ain't I, Rose?" The color drains out of his face. I nod. "Well, I suppose you better marry real quick. You and him get a marriage license. You're going to need me or your momma to sign it. I'll do it. Real quick. Okay, Rose?"

I nod again and close my eyes. The screen door creaks again. Papa is gone.

♪♫

I lay Grace down for a nap and drop more sweet oil into her ear. I shudder from being hungry, but I'll feel even worse if I ain't done cleaning those collards pretty soon. I look for Momma's apple pie because it's the onliest thing that sounds good right now, but all I find is an empty pan ready to be scrubbed.

"You should a put the greens on by now, Rose. They're going to be tough," Momma growls.

"Momma, I'm real sorry."

"Sorry? Sorry ain't nothing but sorry, Rose. Ain't you got more to say? Ain't you ashamed?"

"Yes, Momma."

"And sorry about what? Dirty, tough collards? Or bringing shame on your family?"

"Both, Momma."

"The whole town's fixing to talk bad about you, Rose Monroe. About us, about *me.*"

"I'd do anything to make up for it, Momma."

"Good. Then you'll get out of my house, Rose." She stands, one foot in front of the other and one hand on her hip. Her face is redder than a summer tomato.

"Get out?" I must have heard her wrong.

"Yep. I'll help you leave here." Momma hurries into the room where me and my four younger sisters sleep, with me close behind her. She snatches a pillow off one of the beds, dumping it out of its case. "Put your clothes in here," she says, handing me the pillowcase. Momma turns to the dresser and starts to yank open one drawer right after the other, until she finds my underpants.

"Here you go," she says. "Guess there ain't no use anymore in telling you to keep these on. And don't forget your clothes on the hangers." I turn to the chifforobe and take my other skirt, my blouse, and my two sweaters down.

Momma hands me my coat from a wall hook. "Looks to me like you have it all. You're ready."

She's throwing me out, and I ain't got even a notion about where I can go. "No, Momma. Please! I ain't got any place else to go. Ain't I your own flesh and blood?"

"Go on now, Rose. That boy'll marry you if you ain't got no home. He can't leave you out on the street. If he does, your shame'll be pinned onto him, too."

Grace, Delores, Mark, and Mickey wake up from their naps, eyes big and watching me. Momma puts her arm around my shoulder, real gentle, but I jump, thinking she's going to smack me.

"Wait here, right here," she says. Momma scuttles out of the room, giving me another chance to study the faces of my little brothers and sisters. I wonder who's going to take care of them. Momma sure ain't never seemed to want to.

"I love you, Grace, Delores. Mark, Mickey, I love you." But saying it twice ain't enough for me. I've got to make them know I mean it. "I love you. I love you so much." I repeat myself, the same way Momma does.

"Lub you," Mickey says back to me.

"I love you, Rosie," Grace whimpers. She gets to crying, and Delores and Mark bawl, too.

"Here it is," Momma says from behind me. "You're gonna need this." She shoves a wrinkled piece a paper toward me. It's got *Certificate of Birth* printed at its top.

"What in the world is this for?"

"When you and him go to get married, the people at the courthouse'll ask for it."

"Oh. Momma, please. Please don't turn me out." My knees are just a shaking, my hands, too.

"I ain't sacrificing the rest of my family for you," she says. "Things'll turn out all right for you, Rose. I love you, but this ain't your home no more."

I love you, she said. *I love you.* Even if Momma don't mean it, she said it. I tuck the words into my heart, wanting to hear her say it over and over. But she pushes me a wee bit in the small of my back. And somehow I'll get myself outta here. I pass through the bedroom, living room, and out to the front porch. A board squeaks under my foot, sounding like a guitar string that's broke after it's been plucked too hard. Momma stands at the door.

"Go on, now. Don't be looking back, girl. Go and finish making that family you got started."

Quicker than a quarter note, my feet turn into bullets, a racing away from the back of Momma's hand and her telling me I ain't doing anything right. Running from Papa, how he ain't ever home to protect me from her. Running from that old sagging torn mattress I sardine into at night with my four sisters, its metal coils a tearing through its outer cloth and digging into my thighs and back. Running from the outhouse and how it makes me wretch every time I open its door. Running from the rusty washing machine full of dingy water and worn-out soap, just a churning out dirty clothes, no matter how hard you try to get them clean.

About a mile from home, my feet burn like the dickens and won't go even a wee bit more. I hobble to a fallen down tar shack. Sitting down on an old log, I take my shoes off and get sick all over again after. Blisters, red and bleeding, hang onto my feet by threads of skin. I'm in the middle of nowhere. I need a ride, but there ain't another soul who knows it.

No matter which a ways you go from here, it means two more miles of walking. The store's about the same piece as Maggie Ebbing's house. And if I walk to the store, I ain't got a nickel to call her. Maggie's got a bad name for getting into *trouble*, but you ain't allowed to be picky when you're Rose

Monroe. I stand up, trying to catch my breath. The cold leaves feel good against my fiery blisters.

Walk, Rose, walk. Real slow, I make my feet take a few steps. A pebble gets under one of them blisters of mine, hurting so bad I think I ain't going to make it. I hear somebody playing a piano, a song I don't know. Whoever's playing keeps making the same ole mistake. I hear the kerplunk over and over, trying to get the notes straight. Through the trees is a white sign with black letters: Thankful Country Church. Welcome! Pastor: Brother Jeremiah Little.

The piano music starts up again, and I spot a church way back from the hard road, behind some birch and pine trees. The little white building has a steeple and red double doors, and one of them is open. It ain't far, but a hammer is pounding the inside of my head. My empty stomach growls so hard, warring with my feet for attention. I look around for another log or a stump to sit on when the piano stops. *Be brave, Rose, be brave. Don't stop till you get yourself some help.* Slow and quiet, I shuffle to the church steps and plop down on the second one. I hug the pillowcase in my lap.

"May I help you?" a woman's voice echoes down the steps. A short lady, with a round face and short, curly black hair, looks down from the top of the stairs. Oh no. Here she goes poking herself into my business.

"Thank you, ma'am. Would it be all right if I sit here a minute?"

"Of course. May I get you something?" She hurries down the steps. "Oh my. Look at those blisters!"

I try to smile. "These shoes ain't meant for running." *Dumb ole Rose. You shouldn't a told her that. She might think I'm trying to get away from the law.*

"I think you're right. Your feet must hurt terribly, young lady. By the way, I'm Daisy Little. My husband, Brother Jeremiah Little, is the pastor here." She bends down a wee bit and smiles at me.

I ain't about to get friendly with a preacher's wife. She's liable to tell her whole church about me being *in trouble*. I can picture her right now, just a singing Frankie Laine's "Jezebel," looking around at me and thinking *whore*. *Floozy*. Or maybe she'll sit at the piano, but in place of sheet music, she's eyeballing a picture of me in a humiliating pose.

"Young lady?"

"Ma'am?" I ain't listening too good, I guess.

"Are you on a journey?" Her face breaks into a grin.

"Yes, ma'am, and I'll be on my way now." Slow and easy, I try to slip my shoes back on.

"Honey, let me help you." She takes a step closer. "How about some Band-Aids?"

"Thank you, ma'am, but I'll be all right." I look down at my feet, just a wondering what to do next. *I ain't all right.*

"Well, may I give you a lift?"

"A lift?" I must sound surefire stupid. Everybody knows what a lift is.

"Yes, a ride. Sweetheart, may I ask your name?" She takes another step closer.

"Rose. Rose Monroe." I close my eyes. Maybe when I open them, she'll be gone.

"Such a lovely name, Rose. Another flower. I'm not sure you caught mine. I'm Mrs. Jeremiah Little, but my friends call me Sister Daisy."

In spite of my hurting feet and hungry stomach, I open my eyes and smile. *My friends call me Sister Daisy.* It's like she's hinting a wee bit about her and me being friends. That's cause she ain't got a notion that I'm *in trouble*. I ain't going to tell her, either.

"Thank you, Sister Daisy. A lift would be nice."

"Wait here, Rose. I'll have to get my keys and let my husband know. Where am I taking you?"

How in the world can you tell a preacher's wife you're going to Maggie Ebbing's house? This whole county knows about Maggie, her drinking, and her wild ways.

"Just over to a friend's house. A couple of miles from here."

"All right. Hold on a minute. Okay?" Sister Daisy hurries up the steps and closes the front door from the inside. Frankie Laine's song dances through my mind. I put my own words to it. *Jezebel! A demon of love turned Rose into Jezebel.* Pure old panic wraps itself around me. Them gumballs in my gut start a churning again, and my hands feel wet with sweat. My bones feel cold, like wind has blowed right through my flesh.

A shiny maroon Chrysler Windsor turns in my direction with Sister Daisy behind its wheel. *Keep your mind straight, Rose. Don't conjure up more fear.* The car stops, and I hop into the passenger's side, my shoes a dangling from my left hand. I close the door, and Sister Daisy hands me some bandages. We pull up to the hard road.

"Right or left?"

"Left, then turn right on Chestnut Road, ma'am. It's the third house on the right."

"Okay." We drive along, both of us quiet. "That's it." I point to Maggie's mailbox. She's got a white picket fence around her green shotgun house, and her powder blue Buick is parked in the front yard. Sister Daisy's car stops, and I jerk on the handle of the door to push it open. Before I can jump out, Sister Daisy puts her hand on my left arm.

"Rose, if I can ever do anything for you, please let me know. Will you? We're in the phone book, under Jeremiah Little."

"Yes, ma'am. Thank you," I say, trying to scuttle out of the car.

"The Lord knows all about what you might be going through, Rose."

"Yes, ma'am. Thank you." I hop out, closing the door of the Chrysler behind me. *The Lord surefire knows.* And he's bound to be even madder at me than Momma is. He knows it ain't really Mother Nature to blame. It's me, *Jezebel Rose*.

Chapter 2

Dear Father God

Sister Daisy

I reach for Rose's hand, hoping to give her some reassurance, but she jumps from my car and begins to hop like an injured bunny. Rose looks back at me and shoos me along with her hand. My intention of waiting until she has been invited inside is in vain. I back out of Maggie Ebbing's driveway, hoping no one in the congregation will see me.

What an inquisition that would be, rife with judgment and condemnation and bereft of compassion and love. Jeremiah and I were warned about the Ebbing woman a few days after we arrived, how we should turn her away if she should show her face at our place of worship. "How Christ-like," I had said to the deacons. I expected them to be offended, but the truth soared past their deceived hearts, unaware of my protest.

Six months into life at the Thankful Country Church, and I am ready to flee, just like Rose. How desperate a young girl has to be to seek refuge at

Maggie's. On the drive back to the parsonage, Rose's beautiful face, still bearing traces of tears, haunts me.

I wince, visualizing the parsonage in which we live. "Quaint," I told my husband when we drove up to the property. I take a deep breath.

Father God, please help me get through this day. You have given me a wonderful husband, and I thank you for him. Help me see the best in everyone. And dear God, please help Rose Monroe. I don't know what her needs are, except a pair of properly fitting shoes. Amen.

Chapter 3

Tayki: Woman

Ma-Ki

What a mess Rose's feet are, some of the worst doggone blisters I ever seen. I reckon she outgrew her shoes a year ago. Every time my razor blade gets close to her foot, the girl cringes. But I got to trim away her dead skin.

"You got to buck up good, Rose. This hurts, and that's all there is to it. I'm near about done. Close them pretty eyes of yours and think on something nice."

"Thank you, Mz. Ebbing. I sure do appreciate you doctoring me."

"Ain't no use in calling me 'Mz. Ebbing.' Nobody else does. How about Ma-Ki or Ma?"

"Ma?" I reach for Rose's left foot, but she jerks it back.

"Yep. Ma-Ki is my given name, but most everybody calls me Ma these days. Ain't never been called mother or mama. Just plain old Ma." I hold tight to her underfoot, where there ain't any sores.

"Yes, ma'am."

"You stay put, and I'll finish taking care of them feet of yours." Putting the old pail in the sink, I run water into the kettle.

"Buster!" Hearing his name, my grandson barrels up the back porch with his dog beside him. His hair drops onto his forehead, not a drop of pomade to stop it or to dampen the red in it. He got that red from his granddaddy Burl. Maybe them freckles, too.

"If we got some roses blooming out there, pick me one with the strongest color. Watch out for them thorns."

"Yes, ma'am." He looks over at Rose.

Her mother, Emmaline, did a good job picking a name. The girl's got pretty green eyes, the color of a rose's stem. Got pretty hair, too, with red, orange, and yellow, near about the shade of maize, in it. But Rose don't know she's beautiful. She's the type of girl who no-good men seek out, sweet and comely, but don't know their value.

I pour boiling water into the bucket, add a drop of lavender oil, and pinch some dried sage into it. The front door creaks open.

"It's getting cold out on the porch, Ma. You care if I take a nap on your bed?" my daughter Maggie asks. Her eyes show traces of red. I wonder if she's drunk, been up all night. Maybe both.

"All I ask is leave it like you find it."

"Uh huh." Maggie heads to my bedroom.

A fresh rose, deep red, lays by the sink. Buster slipped in, me not knowing it. "We're near about done, Rose."

"Thank you, Ma. Hey, there's something I don't get. Is Buster your son or grandson?" Her mouth hangs open a little, and she fidgets, playing with her earlobe.

"He's Maggie's, but I raised him like my own. You didn't know that?"

"I heard he's Maggie's boy, but she ain't never mentioned him. It's a wee bit confusing."

"I reckon so. Like my name. People get Ma confused with Ma-Ki, but we're the same woman." After pouring a little cold milk in the lavender water, I pluck scarlet petals from the bud, dropping them in, so the liquid'll soak up their perfume and medicine. Aw shaw, this girl's known a lot of sorrow, needs all the cure she can get. Healing's got to start somewhere, maybe her feet first and on up to her heart.

Her family ain't never had anything, almost as bad off as some Seminole families I knew as a girl. When Maggie told me Rose don't have anywhere to go, I wasn't took aback.

"Rose, women carry all the blame, but it ain't right."

"I don't know what you mean, Ma."

"You been running. Emmaline tossed you out?"

"Yes, ma'am." Rose shuts her eyes.

"Only one reason I can think of. You must be *in trouble*." Rose leans over close to me, hugging herself.

"Yes, ma'am. I turned into a bad girl."

"Well, I ain't about to call a nice girl like you bad. You and that boy, sure young and foolish. But what you'll reap in this world—it's bad. You're only a young'un who's ready to have another young'un." I pour more milk into the water. "Here we go." I slide the pail under Rose's feet. She eases in one foot and then the other.

"Oh, Ma, it's so pretty, and it don't even sting!" Her green eyes open wide, sparkling like dew on a primrose willow. "They're in a garden, Ma." She giggles. "My feet are in a rose garden! Where'd you get this idea?"

"My ma taught me. Her and Pa were half Seminole, both of them. We made our medicine from what grows wild." I pick up a fallen petal from the floor, hold it next to her hair before I drop it in the pail.

"How about your children, Ma? Are they?" She rubs her hand over her stomach.

"A quarter Indian."

"That's still a lot. Ma, did you grow up here in Bradford County?"

"In Osceola County, like the Chief. By swampland." I lean my head back, close my eyes a little, like always when I recollect being with Ma and Pa.

"A swamp? What's a swamp like?"

"Well, when floods rolled in, we looked for high and dry land, reaping corn and potatoes. My ma taught us to bead." I run my finger over coral and shale beads on my necklaces. "We traded our jewelry, and most of it went down south to be sold. South Florida's where most of my people live."

"We learned about the Everglades in school, but not about Seminoles. I'm learning better from you." Rose swishes her feet, near about knocking some water onto the floor. "Did you live in a teepee, Ma?"

"Nope. We lived in a frame wood house with a chickee roof, thatched. We had walls, but our people way down south live in real chickees, no walls. Our place was built up on posts. No electricity. The swamp makes for a hard life, not fit for people. We all got better houses here. Your ma's from North Carolina, ain't she, Rose?" Uppity Emmaline, she'd brag all over town about being from Charlotte.

"Yes, ma'am."

"And where is your pa from?"

"Tennessee."

"Unless somebody's family has lived here a long time, what we call Old Florida, it's easy to get shook up a little bit, hearing about how we lived. But Pa had a shotgun, and he used it on them gators. He didn't wrestle them, like some Seminoles." I teehee like a young girl. Rose breaks into a grin, and I want to take this sweet flower into my home, love her like she's my own. I can't figure how in the tarnation Emmaline threw her out.

"Ma, you made me laugh so hard I forgot about my hurting feet." She bends low, her nose sniffing the liquid. "I bet they smell good." She laughs again.

"This here's a *tayki* foot soak. Tayki. Seminole for woman."

"Tayki? You still talk in Seminole?"

"Miccosukee Seminole, the tongue of my people. We talk a little Creek, too. Some call it Muscogee. Keep soaking, Rose, and I'll be back in a snap."

I walk to my bedroom where Maggie lies across my bed, face up and snoring. From a drawer in my chifforobe, I pull out a drawstring bag made of buckskin, some gauze, and a tin of salve and fetch a pair of clean white socks from my chest of drawers. I peek at Maggie again, looking peaceful, plumb innocent, the way a doe looks before the spear strikes. She rolls to one side, and I hurry back to the kitchen.

Teardrops hang off Rose's chin and nose. I hand her a clean cloth from the sideboard.

"Rose, girls *in trouble* get scared, wondering how they are gonna survive. But what young'uns need most is love. When they ain't gotten enough love, they grow up mean."

"Yes, ma'am."

"Love is powerful, Rose. It can heal if you let it, one step at a time. Young tayki, we took a step today, doctoring them blisters. Them feet are important. A woman can't make her footprint without them. And know this: it's footprints the eye ain't able to see that matters most." Taking more clean cloths, I sit in the kitchen chair and put them in my lap. Bending down, I lift her right foot.

"Ma, do you talk much using them Seminole words?"

"I used to know more, but I ain't spoke it in a while. I can't recollect how to string together a sentence, but being half-white comes in handy. I speak English. Near about everybody understands me when I talk."

I expect Rose to giggle, but she's real serious, her face looking like it's fixing to crumple. "Ma," she says, almost whispering. "I ain't never thought about being half one thing and half another. What's it like?"

"Now that's a question I ain't been asked too often. When I was young, folks called me a half-breed, but I don't hear it too much anymore. They probably still think it, though. But I'm not bothered anymore by strangers who try to show off, thinking they're better than everybody else."

"But sometimes the truth hurts real bad, Ma."

"Yep, especially when you're tayki."

Rose teehees again, her face losing its sadness. I reach for another clean cloth to use on her feet. Her blisters have lost some of their redness, and her skin feels softer. I run my finger under her foot. She jerks a little and laughs.

"Tickle easy, huh?"

"Yes, ma'am."

I dry her feet and put salve on them. Real careful, I wrap them in gauze and put socks on her. "Rose," I say, picking up my buckskin pouch, "these here ain't new, but they ain't been worn, either. I been keeping them, waiting for somebody special like you." I pull out a pair of moccasins, big enough to fit Rose without pinching her toes and heels.

"Oh, Ma! I can't take your shoes!"

"They're yours now." Slow and careful, I slip them on her feet.

"They feel so soft! Ma, I ain't got any way to do something special for you."

"One day, Rose, you will. I feel it deep inside." I haul the bucket to the back porch, empty it into the yard, and leave it. Back in the kitchen, Rose ain't moved. "Rose, I been up since before dawn. It's time for my nap. Maggie's got my bed, so I'm fixing to go upstairs. If you're tired, you can stretch out on the settee."

"Yes, ma'am. I will." She gets up and walks around, real careful. "These shoes sure do feel good, Ma."

"Good. I'll see you after a while." I give Rose another smile. It's not easy to climb them steps these days, but it's a lot easier than walking in shoes way too small. Rose's blisters ain't nothing compared to the torment she's fixing to face, just like Emmaline did. Everybody knows Avery Monroe ain't the father of the oldest boy, making Emmaline's hell a little worse.

Young Emmaline was a bird of paradise: orange hair flamed, showing off her emerald eyes. Took up with the son of the sheriff, from a family who had ideas about who belonged and who didn't. But Grainger Tannen didn't let her stay in his paradise very long. He got done with her pretty quick, and she learnt she wouldn't be a part of his moneyed family. Eden belched her out and right into Avery Monroe's arms.

Gossip was on near about everybody's lips. Emmaline looked like she was in her sixth month, living with her folks, when she became a wife. After Avery married her, he took her to town, his arm around the big-bellied beauty. His proud smile showed he was glad to have her, but her own pride was gone. Her first wing shattered by Grainger, and soon the other one broke from lack, never enough of anything.

I reckon I done the same thing, broke them wings of my girls, my son, too. Shame rests on their shoulders and lives behind their eyes. I see it on Bessie near about all the time, even when her husband stands beside her. And instead of marriage, Maggie got a baby. Her shame done turned to anger a long time ago. Lily and Dora, the two girls I got left at home, they watch Maggie drinking and carousing. They wonder aloud who she's fixing to take up with next. And my son Percy runs to every juke joint he can find, from woman to woman. But he works hard, takes care of this house, me and his sisters, too.

It's that sweet Rose who's got me puzzled. Such a good girl, she is, with a mother vexed like a rabid fox. I ain't got the heart to tell her what it is like to be half-Seminole, how people shunned me, no matter where I went. I could tell Rose how hard it is to carry a lifetime of shame, but I won't. She's got enough troubles. And how she'll get that baby's father to marry her is a doggone mystery.

Chapter 4

The Howling House

Green Cove Springs
January 1953

Janie

"1953! Happy New Year!" Grown-ups whoop it up from our front porch.

"Happy New Year!" the crowd calls back. They're bundled up and huddled together. "Y'all are sounding real good tonight."

Mama sings so sweet and high while Daddy strums his guitar. A couple of men who work for him have been playing the bass fiddle and the harmonica. Daddy's brother T-Bo is here from Georgia. My uncle picked up his dulcimer a minute ago to play "Jolie Blonde." That's how I know when Mama and Daddy are calling it a night. Daddy sings it with Mama, real soft and quiet.

I listen to the words, not sure I have them exactly right. *Eh a ha! Eh a ha! Jolie Blonde my tea feet crinoline.* There's always a song with words I can't figure out. I don't have a big crinoline, but "Jolie Blonde" always makes me wish for one. Daddy says the song is about a pretty blonde girl, but nary a one of us has light hair. Mama's family is black-headed because they have so much Seminole in them. My daddy's people are French, and they have dark hair, too.

People say that movie stars bleach their hair blond. I don't know how they can stand it, stinking the way it does. A couple months ago, Mama spilled bleach on my favorite dress, one she made me for my thirteenth birthday. I still have to wear it, but I always feel goofy with a big old white splotch on the knee of my fancy blue frock.

The thought of my not-so-special-anymore ruined dress and the noise on the porch makes it hard for me to get back to sleep. Uncle T-Bo announced earlier that he's sleeping on our settee tonight and heading out early in the morning. He has a wife, but he didn't bring her with him. I've learned not to ask grown-ups where the husband or wife is. No sir.

Mama and Daddy settle into their bedroom, right next to mine. They don't sound so happy now that we're an hour into the New Year.

"Bessie, you know plumb good how my kinda work ain't gonna let me stay in any place too long. You knew all this when I took the job," Daddy says. Here we go again, Mama and Daddy talking about moving away. I don't know how long we've lived in this cedar house, but we got here before the twins were born. Now they sleep in this tiny room with me. Being so close to Mama and Daddy makes it easy to hear them talking about things they think are secrets.

"We've been here a good while, Willard," Mama says. I can hear her voice quiver, meaning she's about to cry. "It's been good for me, not too far from Junior's. You know how much I love to dance. All week long I wait for Saturday night."

"Bessie, you had your bad times at Junior's, too. No place is perfect. 'Sides that, life ain't about dancing. I've got to make a living for this here family. You're something special, but we can't stay here in order to be close to Junior's." Daddy is a quiet man, but when he talks, you can count on what he says. He's a foreman over the heavy equipment operators for Hercules Powder Company. He and his men dig up minerals from the ground to make gunpowder.

"Willard, this house has got a real good yard and ain't so close to the train tracks like the other places we've lived in."

"I've got a house lined up. It ain't so close to the tracks. Stop worrying so much, Bessie." The bedsprings creak. It's quiet for a minute, and I wonder if they've gone to sleep. "Don't cry, honey," Daddy says. "I reckon something else is bothering you. Come here."

I imagine Daddy with his arm around Mama, her head on his shoulder, the way I've seen them a hundred times. It's how Daddy dries Mama's tears right up. "Bessie, honey, we ain't leaving Tommy. Our little boy left us a long time ago. He ain't in this house anymore."

I hear Mama squalling, pretty near as loud as the night my brother died. Thinking about it makes my heart beat fast and hard, like it's going to jump from my chest into my throat.

"Willard, I wish you would listen." Mama's voice sails through my room, high and loud. "I dread moving with Kenny and Benny. Who's gonna watch them while I pack up?"

"Same one who watches them when you sing," Daddy says with a sigh. "Janie will."

The moon hangs above my window, a light that won't let the darkness take over. A blast of cold air makes its way through the cracks of the wall, through the spots I stuffed with old rags to keep the wind out. I shudder and think about how Mama's right. It's been nice living here. Having Kenny and Benny to look after is fun. They weren't born when my other brother, Tommy, died. He was two years younger than me and got sick with a fever.

I remember how Mama sat in the front room of this house, on the settee, holding Tommy in her arms. It was cold, and the wind made the house howl. Daddy kept a fire going in the fireplace, brewed Maxwell House, and smoked Lucky Strikes. Mama stayed real still, though, not wanting a thing. I brought her a glass of water, and she drank a couple of sips real fast. Then she shook her head.

"No, honey," said Mama. "If I drink too much, I'll have to go to the bathroom. I don't want to get up, just want to sit here with Tommy. But I sure appreciate it."

Sometimes I feel real stupid, and this was one of those times. My cheeks felt hot with shame, bothering Mama instead of helping her.

"Janie," Daddy said, "I sure would like some of that water." I took it to him and stood with him while he drank it. He rubbed my back a little bit with his free hand.

"The fever's gone," Mama announced. "Gone, gone . . . gone." Then she cried. I mean, she wailed, louder than a dog I had seen right after it got run over by a car. Tommy's face turned white. I couldn't figure out why Mama was crying so hard when my brother's temperature had gone down. I went over to talk to Tommy, but Mama stopped me. "No!" she yelled and held onto him tighter. I stood still and watched her cry. After a while, Daddy walked over to Mama.

"Let me have him now, Bessie." He stood in front of her, but Mama wouldn't let go of Tommy. "He ain't with us anymore, honey." Mama didn't try to stop Daddy when he scooped Tommy up in his arms and headed out to our truck. I heard the door slam, not knowing the next time I'd see Tommy he'd be in a pine box.

♪♫

The twins are gone from their bed, making me wonder if the boys are still alive. The sound of Mama's soft moccasins, scuffing against the wood floor, comes toward my room. She totes one of my little brothers in each of her arms. They're wearing miniature dungarees, their faces smudged with oatmeal. I hope they don't get Mama's hair dirty. It's still down, black silk flowing past her shoulders. Mama is the prettiest lady I've ever seen.

"Janie, you need to watch these boys today. Me and your daddy are going to be real busy." From the frown on her face, I know better than to ask any questions.

"Yes, Mama." She leans over to put the boys on the bedroom floor and heads to the back of the house.

I don't get how twins can be so different. Kenny, who is fourteen minutes older than Benny, is a lot bigger. He's a serious boy, but Benny is what Mama calls happy-go-lucky. He smiles all the time. I can't pick a favorite, but if I had to watch only one of the boys, I'd pick Kenny. He doesn't smile as much, but he gazes into my eyes like he reads what I am thinking. It's like having a secret with someone who can't tell it no matter how much he wants to.

"Janie!" Mama calls. She sits at the kitchen table with her arms folded on the tabletop and her head buried in them.

"Yes, ma'am?"

"Come here." I walk over to my mother, and she lifts her head. She puts her arm around me and strokes my hair. She sings "You Are My Sunshine" to me like I'm still a little girl.

I'm not going to tell Mama it hasn't been my favorite song for a long time. I think she hasn't noticed I'm not a little kid anymore. I've been thirteen, *a teenager*, two whole months, and I'm liking different songs now, grown-up ones. But no matter what Mama sings, she touches me deep inside. When something feels upside down, Mama knows how to turn it right side up. It's the sound of her voice, singing even when she talks. She hugs me, tender and slow. I go outside to play tag with Kenny and Benny.

Before long, our Chevy truck is loaded. I take my brothers out to the porch while Mama uses a garden hose to spray the floors clean. Daddy leaves the house key on the windowsill, and I follow him outside. "Daddy, should I get the rags out of the walls so we can take them with us?" He looks at me, his head cocked to one side, a Lucky Strike hanging from his lips, and his eyebrows scrunched together.

"Don't you remember?" I ask, pointing to the walls of the house where some of the rags stick out from the cracks in the cedar. "The wind made the house howl real bad, so I jammed rags into the cracks, trying to get that noise to stop. You helped me."

Daddy smiles, letting the cigarette drop on the ground. He smashes out the fire of the Lucky Strike with the bottom of his brown brogan.

"You know what, Janie? The rags worked real good. I forgot all about the noise this here house used to make. What do you say we leave the rags right where they are? It'll help out the next people who live here."

"If you want, Daddy." He winks at me and breaks into a grin. Shoot, I wish Daddy liked to hug, so I could throw my arms around him right now.

In the back of Daddy's pickup is Mama's brand new white washer. Her Singer sewing machine is folded into its oak case, sitting next to a bunch of cardboard boxes. Another pickup, belonging to Daddy's friend Earl, is packed with our furniture. "Come on!" Daddy calls. I squeeze into the cab. Kenny crawls into my lap, and Benny climbs into Mama's.

"I sure will miss this place," she says.

"Yep, some good times here. Some bad ones, too," Daddy says. He starts talking to Mama about his work, and in a few minutes, we pass Spring Park, right in front of the St. Johns River.

"Hey, y'all," I interrupt. "Do you think those pennies people tossed into the wishing well yesterday will bring good luck?" The wind blows hard today, making the water choppy as it flows north, not south. We've got something special right here in Green Cove.

"I reckon it depends on what they wished for, gal," Daddy says.

"There's no place to go shrimping in Starke," Mama says. Her voice quivers again.

Daddy likes to take us out to catch shrimp for our supper. We would stand on the edge of the bridge, waiting for him and Earl to bring those ugly critters up in a big net. I love to snap off their heads, getting rid of their big bug eyes and antennae. A good rinsing and they're ready to get thrown in boiling water. All we have to do is add some salt, and they taste real good.

"I'll take us fishing, Bessie," Daddy says. He turns the corner, passing by a red brick general store with a peeling black roof. "We'll fry up some catfish."

I press my forehead to the back window and wonder how long it will take us to move back to Green Cove, to the place me and Mama love. I whisper to my heart: *we'll come back home.* We will.

Chapter 5

Slipping Around

Starke, Florida

Rose

"Maggie, you think I ought to go to a doctor?"

"What for?" Maggie shifts her new Buick into a higher gear and starts a humming along with the radio to Ernest Tubb's "Slipping Around."

"To be sure I ain't mistaken." Maggie cuts her eyes over to me, keeping her face straight ways. Her half-smoked cigarette's a dangling from her strawberry red lips.

"Is that what Ma said? To see a doctor?" She slows down the car and turns her whole head to me this time. It ain't hard to figure out why some people say Maggie's the prettiest woman in Bradford County. When *A Place in the Sun* came out, everybody who saw the movie talked about how Elizabeth Taylor reminded them of Maggie. Especially her eyes. Violet. I ain't seen anybody else with them eyes.

"Ma? Who is Ma?"

"*Ma.* Ma-Ki. My mother." Smoke is coming outta both her nose and lips. "Did she think you might be ailing?"

"No, I'm just a hoping I'm sick instead of . . ." I push the back of my head into the Buick's padded upholstery and close my eyes. When pain goes to slicing through my little toe on my right foot, I look down and see the moccasins Ma gave me. Deep down, I know I'm *in trouble.* Ain't no sense in thinking I'm sick with something else. "Well, if a baby's on its way, I hope it's born before it gets so hot."

"Heat comes and goes. Young'uns don't. You're good and stuck," Maggie claims. She takes another swig of whiskey.

"I know it." Like my momma's stuck with me and them brothers and sisters of mine. Maybe it's why she's been mad ever since I can remember. I see her slipping an ounce or two of whiskey most every afternoon. I wonder if Papa knows. If he does it when I ain't looking . . . if Ma drinks it, too. Maybe I'll find out. "Your ma sure is sweet, Maggie."

"Well, she ain't perfect, the way some people think, Rose. But she sure enough took a liking to you."

"She treated me like a good girl."

"Sometimes good girls wind up in trouble, Rose. Ma's done got human nature figured out."

"You ain't surprised I'm *in trouble.* Are you?"

"Nope." Maggie's answers get shorter and shorter. She lets loose with Ernest Tubb. "*Slipping around, afraid we might be found.*" My tears start falling. Maggie tucks the flask under her skirt and looks my way. She gives my shoulder a squeeze. "Look, Rose, it ain't like you're some church girl."

"No, I ain't. But there ain't been nobody else. Just one. And it ain't happened just three times. And I can't help it if Momma and Papa ain't a mind to take us to church, Maggie." My mind leaps back to Sister Daisy, nice to me, like Ma.

"See what I mean? Rose, you been running around with the Bradford County Casanova. Church girls might stare a lot and flirt a little with him. But it stops there."

"Casanova? What's that?"

Maggie slows down, turns toward me, and starts a puffing real hard on her cigarette. She coughs a wee bit and shakes her head. "Rose, don't tell me you ain't got a clue who Casanova is. He was a lady's man, had a bunch of women at one time. Love 'em and leave 'em. Now you learnt what a Casanova is." She speeds up again and starts watching the road. It's a good thing because I don't want her looking at me. My broke heart, I know it shows all over my face. I feel my bottom lip tremble, and my nose starts to drip. I ain't got a hanky or Kleenex. I ain't got a thing in this world.

"Maggie, he ain't like a Casanova. He loves me, only me! He tells me every time I see him."

Maggie chuckles. "Uh, you fell for that line?"

Casanova? If Maggie's right, it means he's a running around with all kinds of women. I remember what Momma said. *That boy'll marry you if you ain't got no home. Your shame'll be pinned onto him, too.*

"You think he's cutting out on me, Maggie?" My right eye starts to twitch, but I don't want Maggie to know. I cup my hand over it.

"Sure is a good chance of it. Where was he last night? He didn't come looking for you at my house."

"Well, he didn't know I was at your house. Maybe he went over to mine. Except it ain't mine no more."

"Rose, if a man wants to find a woman, he'll find her. Especially one who's carrying his young'un."

"But he doesn't know I'm *in trouble!*"

"Uh huh." Maggie takes another swig.

"Maggie." I cover my face with my hands, hoping to hide the twitching. "I'm going to pieces!"

"Well, I got the cure." Maggie turns her head toward me this time. "Let's ride over to Buddy's Bar."

"Oh no . . . I feel a little sick, Maggie." Sick at the thought of *Casanova*. My head is just a spinning. Maggie's right. It ain't like I'm some church girl. It's how I got in this mess.

"Well, I can leave you at my place before I head over to Buddy's."

"Maggie, would you be mad at me if I wanted you to take me to the Thankful Country Church instead?"

"Church? *That* church, Rose?" What's left of Maggie's cigarette falls outta her mouth and onto her skirt. She picks it up real fast and throws it out the car window. Before I can answer, Maggie spins her car around, and we start a heading to the church. She keeps quiet and doesn't make fun a me. "You can get your own ride back to my place?"

"Surefire will."

"Good enough, Rose. If I got a caller when you get to my place, ease in quiet. Go straight to the spare room. You hear?"

"Yep. Thanks, Maggie. Would you do me one more favor? If you see him first, would you tell him? So I don't have to?"

"If you want me to, okey dokey."

I nod. She stops in front of the church, and I get out slow, hoping Sister Daisy will be home. I wave to Maggie and walk up the path. Sister Daisy is just a hollering while she plays the piano.

"Hallelujah! Hallelujah!"

I climb the church steps, nice and easy with my sore feet, until I reach the open door. I knock, but Sister Daisy don't answer, so I push the door open a wee bit. Her back faces me. I ease over to the piano. When she looks up, I make myself smile.

"Rose!" Sister Daisy jumps up. "I didn't see you come in."

"Hey, Sister Daisy." I keep my voice real quiet and soft. I got a lot to be ashamed of.

"Well, how are you, honey?" She smiles and reaches to put her arm around me.

I ain't able to answer. I ain't smiling anymore. I'm *in trouble*, and I ain't got a husband, a home, a dollar, or anything you need in this world to get by.

"I'd offer you a seat on the pew, but it's time for me to take a break. I see you got yourself some moccasins."

"Yes, ma'am. Somebody gave them to me."

"What a nice gesture. You certainly needed them. Why don't we get you off your feet? I'm hungry. Would you like to join me for a sandwich?" She squeezes my shoulder a wee bit.

"Yes, ma'am. I sure would." Mama taught me to always say no when people offer you something. But my stomach is aching for food. I got a notion that Maggie ain't cooking tonight. I better grab ahold of what I can get.

"Follow me." We head out the side door, and Sister Daisy crosses her arms and rubs them with her hands. "It's still chilly today, isn't it, Rose? You didn't walk over here, did you?"

"A girl dropped me off. And yes, ma'am, it's surefire cold." Sister Daisy takes us along a flat stone path, up to a white frame house. She slips her arm through mine. It's like we're two friends, not a preacher's wife and a girl *in trouble*.

"My husband and the men from the church refurbished this house a few months ago," she says, opening her front door. Inside, I hear Sister Daisy's cuckoo clock keeping time. She's got fancy rugs on the floor, and her sofa ain't got even one hole in it. "Jeremiah, my husband, he is out for the afternoon." She turns into her kitchen. "Do you like chicken salad, Rose?"

"Yes, ma'am." Chicken salad? I ain't never had it, but it sounds real good. "Can I help somehow?"

"Why don't you pour us some tea?" Sister Daisy points to the cupboard. I open the white cabinet door.

"Oh! Look at these glasses. They've got daisies on them! I ain't seen such fancy things anywhere."

"You'll see all kinds of things around here with daisies. Jeremiah goes a little bit overboard, bringing things home with what he calls 'my name all over it.'" Sister Daisy giggles, while she spreads chicken salad on the bread.

My mind flashes to the red rose petals Ma put in to soak. *Rose.* You see what-nots everywhere with roses on them. I wonder why in the world Casanova ain't never brought me a rose on a glass, a rose on a scarf, or a rose on an apron. He ain't bought me a fake rose inside a plastic ballpoint pen holder like I saw at the dime store. *Not even just one old plastic rose.*

"Rose? Are you doing all right, dear?"

I ain't able to answer. I'm hungry. I'm *in trouble*, and I ain't got a notion about whether or not I can trust Sister Daisy.

"Rose, honey." She puts her hand on the back of my right shoulder. I lay my forearms onto the kitchen counter. Sister Daisy brings her arm down, wrapping it around my waist.

"I knew the minute we met, Rose, surely something is bothering you," she whispers sweet and soft.

My hand finds its way to my stomach, just a begging Sister Daisy to uncover my secret.

"Honey, are you telling me you're with child?" Her dark eyes hold tears. I nod my head. "The Lord knows all about it, Rose. He does."

"I ain't got any idea what that means, Sister Daisy!" I bring my fists in front of me, ready to fight God, Momma, and even Sister Daisy.

"It means you and I don't have the answers, but He does." She strokes my hair.

"Answers?"

"It means the Good Lord wants to help you, Rose. Honey, have you prayed about this?"

"Prayed? God's mad at me. Ain't He?"

"No, Rose, He's not mad. He's a forgiving God, one who specializes in love, not anger." She gives me a wee smile.

"But I'm a Jezebel!" I hug my waist, thankful it ain't already big and showing the world what I done.

"Rose, as surely as we're standing here, you're no Jezebel. We've all sinned, and we all need forgiveness." She gives me a wee smile.

"It's real hard to imagine you sinning, Sister Daisy."

"How sweet of you to say, Rose, but I've sinned my fair share." She leans closer to me. "Rose, have you ever asked Jesus into your heart?"

"No, ma'am," I gulp. "Will He help me if I do?" I've been a wanting to shake my fists at God, but maybe I should start begging for His help.

"Yes, somehow He will."

"Okay then." I don't know how in the world to start a prayer. All of a sudden, I can feel the tears, just a pouring down my face.

"Would you like me to pray with you?"

"Yes, ma'am." Sister Daisy tucks her arm into mine, leading me into her living room.

"Let's kneel here and talk to the Lord." We get on our knees in front of her pretty blue couch. "Dear Lord . . ." Sister Daisy begins. I can't think of anything to say to God. I got plenty I could say to *Casanova*, though. When Sister Daisy stops praying, I whisper an amen.

"The Lord loves you, Rose, and He loves your baby." She gets up and sits on her couch, patting the cushion next to her. I get up and sit there, too. "Do you feel any better?"

"It still don't seem real, any of it, Sister Daisy, except when I'm sick every morning." She goes to the kitchen for our sandwiches and brings them back.

"How old are you, sweetheart?"

"Sixteen." I gobble up my food real fast, but she ain't even touched hers.

"Rose, you're still a girl, a girl someone should be taking care of. What about your young man?"

"I don't know. Sister Daisy, I'm afraid I've gone and fallen in love with a Casanova."

"Oh?"

"Yes, ma'am. He tells me he loves me, but I can't figure out why I ain't seen him in two days."

"Rose, try not to panic. Sometimes it takes people a little while to sort through things. What about your parents? Do they know?"

This part of the story might take all day. "Sister Daisy, how 'bout we eat some more food, and I'll tell you then."

"What a great idea, Rose. I'm getting hungrier by the minute!"

♪♫

Me and Sister Daisy talk about my momma and papa until it's almost six o'clock and dark outside.

"Rose, would you like to spend the night with us?"

"Thank you, ma'am, but I better be getting back over to Maggie's." *Maybe he'll come looking for me.*

"Let me get my car keys and write Jeremiah a note. He'll be back any time." I walk outside in front of Sister Daisy. The front door light shines in the darkness, showing a man leaning up against a tree. I start to holler, and then I hear Casanova's voice.

"Rose, Rose, it's all right." He steps my way.

Sister Daisy stops real fast and clutches her pocketbook. "Rose?"

I touch my belly and point at him. Sister Daisy's mouth forms a big *O*.

"Rose," he says, "I been trying to find you." He moves a wee bit closer to the tree again, slow like a buck that knows a hunter's watching. What in the world is wrong with him, showing up at the preacher's house? I don't want Sister Daisy to see him talking to me.

"I ain't in need of a ride after all, Sister Daisy."

"I'll be inside if you need me, honey."

"Yes, ma'am. Thank you." Sister Daisy reaches out and squeezes my hand before she walks back inside.

I turn to *Casanova*. I'm glad it's dark, so he don't see shame a turning my cheeks red.

"Rose, come on." He's a motioning for me. "I been waiting for you a good while. I got my car out by the hard road." He walks quick. With my sore feet, it ain't easy to keep up with him, but Casanova don't seem to notice.

"How'd you know where I was?"

"Maggie told me." He walks faster.

"My feet hurt. I ain't able to keep up." I try to hurry to the car. He opens the door for me, something he ain't done before. I get inside, and he leans into me.

"Rose, Maggie told me you've gone and got yourself *in trouble*."

"Well, it ain't something I did all by myself." He closes my door and hurries over to open his.

"I reckon you got a point there, Rose."

"You helped me get *in trouble*." I look straight at him, but he looks away.

"Oh come on, Rosie." He pounds the steering wheel. "Your baby can't be mine!"

"What makes you say such a mean thing?" I close my eyes and slump down into my seat. "I ain't been with no one else, so it has to be yours."

"Listen, Rosie! I've been with a whole lot of girls, and nobody's gotten *in trouble*, so it must be somebody else's baby you got."

Casanova's ditching me. I ain't got nobody. Nowhere to go. Them gumballs get a popping in my gut again, and I feel ready to hurl. "You know there wasn't nobody before you!" I'm *in trouble*, and I ain't got a chance of getting married, a place to live, money, or anything you need to live in this world.

My hurt's been butchered and stewed, put away in glass jars. I close my eyes, and I can see them, sealed shut with Mason lids. They're just a sitting on a pantry shelf that ain't strong enough to bear their weight. Every jar shouts: *I've been storing up Rose's hurt, and it's time to open me up!*

"First don't mean only, Rose!" *Casanova.* He slumps, a looking me square in the eyes.

Lids are a waiting to pop. "Take me to Maggie's. Now!" I holler.

He reaches down and turns the radio up real loud. Casanova don't say another word, and me neither. When the car stops in Maggie's driveway, "Too Young" by Nat King Cole starts a playing on the radio. I climb out and watch him leave. This is the first time I've been in the car with Casanova, and he ain't touched me. *Anywhere.*

Chapter 6

Why Not Me?

Sister Daisy

I turn off the inside light and stand with the door ajar, making sure Rose truly does have a ride. How that miscreant of a man found her here, I don't know. But it's a small town in which we live, and word spreads quickly. After hearing two car doors slam, I lock the door and turn the lights back on. As hungry as I was, I somehow forgot to eat my sandwich. I begin to devour it when I hear Jeremiah coming through the back door.

"Well, good evening, Sister Daisy," he teases me. My husband wraps his arm around my waist and draws me close to him. I put my sandwich down and turn to him.

"How was your meeting?"

Jeremiah shakes his head and sighs. I know what that means: no progress. He walks over to the coffee table and picks up the plate and glass Rose used. "Did you have company?"

"Yes, Rose Monroe, the girl I met yesterday."

"How did it go?" Jeremiah gathers the few dirty dishes and begins to wash them.

"Jeremiah, you're doing my job." I try to wedge in, but he won't let me.

"Well, how was your time with Rose?"

I prop my elbows on the counter and look into my husband's eyes. "She is sixteen and pregnant and has no place to go." My voice breaks.

"You know we can't take her in, don't you, Daisy?" Like always, Jeremiah knows what I am thinking.

"Yes, I know we can't, but how I wish we could." And tears, pooled in my eyes, break free, two rivulets falling down my cheeks. Rushing rivers of regret. Jeremiah returns to my side.

"Honey, we tried so hard for a baby. I've sent up more prayers to become a father than any other thing on this earth. I don't know why the Lord didn't give us children. You'd be the best mother on earth." I nod my head, unable to speak. Here we are, clinging to each other in this tiny, rural town.

Father God, thank you for sending Rose to me today. Please help her and the baby she carries. But why not me, Lord? Why no baby for me? For my faithful husband? I'm still trying to understand. Amen.

Chapter 7

The Leaning House

Starke, Florida
January 1953

Janie

"Look ahead, Bessie," Daddy says. "It's gonna be a good year." Benny, who's all stretched across Mama's lap, starts to wiggle. Kenny doesn't move nary a bit. His head gets heavier and heavier on top of my arm. "Look ahead, Bessie," Daddy repeats himself. "How many heads, Bessie? Fifteen? Twenty?"

A bunch of Mama's kin people spread along the front of the house. "Aw, Willard," Mama says, a smile exploding across her face.

Before I can get the door of the truck wide open, two of my aunts reach in for my little brothers. My cousin Buster runs toward us, whooping like a Seminole who's doing a rain dance. Thirteen like me, I've played with Buster since I can remember: marbles, slingshots, wildflowers, and songs.

"Go on," Daddy nods. "You can help us unpack after a while."

"Come on!" Buster yells out. He runs to a big oak tree that's circled by some old inner tubes. We jump from one to the other while the grown-ups make music on the front porch of our new home. Mama, whose voice is prettier than a house wren's, sings.

Buffalo Gals, won't you come out tonight . . .

"Here it comes," Daddy yells out. Mama stomps her foot, and with her hands on her hips, she hightails it back into the house.

I danced with a gal with a hole in her stockin',
And her heel kept a-knockin', and her toes kept a-rockin'.

Sometimes this verse makes Mama mad. A long time ago, she told me why. I remember the sad look on her face, how her shoulders slumped, and how her dark eyes lost their sparkle. "Don't tell your Daddy, Janie. I'm ashamed. White people talked bad about my ma and me because we didn't wear stockings."

"But I thought it was because you're Seminole, Mama."

"Partly. See, Janie, Seminoles go barelegged. Proper white women wear stockings, and they look down on women who don't."

"Mama, if that song hurts your feelings, why don't you tell Daddy? He'd stop singing it."

"Janie, Seminoles are real good at keeping secrets. Remember what I am telling you: real good at keeping secrets."

"Mama, are you more Seminole or white?"

Mama stopped folding clothes, stood still, tears rolling down her light brown face. I couldn't figure out what was hurting her, but I wanted to make it stop. So I asked again.

"You *are* a Seminole, *aren't you*, Mama?"

She didn't look at me, just picked up the basket of unfolded clothes, walked to the back porch, and threw them into the wind, one piece at a time. I ran into the yard, grabbed them up, and toted them inside. Before I could get back in the house, I saw Mama driving off without Tommy or me. I couldn't figure out what I said to hurt her. Scared I'd never see her again, I sat still and held my brother tight till Daddy got home from work.

"Hey, race you to the swing," Buster says, reminding me how much fun we're having and helping me forget the sad days. We gallop to another oak tree with a tire hanging from one of its limbs. I grab the tire the same time Buster grabs the rope. I climb inside, elbow him out of the way, and push my legs as far back as they'll go.

"You're gonna get it, now!" Buster yells out. He pulls the sides of the tire way up high. I work with him, holding my legs straight out and leaning back so I can go higher. I pretend I'm that swimmer-turned-movie star, Esther Williams, rolling down the highway in a Cadillac convertible, top down, the wind fluttering my hair.

"Janie! Buster! Come on and eat dinner," Mama yells out.

We make a run for it, and this time nobody is on the porch or standing in front of it. Clear as a cloudless sky, the house stands in front of me. *Or maybe it doesn't stand.*

Great day in Green Cove. I can't let Mama live here. My heart shuts down, turns off, and near about stops ticking.

Somebody played a joke on this house. It leans to one side, like the home that belonged to the old man who walked a crooked mile. Mama's going to squall all the time if we stay here. People will talk bad about us, the way they did with Ma's bare legs, her Indian ways, and her not knowing if she's Seminole or white. *Or how she doesn't know her real daddy.*

"You think everybody is standing over to just one side of that place, Buster?" I hurry up the porch steps, but Buster grabs my arm and stops me.

"Bitin' bass, Janie. Were you thinking it's people who are making the dadgum house lean?" He hoots again, throwing his head into the air, slapping his hands on his thighs, and poking his rear end out.

I try to kick him in the shins, but he dodges my foot and uses his elbow to nudge me inside. I run through the front door and take a close look at the fireplace. The top of it has pulled away from the plaster wall, leaving a space for critters to come in, and thick cobwebs have clumped together in it. An unfinished oak mantle, that could be pretty if it wasn't lopsided, begs for a coat of paint. A fire burns in the hearth. I fan it with my arms, wanting the embers to jump onto the floor. *I hope this place burns to the ground.*

"Get in here, gal," Daddy yells out.

The smell of Ma's baked ham and sweet potatoes drowns out the stink of the cabbage field out back. I hurry into the kitchen.

"Ma came over and cooked before y'all got here," Buster says.

"Yep," Ma says. "Black-eyed peas and hog jowl." She stands at the stove, turning a cast-iron skillet upside down to shake out the cornbread.

"Peas and hog jowl for good luck on New Year's Day," Mama says.

Like a lucky housefire.

Mama looks at me and then nods at the twins, signaling it's time for me to get them cleaned up for dinner. I wipe their hands real quick, and we hurry back out to the table.

"Thunder and lightning, them boys," Ma says. Ma's been talking about it since the twins were babies. At first, she'd shudder all over. Mama told me that Seminoles believe twins can be real trouble, thunder and lightning, a dangerous storm. But today Ma's dark eyes sparkle, and her cherry lips form a little smile. She wears her black hair in a single braid.

Daddy's fair skin stands out, next to Ma and Mama. His hair is as almost as black, but his eyes are as blue as the St. Johns River. Mama's nose is broad, her cheeks are high, and she has big dark eyes.

Back when Tommy was still alive, I figured out that Daddy is shorter than Mama. They were barefoot. Daddy was gazing up into Mama's eyes, and she leaned her head down to kiss him. Way back then I learned big sloppy kisses don't just happen in the movies but in real life, too.

♪♫

The twins give in to a nap as soon as I put them on the bed. Mama, Ma, and her sisters unpack while me and Buster play outside. He stashes his jumping jacks into his pocket, ready to switch to marbles.

"Race you back to the swing!" I yell out. I take off but stop real fast. Buster leaps ahead, pretty near smashing into a water oak. "Look!"

Buster walks closer to me. "Look at what, Janie?" He slaps his hands on his hips. "I don't see nothing but a big ole fieldstone."

"Yeah. Help me pick this up, Buster. It's too heavy for just me."

"What are you fixing to do?"

"I'm going to haul some of these and put them on one side of the house, the side that's higher up, to weight it down. You know, to make it stop leaning."

"Janie, you've gone plumb crazy. There ain't enough rocks in all of Bradford County to level that ole place." He shoves his hands into his pockets and looks up at the oak. Why don't we build a new tree house instead?"

"Buster, how can I even *think* about building a tree house when Mama is living in a place pretty near ready to fall over?" I point back to the house. "And everybody who sees the place will make fun of us."

"Cause of a house?"

"Yes. Houses are a big deal, Buster. And so is being laughed at."

"You stay right here, Janie. I'll go get a wheelbarrow."

"What kind of crazy notion have you two young'uns got now?" Daddy cuts his eyes at a wheelbarrow with three big ole stones in it. It sits smackdab in the middle of the kitchen.

"We're trying to stop this house from leaning, sir. Buster is helping me. We're going to level the place with these big old stones."

Slower than a turtle crawling out of a pond, a grin spreads itself across Daddy's face. He leans his head back and laughs like he's heard the world's funniest joke. I hold my breath.

"Willard, what in the world is so funny?" Mama walks into the kitchen.

"Tell her, Janie. Tell her what's so funny," Daddy says, nodding.

"I'm putting fieldstones on the west side of this house, trying to stop it from leaning."

Mama's mouth turns up at the corners, and her eyes start to glow. "That's a real good idea, Janie. Mighty fine." She turns and looks at my father. "Willard, that's enough," Mama hollers out, even though she's only three feet away from him. And right behind her stands Ma, hugging her hips with her hands. Her jaw juts out, and her mouth is a straight line. I can't tell whose side she's on.

"Finish up, gal," Daddy says. "Be done before me and Percy get back from the fishing hole." He shuts the door, his grin gone.

"We can get started with them three," says Buster. He carries one big rock to a corner of the kitchen, setting it down real careful. Then we haul the others, heavy like boulders, to the bathroom and into the corner of the front room.

"Buster, I'm downright proud of you. You and Janie done fixed the house. Wait and see," Ma says.

"Yes, ma'am. Thank you," Buster says.

Me and Buster plop down on the front porch steps. Sometimes I want to hug him, but he won't let me. He won't let me draw him, either. My cousin has got dark green eyes, freckles, and a pointy chin. When the sun hits him just right, it shows off the red in his hair. He doesn't look a thing like his real mother, Aunt Maggie, or even like Ma, our grandmother.

"Janie, I reckon we ain't going to know for a while if them rocks work or not, huh?"

"It's got to work fast, Buster."

"You're crazy, girl. Hey, how about me and you play our song game?" Buster stretches his long legs out in front of him and leans back on his elbows. "My, heart, jumpin'."

"'Babyface' by Art Mooney. My turn." I sing one word at a time: "Note, frog, throat."

"Pure easy. 'Woody Woodpecker' by Kay Kyser. Give me one ain't so simple, Janie."

We go on like this for a while, not missing nary a one. Buster and me, we know our music.

♪♫

"Come on, Janie. I got something to show you," he says. He points to a black car. It used to belong to my aunt. "Maggie got a new Buick and gave this old one to Ma. Ma don't know how to drive, so Dora and Lily carry her places."

Buster motions for me to get in. I hop into the driver's side and slide up against the passenger door. He starts the car, sports a big grin, and punches the gas pedal with his foot. Next thing I know, we're driving down the dirt road that runs along the front of the house. Plumb amazed, I can't take my eyes off Buster.

"Percy learnt me how to drive," Buster says. "I been waiting all day to take you for a ride."

"Faster, Buster!"

He shifts into high gear. We're the only car on the dirt road, so I pretend I'm in a parade. I wave at cows, an old horse, and a barn. Buster slams on the brakes so hard my head jerks back and forth.

"Oh no! No!" he yells out.

Buster throws open the door and runs to the rear bumper. He hurries back, holding his dog, Pistol, real tight. That dog looks deader than a doornail, tongue hanging out, eyes open, and still not moving. And Buster cries so hard his shoulders shake. I lean over to look at Pistol, hoping not to see any blood or guts.

"He's alive, Buster! I can see him breathing."

"Janie, drive us to the fishing hole!" Buster yells out, even though he's right next to my window.

"Are you crazy? I don't know how to drive."

"You ain't getting it, Janie. Drive! Pistol's all I got." Tears drip down Buster's cheeks. "And I forgot all about him while you were here. He's been out here sick, all by himself. He may die."

I climb into the driver's side, pull the knob, press the button, and turn the key. The car sputters and shuts off.

"You forgot to work the clutch and the brake!" Buster yells out.

Great day in Green Cove. "I didn't forget, Buster. I don't know how!"

"Janie, push down the clutch. Put your feet on the brake. Let go of the clutch and slide your right foot over to the gas pedal." After Buster shows me which pedal the clutch is, I do exactly like he says, but the car still won't go. "Pull the choke! Don't flood it! Choke it!"

He reaches over and pulls a knob on the dashboard. The car jerks, lurching forward. I'm a lot shorter than Buster, making it real hard for me to see out over the windshield. The car stalls out when the tires sink into holes, but I get it started up again.

"Go on to where Uncle Willard's fishing."

I drive real slow to the lake, so I won't have to mess with the gears too much. Around the curve sits Daddy's truck. I brake and the car quits. Still bawling, Buster hangs his head out the open car window and yells out for help. Daddy and Uncle Percy bring their lines in and come running.

"Boy, what's wrong with you?" hollers Uncle Percy. Then he catches sight of the dog. "What happened to Pistol? He dead?"

"Near about." Buster's voice shakes real bad. "I found him laid out on the side of the road."

Uncle Percy opens the car door, squats down, and whispers something to Pistol.

"Let me get a look at him," Daddy edges in. He leans over, and Pistol whimpers as Daddy opens its mouth and pats its belly. Daddy looks straight into the dog's eyes and then at Buster.

"I think he got ahold of something poison, but I ain't convinced all the way. Or it could be something bit him. We're going to keep a close eye on him." Daddy straightens his straw fishing hat. "Percy, I think we better get these young'uns and this here dog back to the house. Percy, you drive Buster and that dog."

On the way to his truck, Daddy stops to fire up a Lucky Strike. He opens the passenger side for me. "Janie, your mama's gonna be real aggravated if she finds out you drove Ma's car."

"Yes, sir," I reply.

"I ain't about to tell her." He takes a long drag from his cigarette and turns to look at me. "That dog of Buster's, he probably ain't gonna make it. We'll keep that just between me and you, too. Buster may need you a whole lot these next few days."

I nod but don't say nary a word. We drive into the front yard, where Buster sits on the porch swing with Pistol and Ma.

"Can me and Pistol stay here tonight with Janie, Ma? I'm scared to move him."

"I reckon it'll be all right. You behave, now, Buster," Ma says, pointing her finger at him. Pistol lays dead still.

But Uncle Percy stops, on his way to leave, to check on my cousin. He squeezes Buster's shoulder. "I hope that dog of yours'll get over what's ailing him."

Buster sleeps out on the porch swing with Pistol because Mama won't let dogs inside. The chilly night creeps along, and I wake up a bunch of times, wondering if Pistol's alive and if Buster is freezing to death.

When night seems its darkest, I hear whimpering. I get up and take my favorite quilt to Buster and Pistol. Mama has put a little kerosene heater near the porch swing. I spread the quilt on top of the other blankets covering Buster and Pistol. It's my cousin, not his dog, who's been crying in his sleep.

Chapter 8

Happy New Year

♪♫

Buster

"You can take this out to your dog," Aunt Bessie says. She passes me a plate of biscuits and fried taters.

"Anytime your dog's feeling puny, you bring him around," Uncle Willard declares. "This here family likes dogs, but we move too much to have our own."

Janie bites her bottom lip and looks down at the table. I feel sorry for her. She moves every whipstitch and has to look after them brothers of hers. No wonder she aims to fix one thing right after another. Some things about her life seem hunky-dory, like having both a mama and a daddy. But I reckon I ain't the only one who's got troubles.

I grab another biscuit for myself before I head out to give Pistol his ration.

♪♫

Bitin' bass. Maggie's Buick is parked at the edge of our front porch. I walk out to the porch and watch my dog grub for worms and bugs. Aunt Bessie walks out and stands at the door.

"What you so smiling about, Bessie?" Maggie hollers. She gets out of the car, a cigarette hanging from her lips.

"Pistol," Bessie says. "Look at him run. We thought he wasn't going to make it."

"Who cares about an old dog?" Maggie says. "Hey, Ma! I need Buster for some chores today."

"No, Maggie." Ma stands her ground. "You ain't taking him to do your dirty work."

The front door slams, and Maggie stomps toward me. I jump off the swing and the side of the porch. Maggie's right behind me. Maybe she'll fall and break something.

"Hey, boy." That half-drunk she-goat grabs my arm, twisting it. "Happy New Year."

"Hey boy? I got a name!" I jerk my arm away from her.

"Watch how you talk to me, boy." She brings her hand in the air, stopping stiff, looking like an Indian in the movies saying, "How!" Maggie takes her hand down and starts walking back to her car.

"Buster." Janie runs to Bessie's side, calling for me over the purr of Maggie's engine. "What's got her so mad?"

"Who knows, Janie? She's drunk, I reckon."

"You think she's all worked up because Mama's back?" Janie won't stop with the questions. "Maybe they're arguing again about who's going to get Ma's house when she dies," Janie says. "You know, Mama's *just half* with her sisters and Uncle Percy."

"Yep. That's how I heard it." I break into a good clip. All my life my aunts and uncles have been fussing over this farm, who's got more right to it.

Makes me think of my own father. Alive but I ain't never seen his face. Ashamed of me, I bet. I got that in common with Aunt Bessie, not knowing who our daddies are.

"Buster, isn't it weird how Ma married a white man?" Janie speeds up, too. "And had a baby for a white man she never married?"

"I dunno." *Questions.* I barrel ahead. Next she'll be asking about my daddy and more things I ain't ready to think about. Maybe Janie moving here ain't fixing to be too fun, after all.

"Does it make you feel weird about me, Buster?" Janie runs at my side, sputtering out the words. She puffs out plenty of air, trying to keep up with me. "Being *just half* cousins."

"Nope." *Bitin' bass. I wish she would hush.*

"Your grandaddy Burl was a white man, too, right?"

I nod my head, catching sight of the barn. I ought to sprint in and lock Janie out. Till she gets quiet, anyway.

"Isn't it crazy that both of them were dead before we were born?"

I can near about touch the barn door.

"Buster, Mama won't answer me about our granddaddies. How much do you know?"

I grab hold of the barn door, Janie right behind me. Holding it open a crack, I glimpse Janie's nose, mouth, and pointy chin. "There's a rule, Janie. Only boys in the barn the first week of the year." She busts out crying. I jerk the door shut, making sure Pistol made it in.

Aw man. Girls and women. They know how to take the happy out of New Year.

Chapter 9

Poor Pitiful Janie

Janie

"Mama, did you know this is the first time in my whole life I've started a new school when Christmas break is done?" I gobble down my Cheerios while Mama sits next to me at the table, hugging her stomach.

"Janie. I need you to watch the twins. You'll be starting school tomorrow." Mama closes her eyes. Good. *Now she won't see if I cry.*

"Yes, ma'am."

Great day in Green Cove. If I go back today, they'll barely notice me. They'll be talking about what they got for Christmas and who got run out of the house for drinking too much or who stuck their nose too far into somebody else's business. But tomorrow will be like any old day. They'll take notice of a new girl, staring at me and maybe making fun of my dress or my hair like they've done before. I hate to change schools.

"Keep them boys real quiet. I'm feeling puny today." Mama cries real gentle again.

"Mama, don't worry." I take the boys to the front yard and grab a rope. "Here. Pull!" I toss them an end to tug on. The boys yank hard, I give in a little, and let them think they can bring me down.

The sound of a house wren, staccato and real high-pitched, comes from the top of some oak trees. Now she flies low, lands on the ground, and a bunch more join her. Their sweet music fills the air, sounding every bit as pretty as Mama's singing. Kenny and Benny jerk harder on the rope, breaking the birds' spell on me, and I'm flat on my behind.

"Fair and square!" Kenny yells out. Benny runs toward me and puts his little foot on my stomach.

"We won, me and Kenny!" Benny spreads his arms wide.

"Yes sir, you did." I wish my brother Tommy could be here to play with us. We'd have even sides. Kenny runs toward us, his soft brown curls bouncing in the breeze.

"We beat you, Janie!" Benny plops down on my stomach, and Kenny stretches out next to me. The smell of ashy blackjack oakwood rises from the chimney, messing up the crisp morning air.

"Janie, I wanna play cops and robbers," Kenny says.

"Me too!" yells out Benny. He stands up too fast, loses his balance, and lands hard on my belly.

"Ouch! Be careful." Sitting up on one knee, I grab Benny's sides and squash them. Both boys tackle me, giggling while they pinch and poke. The screen door opens and shuts. I stand up to see what Mama wants, but she's not there.

"Help! Help me!" Mama's voice rings out. A big thud comes next, and I race up the porch. In the front room near the door, she lies on her side. Blood seeps through the back of her skirt, making a puddle.

"Mama! Mama!" I holler out. Her eyes are shut tight. *God, please don't let her be dead!* "Wake up, Mama!"

"Get Ma." Her voice isn't much louder than a whisper. "Quick."

I snatch up Kenny and Benny and put them in the truck. Benny wails. Pushing and pulling the buttons on the dash, I try to work the clutch and the gas pedals. The truck sputters, jerks, and snorts. "Choke! Choke it!" And the harder I yell, the louder Benny cries.

"Huuusssssh! Benny, you're supposed to be the happy one!" Benny calms right down, his eyes wide and his mouth open. The engine fires up, and I get the truck out on the road.

"Choke it! Choke it!" Kenny says. He shakes his shoulders, tosses his head, and grabs the air like he's got somebody by the throat. I nod and keep driving, too scared to look anywhere but straight ahead.

Kenny stands right by me on the seat like he's protecting me. A light ahead turns yellow, then redder than Ruby's lips. I brake and the truck dies. I pull the knob and work the pedals, trying to bring it back to life. A horn honks as the light turns green. I sit up high, trying to see over the steering wheel, but my feet won't reach the pedals. Somebody honks the horn again. Great day in Green Cove! I jerk the knobs, squash the pedals with both my feet, and the truck starts up.

"It'll be all right, boys." I try to sound like I believe what I just said. "We're going to see Ma and Buster."

"It's awright, Janie," Kenny says. "This here truck's choking! Vroom . . . vroom." He holds his arms out and steers an imaginary wheel.

"Vroooooom!" Benny yells out.

I move my feet, pretending I'm Mama at a square dance, sliding my feet along the pedals. No sputters or stops, we're on our way. *God, please keep her alive.*

I jump out at Ma's. "Ma! Ma! Mama needs you!"

In her front yard, Ma drops the basket of oranges she's toting. "How'd you get here?" she yells out.

"I drove. Mama fell. She's bleeding!" I holler back.

Ma jumps into Maggie's new Buick and honks the horn from the passenger's side. Maggie gets behind the wheel, and I run to them. "We'll take care of Bessie," Ma screams at me. "You and Buster watch them brothers of yours."

I remember how Mama passed out cold while she was cooking supper, back when Tommy was little and before the twins were born. Blood gushed from her privates, worse than I saw today. I screamed until Daddy ran in and scooped Mama up in his arms. He put her in the car and took her to the hospital. I was seven years old when I learned about losing babies, how it rips a lady's heart out when she never gets a chance to give her baby a kiss, a hug, or a name.

♪♩

"I pick 'em up," Benny says with a giggle. He plays jacks with Kenny and a girl older than me, somebody Ma and Aunt Maggie left here. Her name is Rose. She did her best to smile at me a few minutes ago, but I looked the other way.

"You want to play?" Rose wants to know. She looks at nobody, just the floor.

Mama taught me not to trust somebody who won't look at me straight. I shake my head. No matter what, I'm glad she's keeping the twins busy. I don't want to do anything except watch out the front window for Aunt Maggie's car.

Out of the blue, here comes Aunt Dora running up the dirt road. She busts through the door. "Janie, what in tarnation? You been driving through town, child. Word's done spread all over Starke!" Aunt Dora yells out.

"I found Mama almost passed out on the floor of the front room. I think Mama's lost another baby."

"Oh my, it can't be!" Real fast, she starts pinning up the hairs that have fallen from the bun on the back of her head.

"Aunt Dora, did you walk here from Crowley's Drug Store?"

"No, girl," she says, fanning herself. "A customer drove me home. Lily's on her way." Aunt Dora flops into a wicker rocking chair and calls for Kenny and Benny. They climb into her lap.

Aunt Lily, who answers the switchboard at a car lot, jumps out of a new white Chevrolet with a sticker on the back window of the driver's side. She dashes into the front room.

"Sister! What are we going to do about Bessie?" Aunt Lily wonders.

"How did you know it's Bessie?" Aunt Dora's eyebrows teepee together, making her look confused.

"Dixie Whittington got a job at the hospital and called me from there. What are we going to do, Lily?"

"Nothing except look after these young'uns, Dora. There ain't a thing we can do."

Benny grins as Aunt Lily folds her arms around him. It must feel good to get scooped up and held. I go back to the front porch looking for Buster, who got to stay home because Ma ran off to my house.

"Hey, Janie, you want to go scoutin' with Pistol and me?"

"No. I'm going to wait here, so I'll know about Mama when word comes."

Buster shrugs his shoulders, picks up a softball, and walks toward the barn with Pistol by his side. My stomach gurgles, reminding me all I've eaten today is a bowl of cereal. I head to the kitchen to make a peanut butter and jelly sandwich.

"Janie's got way too much on her." Aunt Dora's loud voice bounces through the house. "I felt so sorry for that girl when her little brother died. She worries more than an old woman. Poor Janie."

"Never had a birthday party that I know'd of," Aunt Lily says. "I thought maybe when she turned thirteen a few months ago, but still no party."

"That's right," Aunt Dora says.

"She's always a bundle of nerves, afraid Bessie'll up and die any minute. Poor pitiful Janie," Aunt Lily says with a sigh.

I put my hands over my ears. *I don't care about dumb old birthday parties.* I have plenty of fun, like having my mama and daddy to sing with. I close my eyes and try to hear my daddy's voice and guitar, but the sound of my aunts' words echo. *Poor pitiful Janie.* I run to the back porch and find Rose stooping down, her green skirt tugged over her ankles. She hugs her knees and wipes her eyes with her sleeve.

"Hey there, Janie." Her trembling lips smile.

"Hey." I hug my stomach, too hungry and too hurt to smile back.

"I'm so sorry about your mama being sick. You did a brave thing today, driving over here to get help."

"Thank you."

"I hope Bessie'll be all right. I always liked her a lot."

"You know Mama?"

"Yep. A long time ago, we lived on Baker Road, when y'all did."

"You're Rosie? Kathryn's big sister!" How can this be? Kathryn, who had eleven brothers and sisters, liked to come to my house because her family, the Monroes, had nary a toy. We played Candyland, dress up, and Old Maid. Mama felt sorry for them because they were real poor. She made Kathryn a Seminole doll. Mama used an empty toilet paper roll for the body and cut a skirt and cape from shiny bright cotton material.

Kathryn took her doll home, and the next day Rosie came knocking, all her littler brothers and sisters standing around her on our front porch. Mama took me and all them back to the kitchen and started teaching Rosie how to craft. We cut out big circles of black construction paper to make hair and followed Mama's pattern to cut out clothes. Me and Kathryn glued rickrack onto the material, in strips to make it look like it was quilted. Mama painted faces and strung tiny beads.

"Surefire am, Kathryn's big sister," Rosie says. "And now here you are driving, like a grown-up." She stands up and holds her open arms out to me.

I walk into her hug and feel those things deep inside me, hurting things. "I was scared, driving Daddy's truck. Scared I couldn't work the choke just right. But now my heart is choked, Rosie. It's flooded!"

"Oh, honey. I know exactly how you feel." She looks into my eyes and hugs me again. "I'm sorry, Janie, I'm so sorry."

"Too much hurt has got pumped into me today, Rosie." Cradled by somebody I'm not even kin to, I gush big tears like the ones Buster cried for his dog. But I'm not pitiful or poor. *I'm going to show everybody how strong I am.*

Chapter 10

I Love You So Much It Hurts

Janie

I stir cocoa, milk, and sugar in an old pot over Ma's stove. Taking a big whiff of its sweetness, I make sure it's not ready to boil.

"How's my gal?" Daddy smiles, walking into the kitchen. His belly pokes out, like it's stuffed with a pillow.

"Fairly well, Daddy. How are you?"

"Sure is good to see you." Daddy bends over, and I put my head next to his. Lucky Strike smoke clings to him.

"How's Mama?"

Daddy scratches the back of his neck. "She's gonna be all right, so don't you worry." He gives me a wink before sitting down at the table. "Don't forget to turn the stove off."

"Yes, sir." I turn the knob, watching amber, crimson, and cobalt flames disappear. Is this what it's like when somebody dies? Does color leave just the body or does it flicker out of a spirit, too?

"Daddy, was Mama's baby a boy or a girl?"

"Well, it weren't far enough along to know that sort of thing. This here's some bad news, Janie. You won't get any more brothers or sisters. You got Kenny and Benny. That's gotta be enough."

My heart starts to choke again, but I stop it. I lift my chin and hold my shoulders square.

"Gal, I need your help to get your mama cheered up. You can do that, can't you?"

"Yes, sir." I know what Daddy means. Mama will be squalling a lot more, like when Tommy died.

"It got cold quick out there, didn't it? Hey, I remember how sad you were on Christmas when you didn't get one of these." He unzips his jacket, takes out a brown tweed coat and hands it to me. It's got white buttons, the size of silver dollars. I look at the tag hanging from its sleeve.

"Daddy, it's brand spanking new! From the Diana Shop."

"Yep, and just for you," Daddy says. He starts singing Eddie Wakely's "I Love You So Much It Hurts." We finish the chorus together. Daddy looks into my eyes the same way he looked at Pistol, like he's trying to see if I will live through what's ailing me.

"I got to go, Janie. You take good of them boys for me."

"Yes, sir."

He winks again, and I follow him onto the porch. Hugging my new coat, I watch the lights of his truck fade as two more sets of headlights drive up to Ma's house.

Aunt Dora runs down the stairs and onto the porch. "Shoo! Buster, Janie. Get inside! Go back to the kitchen," she yells out.

Buster's waiting on me by the stove. We stretch our necks around the door, trying to catch sight of what Aunt Dora doesn't want us to see. Four men march hard and fast through the front room and up Ma's stairs. They're toting a fifth man atop of their shoulders.

"That's Percy!" Buster yells in my ear.

"Great day in Green Cove. What? Uncle Percy?" He's all beat-up.

"Yep, the one they're toting!" Buster yells out so loud, causing one of the men to look our way.

"I know a couple of those boys," I whisper, "and the old man, too."

The whole house twirls around. Everybody's talking at the same time, but I've fallen into a well. Their voices run together, a loud buzz from a swarm of bees.

A lamp on Ma's bedside table shines in my eyes, and Ma's sawtooth quilt covers me. Buster and Aunt Lily stand over me. My aunt waves something smelling like ammonia under my nose.

"Janie, have you eaten anything today?" Aunt Lily wants to know.

I try to remember. Peanut butter and jelly sandwich? No. I was about to make one, but *poor pitiful Janie* got me sidetracked. Cereal. I had a bowl of cereal.

"I ain't seen her eat a thing," Buster says. "Janie, get yourself up, and I'll fix you some bacon."

"Don't get up too quick," Aunt Lily says. Then she turns to Buster. "I'll make her a plate. You ought to learn to cook something besides bacon, Buster."

"Buster, what's wrong with Uncle Percy?" I follow them into the kitchen. Aunt Lily and Buster look at each other, but they don't answer. "Is Percy dead?" I sit down to a plate my aunt made me, full of cornbread, collards, and a pork chop.

"Janie, ain't you had enough thrills for one day?" Buster frowns at me. "Shucks, just a minute ago you was out, colder than a cuke. Now listen to me good. Uncle Percy's alive. You ain't got any business fretting about nothing, not even Kenny and Benny. Dora and Lily got them." He gets up from the table. "I'm staying in Ma's room till she gets back. You and the twins'll have more space in mine." He yawns big, stretching his arms in the air. "Good night."

Stretching myself out on Buster's bed, I can feel myself falling asleep with my dress and shoes on. I spread my new coat over me, snuggle it to my chin, and say a prayer for my mama, the way I learned to pray in school. *Dear God, if you will help my mama, I'll do anything You want me to. I promise to be better. You'll see. You can count on me, Sir. Please make me brave and strong. Not poor. Not pitiful. Amen.*

♩♫

In full daylight, Aunt Dora stands over the bed, her hands on her hips.

"Janie, you're gonna have them twins while me and Lily work today. Buster'll stay with you till your mama gets home from the hospital. Buster's in charge of Percy, you understand?"

I wish she'd let me wake up for one little minute before she starts bossing.

"Don't go near Percy. You hear? Get up now and get to the front room. Kenny and Benny'll be waking up any time."

Like I don't have good enough smarts to know when my own little brothers are going to wake up. "Yes, ma'am!" Kenny and Benny are still snoozing in the other twin bed. I leave them and head to the kitchen, where Buster is frying a big piece of ham.

"Lily learnt me how to cook ham," he says.

"So what, Buster? Anybody can cook ham. Who beat up Uncle Percy?"

"Janie, he's plumb scary looking. Don't go into his room. He ain't able to get around by hisself, so you won't chance running into him."

"Buster, you're getting as bossy as Aunt Dora. So, who beat him up?"

"You want some of this ham or not?" He pokes me in the ribs with his elbow, making it hard for me to get mad at him.

"At least tell me *why* Uncle Percy got beat up."

"Nope. But me and Pistol are fixing to go to the fishing hole. I'll clean the fish if you'll fry 'em. Deal?"

"No. Not fair! You make me so mad. What about Uncle Percy?" Buster elbows me again. I punch him in the stomach.

"Bitin' bass!" Buster yells. His face goes red.

"Besides, I'm ready for another driving lesson."

"Girl, you sure ask for a lot." He shakes his head. "After I get back, I'll learn you more, I reckon . . . if you don't haul off and punch me again." A car door slams outside, and somebody knocks on the door. "I'll see who's here. Don't move." From the kitchen, I can hear him yelling at somebody. "He's upstairs. Ain't able to come down."

Footsteps thump up the stairs and back down again. The front door slams, and Buster darts back to the kitchen.

"Janie, I'm counting on you to clean them dadgum fish. There ain't any other meat, unless you want to kill a chicken." He takes off with Pistol, me with no idea about what's going on. It's like Buster's come up with another boys' only rule, and I can't do a thing about it.

I fry some eggs and make some toast for the twins, but I check on them and they are still asleep. It's lonely in Ma's big house. I find a pencil and a brown paper bag and sit at the kitchen table with them. In a minute or two, I've sketched a schoolhouse. Great day in Green Cove. I'm playing hooky.

♪♫

The sound of car engines rumbling comes from outside, so I peek out the front window. Aunt Maggie leans against her car, and Rose sits in the driver's seat. Homer and some of the other Monroe boys get out of an old sedan. A man and a woman I've never seen before get out of a station wagon. Everybody follows Maggie onto the porch and into the front room. A man carrying a Bible hurries up the stairs.

"Who's that? Where's he going?" I whisper.

"Shhh. Upstairs to Percy's room." Buster elbows me hard.

Rose looks at me, smiling wide. She walks up the stairs wearing Maggie's scarlet suit, and it looks so good with her strawberry blonde hair. Her lips look creamy, almost the same shade as her dress. She's got her hair curled real pretty. Rose could pass for a movie star, except for the beige moccasins on her feet, the ugly kind Mama and Ma wear. What happened to her own shoes? Great day in Green Cove.

"Good morning," says a short lady who rode up in the station wagon. She has short, dark hair curled real fancy, and she's wearing a pretty cobalt blue suit. "I'm Sister Daisy Little, from the Thankful Country Church. Brother Jeremiah Little's wife."

"Nice to meet you, ma'am," I say.

"Yes, ma'am," Buster adds.

We've ridden by the Thankful Country Church. Every time, I try to figure out what the name means. Is it talking about the United States that's thankful? Or is this a country bumpkin church full of thankful people? I want to ask Sister Daisy, but it's the kind of question that's bound to get me in trouble.

The man with a Bible comes back downstairs, and I figure out he's

Brother Jeremiah Little. He puts his arm around Sister Daisy. Rose's three brothers and their father head up the stairs.

"Percy and I just had a good talk with the Lord," Brother Jeremiah Little tells us. "Everything is settled. Are you ready, Maggie?"

"Yes, sir," says Maggie. "I'm a hoping Percy can get down them stairs." She walks to the front door and keeps her back to us.

"Young man," Brother Little leans toward Buster, "don't you have a lake nearby?"

"Yes, sir," Buster says. "About a mile from here."

"Well, that sounds perfect," says Brother Little. Sister Daisy looks at him and frowns but keeps her mouth shut.

Percy hobbles down the stairs and into the living room. Two of the Monroe boys hold him by his elbows and the other two have their arms wrapped around his waist. Percy moves like a piece of china that's scared of breaking. Even though he got beat up two days ago, his face is still swollen and covered with red, green, and purple bruises.

"Easy with him, Homer! Joe!" yells out Rose.

Homer and Joe grab Percy's arms and elbows and lead him out the front door, across the porch, and into the passenger's seat of his car. His legs stretch to one side, resting on the ground. They turn him forward, slow and gentle. Homer lifts Percy's feet onto the floorboard. Percy hollers, and Rose covers her face with her hands. When her daddy sits in Percy's driver's seat, she gets in the back seat of the car.

"Let's go," Buster says. We hop into Ma's coupe and follow them to the fishing hole. Maggie drives ahead of us, alone in her Buick.

"Buster, why are we going to the fishing hole without any poles?"

"I ain't got an answer for that one, Janie." Buster shrugs his shoulders and rolls his eyes. Boys don't ask enough questions. They charge ahead, even when they don't know what they're doing.

♪♫

Rose and Brother Little wait at the edge of the water for the Monroes to help Percy out of the car. Brother Little steps into the lake, motioning for Rose and Uncle Percy. The cold water climbs to Rose's ribs and covers Uncle Percy's waist. His body shakes, but Homer and Joe, who are shivering next to him, keep hold of my uncle.

"In Romans Six, starting with verse twenty," Brother Little shouts, "the Bible tells how we pass from unrighteousness into our Lord's gift of holiness: 'For when ye were the servants of sin, ye were free from righteousness. What fruit had ye then in those things whereof ye are now ashamed? For the end of those things is death.'

"Rose Monroe, as you claim Jesus as your Lord and Savior, I baptize you in the name of the Father, the Son, and the Holy Ghost." Brother Little puts one hand on top of Rose's head and the other behind her back. He dunks the upper half of her body into the water, and she comes up dripping wet and shivering. Her lipstick runs, her eyes are shut, but there's a smile on her face.

Sister Daisy Little sings softly:

Glory, glory, glory
Somebody touched me . . .

She sings good, but not as pretty as Mama.

Brother Little puts his hand on top of Uncle Percy's head and starts again: "Percy Ebbing . . ." Rose's brothers help the preacher lower the back of my uncle's head and shoulders into the water. "I baptize you in the name of the Father, the Son, and the Holy Ghost."

In back of Uncle Percy, Joe gives him a gentle push at his waist. Homer grips Uncle Percy's hands, tugging on him until Percy can plant his feet on dry ground. He trembles like a dog that's gone for a swim on a cold day, shaking the water from his coat. His wet, raven hair falls over his forehead, and his high Indian cheekbones are lost in the puffiness of his purple, bruised face.

"Rose, will you turn toward your groom?" the preacher yells out. Still smiling, Rose turns to face Uncle Percy.

"Romans Six goes on to say, 'But now being made free from sin, and become servants to God, ye have your fruit unto holiness, and the end everlasting life. For the wages of sin is death; but the gift of God is eternal life through Jesus Christ our Lord.'

"The confession of your sins has led you to the mercies of God the Father through His son, Jesus. You freely received salvation a few days ago, Rose, when you prayed with Sister Daisy. Earlier today, Percy, you asked Jesus into your heart. And now, folks, as we gather here, Rose and Percy will enter holy matrimony."

I haven't heard nary a thing about Uncle Percy or Rose confessing their sins, but I have a feeling they've been sinning together.

"In sickness and in health . . ." Brother Little yells out.

"Oh Lord, forgive us all," Mr. Monroe hollers. He looks up at the sky, bites his pale bottom lip, and jams his hands into the pockets of his bib overalls. Tears trickle from his eyes, and Sister Daisy slips a lace hanky to him.

Rose looks at her father, then at the preacher, and back at Uncle Percy.

"In sickness and in health," she says.

"Percy? Your turn," Brother Little directs Percy along.

"In sickness, all beat-up, and in health," Uncle Percy howls.

Sister Daisy gasps, Buster elbows me in the side, and a little smile starts to peek out of Rose's mouth.

"I now pronounce you man and wife," Brother Little says, clapping his hands in the air.

With a bashed-in face, the waterlogged groom stands on the bank of the fishing hole, staring at his bride. Rose, who looked pert and bouncy just a minute ago, stands shivering with her wet hair dripping onto the shoulders of Maggie's suit. This would make a good movie, *The Opposite of Cinderella*, a story about how a pretty girl turned into a river rat on her wedding day.

Sister Little takes a paper out of her pocketbook, signs it, and hands it to her husband. Rose, Uncle Percy, Brother Little, Aunt Maggie sign it, too.

"I'm taking this dad-blasted license right to the courthouse, make sure it gets turned in," Mr. Monroe says. "First, let the groom kiss his bride."

Uncle Percy groans when he tries to move, but Rose leans over and lays a soft peck on his lips. With trembling lips and scarlet smudged teeth, she looks into his swollen eyes and flashes him a smile.

It's easy to figure out why Brother Little mentioned sickness and health. Percy can hardly move without hollering from pain. And Rose, wet and shivering from the cold weather, stands a good chance of catching pneumonia.

Chapter 11

Somebody Touched Me

Rose

Cold water splashes around me, just a washing away the darkness living inside me. *I am free.* Deep down, there's something new. Hope, hope for a better tomorrow, hope for me to become a better girl. Sister Daisy's singing floats over the water, and her words tickle my soul.

When I was prayin', somebody touched me.

Must've been the hand of the Lord.

Brother Little guides my head out of the lake. I've started over, and I ain't got a single thing to be ashamed of.

While I was singin', somebody touched me.

Must've been the hand of the Lord.

Even after Sister Daisy helped me pray, I stayed scared, just a wondering what would come of me or this baby. Even if Percy backs out, I'll be all right. The Lord will help me.

Glory, glory, glory somebody touched me.

Must've been the hand of the Lord.

My brothers cornered Percy and beat the life out of him. He don't look a thing like the Casanova who held me close and looked deep into my eyes. I thought I had to be somebody special to be so close to his movie star face, with its proud cheekbones and eyes like blackberries, wild and ripe.

Girls like me ain't got enough love at home to see us through. I went a reaching out for love a couple of times before Percy, but I used some good sense before things went all the way. I should have waited this time, too, the first-rate way. But Percy's eyes would shine when he looked at me. He ain't been around, until now, since he found out I'm *in trouble*. I love him, anyway. I lean over and kiss my groom real nice and gentle, so I don't hurt him.

The first time I saw Percy was my sixteenth birthday, the day Momma and Papa made me quit school. They needed me at home to take care of my little brothers and sisters. I cried until my eyes swelled up big, when Momma took me to school and signed me out for good. After I put the young'uns to bed later that night, Papa asked me to go with him to Alvin Foster's barn dance.

When Papa opened the barn door, Percy Ebbing was the first thing I caught sight of. He was a playing the fiddle. His strong shoulder muscles moved big underneath his white shirt. I don't know how I got the attention of such a good-looking man, but Percy started coming around, a showing me how to play the guitar. We sat on the porch steps, strumming and singing. Before long, Percy was looking at me like I was a real girl, not just a picker learning about chords and beats.

One evening, he put his arm around me, a showing me how to play a slide. I learned how the Fourth of July can happen any day of the year. The sparks flowing from Percy made me hungry for love.

Percy took the guitar and laid it down on the step in front of us. He put his bronze hands on the sides of my head and brought his face down to mine. His dark eyes swallowed mine, making me feel like I'd become part of Percy and he'd become part of me. He held me until I forgot the hurt of quitting school, about housework and babysitting. It was Percy and me, nothing else. I didn't move or talk, afraid of killing the magic. Percy kissed me, soft, warm, and slow, and I knew he'd have me when he made his move.

Momma and Papa's notion of me looking after the young'uns backfired. I ain't there to take care of anybody, and I ain't heard from Momma since the day she found out I was *in trouble*.

♪♫

Percy's bed is soft and smooth. He opens his eyes after a long nap.

"Percy, do you blame me because my brothers beat you up?" I stroke his forearm, the only place that don't have a bruise on it.

"Naw, Rosie. I'm mad at them but not at you."

"Please don't try to get back at them, Percy."

"I won't." He reaches for my hand. "There's been plenty enough trouble already."

"I'm sorry." I lift my head and rest it next to his. "I didn't know they were goin' after you."

"Rosie, I figured that out by the look on your face this morning when they helped me down the stairs. Your whole body went stiff, and your mouth dropped open, like a bullet had gone straight through your ticker."

"Percy . . ." My tears get in the way, and I ain't able to say anything else.

"It's all right, Rose."

"Percy, I'm ready to take a two by four and bang it up against their rear ends."

Percy chuckles but stops and grabs his ribs.

"But I still love my brothers. I ain't making any sense, am I?"

"Brothers do all kinds of stuff, trying to protect their sisters. Don't hold it against them." Percy closes his eyes. I whisper his name, but he's already back to sleep.

♪♫

After he's done eating on some soft pinto beans and some egg custard, Percy calls me to the side of his bed.

"Rosie, I don't know what you're expecting from me. I ain't a man who makes a lot of money. I wasn't studying marriage or being a daddy, but here we are."

Our last talk was gentle, and I want to keep things this way. "Percy, did you feel something special when you went into the lake?"

"Naw, honey. But the cold water made me hurt a whole lot more."

"I'm sorry, Percy. I love you."

"Sounds good, honey. Real good."

No *I love you, too, Rose.* "Percy, I want to be a good mama to this baby."

"Rose, how do you know this baby is mine?"

His question slaps the happiness right out of me. "Percy, there ain't been nobody but you. You're the onliest one! That's how I know."

"Shhh, Rosie. Shhh. Everything'll work out all right. A man has to know these things. Hey, look at me." Percy takes his thumb and presses it against the tears running down my face. "I hope it's a boy who looks exactly like me. Give me another kiss, Rose, like you gave me today at the water hole."

This time he kisses me back, and the Fourth of July fireworks dazzle me one more time.

♪♫

Janie

Moonlight shines into the dark room and onto the clock. It's almost midnight. Percy's been groaning a while. I wish he'd take a couple of aspirin and get quiet. The boys are asleep in the other twin bed and don't stir. I tiptoe to the hall, hoping to get another look at Percy's beat-up body. He gets quiet again, and his bedroom door is shut. I go downstairs to wake up Buster. I walk into Ma's room and nudge him.

"What is it, Janie?"

"Percy's hurting bad again."

We climb the stairs and stand outside Percy's door. Buster shakes his head and pushes me down the hall.

"Janie, that's him and Rose," says Buster.

"What?"

"They're doing what married people do. You know. Don't you?"

"Look, Buster, I'm not dumb. Sure, I know what married people do, but Percy's too beat up." Yes, sir, I've grown up in houses with walls thinner than paper. That's how I know about married people.

"Shucks, Janie! That's how girls think, Janie, but there ain't no man or boy too beat up for . . ."

"Okay, Buster."

"Janie!"

"Good night, Buster." I race down the hall and jump under the covers, knowing if I'm not fast enough I'll keep hearing Buster make fun of me.

"Them's some good bacon and eggs, Janie," Buster says. "You gonna throw a punch at me if I eat the last biscuit?" Buster shoves what's left of his fried egg into his mouth. Outside the kitchen window, Daddy's truck pulls up to the back of the house. He gets out and hurries up the back porch and into the kitchen.

"Howdy, Buster. Janie, you ready to come home with me?" Daddy's hat is on crooked, and part of his shirttail hangs out.

"Yes, sir. I sure am." Home with Mama. Away from ole Aunt Dora.

Daddy walks upstairs to Buster's room and helps me gather up the twin's clothes. It may not be real cold outside, but I put on my new coat anyhow. We walk back through the kitchen, where Buster waits for us near the stove. On the way out, I give his gut a soft elbow.

"I'll get you back for that one." Buster smiles big.

"You're just tooting a harmonica." I kick the back of his knee, tripping him good.

Rose

Percy wraps his arm around my waist and leans on me. He shuffles through the upstairs hallway.

"If this walking would help my ribs heal, I'd be plumb thrilled."

"I sure am sorry, Percy."

"You done said that, Rosie."

"Percy, when I saw you walk down the stairs yesterday, I thought maybe you were going to die."

"I ain't about to die, Rose, and I would've healed up faster if Ma had been here with her Indian potions, but she's still with Bessie."

"When is she coming back?"

"Owww!" Percy doubles over.

"Careful, Percy. You've got bruises from your eyeballs to your ankles. And last night, when you were a sleeping, you wailed something awful. It's a wonder you didn't wake up the whole house."

Chapter 12

Good Intentions

Sister Daisy

The clack of keys from my Smith Corona never fails to offer me refuge. Composing anything, even a letter to my mother, helps me focus on a world outside Bradford County.

"Daisy, are you still annoyed with me?" Jeremiah smiles in his quirky way.

"Who said anything about being annoyed?" I start typing again, hitting a couple of wrong keys.

"You've been in your own little world since yesterday. You barely said good night to me."

"Jeremiah, I've known you to be impulsive, but *virtuous Virginia*, you took a beautiful bride and baptized her. Beautiful Rose looked a mess when she said her vows, and she was shivering from the cold. What were you thinking?"

"I wasn't thinking, Daisy. I was led by the Spirit. I asked the Lord for guidance, and suddenly I knew why He had impressed upon me to marry Rose and Percy by a lake. I felt it, Daisy. I felt her coming alive in her spirit. Didn't you feel it?"

Did you feel it? And suddenly, I am thrust back to a small chapel in Westchester County, New York, years ago. I was engaged to Wallace Maxwell Gordon, Jeremiah's cousin. Wallace was a cadet at West Point, and I was a senior at Sarah Lawrence College.

One Friday night, Wallace asked if I wanted to meet his cousin, Jeremiah. It sounded as good as anything else my fiancé might plan. When we pulled up to a little chapel in Westchester County, I expressed my confusion.

"Let's go inside," Wallace said. I followed him in, and we took a seat in the back row. "My cousin, Jeremiah, will be up there. He's a country preacher." Wallace nodded toward the front of the church and began to laugh. "Shall we offer up some 'amens' once his sermon begins?"

I could see the family resemblance. Both young men had light brown hair, dark eyes, strong jaws, and broad shoulders. Jeremiah looked our way, nodded, and smiled. I wondered if he knew his cousin was degrading him.

Not long after the choir concluded their singing, Jeremiah began to preach, ever so softly, about Jesus and the Samaritan woman at the well. He spoke about how Jesus had walked miles out of his way, so He could encounter this woman, one whose life had been in turmoil. At the Presbyterian church back in Virginia, I had heard sermons from the same Bible passage, sermons criticizing this woman. But Jeremiah made her so real, so thirsty for purity.

When he asked who wanted to be born again, to drink from the river of life, I found myself standing. Of course, true to his West Point manners, Wallace stood with me. I stepped in front of him and into the aisle. Wallace grunted and shook his head, but I began to walk toward the altar in spite of his disapproval. Each step took me farther from my place in society, farther from the wealthy friends with whom I associated. Warm love was something I didn't have, and I knew I could find it at the front of the chapel.

At the front of the church, Jeremiah led me in the sinner's prayer. When I returned to my seat, Wallace would not look at me, but I didn't care. I was in love with Jesus. The service closed, and Jeremiah was at our pew. He shook hands with Wallace and gave us each his business card. A local number was scrawled across mine.

"Daisy, are you listening?" My husband's voice brings me back to the present day. He pleads with me from the doorway. "Did you feel the Spirit moving?" He begins to pace, three steps forward and three steps back.

"I am doing my best to understand this, Jeremiah." I breathe a long, heavy sigh, signaling I am ready to end this conversation.

"I have one question for you, Daisy. 'Somebody touched me.' What on earth made you pick that song for a wedding?"

"I know it isn't traditional, Jeremiah. But it's what came to mind."

"Well, you can be sure somebody touched Rose," he says. Then he gives me the tiniest grin and waits for me to understand his implication.

Oh my. Jeremiah's right. My face becomes flushed, and I hear my husband chuckle. I open my mouth to respond, but I can't think of anything to say to make me sound less foolish. Jeremiah breaks into full-scale laughter, and in spite of my embarrassment, I join him. He dons his hat, picks up his car keys, and blows me a kiss as he heads out the door.

Father God, forgive me for judging my husband. And please forgive me for anything inappropriate I've done. Thank you for understanding our intentions, Lord. And this letter to my mother, Lord, please help me sound happy about living in Florida's farmland. Amen.

Chapter 13

The Power of *Lhaamin*

Janie

Great day in Green Cove. Furniture's been shifted around the house, and my twin bed is in the living room, where the settee used to be. I head for Mama's room to make sure everything is okay. But Ma stands in the hallway with her arms crossed over her chest. I stop.

"Your mama's in her bedroom," she says. "She's in bad shape, but you go in, no matter."

Mama and Daddy's room is still. Leaning over her bed, I kiss Mama on her forehead, and she jumps like a mosquito who sees a hand-slap coming its way. She's under a pile of covers, her long black hair falling down her copper shoulders.

Mama's eyelids wrestle with waking up, but they finally open.

"Come here." She pats the bed. I hop up with her and put my arm around her waist. I press my cheek next to hers.

"I love you, Janie."

"I love you, too. Mama, I've been worried about you."

"Try not to worry, honey." She puts her hand over mine. "Ma says you drove the truck all the way over to her house when I . . . you know . . . fell."

"Yes, ma'am. I can drive good now. Buster gave me lessons when I was at Ma's. I can take good care of you." I begin to sing "You Are My Sunshine" to Mama, the way she sang it to me when I was little. Her voice has a way of turning upside down things back to the way they're supposed to be. Mama squeezes my hand.

"Janie, Ma will be leaving pretty soon. I'm counting on you to keep them boys out of my room. Go ahead and send them in for a minute."

I climb down from Mama's bed and motion to my brothers, who are standing outside the door. Kenny has his hand on Benny's shoulder. The boys go into Mama's room, and I walk to the kitchen to get a glass of water. Ma follows me.

"I got to learn you 'bout Bessie's medicines, Janie. She's got to take shots." Ma opens the refrigerator and picks up a glass jar with a lid on it. "This is it. The needle's soaking in alcohol. There's pills in the cupboard for when she gets to having bad pain. Bad pain, Janie, not just pain. You know the difference?"

"Yes, ma'am." But I don't really know much about hurting, unless it's the type of pain that chokes the heart.

♪♫

Ma-Ki

Bessie's lost herself, some of her best ways. Her blaze has done gone out. I ain't able to count all the times I wondered if it's my fault she's given up. I can't leave my daughter how she is, a horse with a broke leg. I stand at the foot of her bed.

"Bessie, I raised a strong girl, and you still got plenty of strength."

"No, Ma. I ain't strong anymore."

"When you were a young'un, you bent all the way to the ground, day upon day, picking them strawberries. You recollect that?"

"Yes, Ma."

"We didn't have no money. I'd notice you plucking ripe berries from the ground into your mouth. You wouldn't need hardly no food at home, that way."

"Sure was a long time ago, Ma."

"Who you were then is part of you now. Hardy. Toted full-size watermelons, so big and heavy they'd bend you over backwards. After a day's work, sweat pouring from your brow, you helped clean the house and cook."

"I ain't a young'un anymore, Ma."

"You ain't old, either. Don't let this thing get a hold of you, daughter. You still got plenty of life in you."

"I feel dead." Bessie sighs and rolls over, hiding her face.

"But you ain't dead! Don't forget where you come from!"

"I'm fallow, Ma!"

"Aw shaw! Recollect your history. The day Mammy and Pappy put you on that Cracker horse. You rode her tall and proud, not needing help from nobody. Our people saw you ride by, and they hollered '*Lhaamin! Lhaamin!* That wild creature and you were one."

"One. Lhaamin means one," Bessie mumbles.

Yes, one. I got to get Bessie to turn upward, to remember who she is. "When you and your horse dashed by, cattails and sawgrass saluted you. They stood still, high and tall. No wind could sway them like you did."

"Ma, quit telling me things it'd be easier to forget." Bessie breaks into crying.

"The wrens, mockingbirds, the warblers all held their breath as you and that horse whisked past them. They would sing, *'Lhaamin!'*"

"I remember." Bessie props herself up on one elbow.

"Bessie, what was your horse's name?"

"River Wind."

"That's right, River Wind. *Hahchi Faplihchi.* River Wind. You were the only one she took to. I watched you ride her, your braids galloping in the air, a mind of their own. Both of you, Bessie, a mind of your own."

"I loved that horse."

"And she loved you."

"Ma, I wish I had a picture of my River Wind." Bessie hoists herself higher, leaning against her pillows.

"You do, Bessie. Her picture lives in your mind. Can you see her?" I watch Bessie close her eyes.

"Yeah, I can." Swales of tears flow from Bessie.

"Ride your Cracker again! Bolt through this sorrow, daughter! You've got powerful Seminole blood flowing through you. We don't surrender. We stand, fight to the end."

"I know it, Ma."

"You're as strong as *Hahchi Faplihchi.* Strong as River Wind. Recollect your power."

"I'm sick, Ma."

"People take advantage of a sick woman, Bessie. No matter how good Willard is, he's a man. Don't stay in this bed any longer than you got to."

"Ahh . . . okay."

Pain medicine lulls Bessie to sleep. Janie's standing right behind me. I take her by the arm and lead her to the front porch.

"Janie, you got a right to be worried about Bessie," I whisper, "but every single thing ain't your business. Sneaking is meant for harm, not good." She hangs her head and puts her face in her hands. "You're strong, too, Janie. Womenfolk need to be."

"Ma, I'm just a girl."

Not for long, Janie.

♪♫

Janie

I've got the husks off most of the corn when Daddy walks in our front door.

"In here, Daddy! I've got a ham sandwich for you."

We take our sandwiches into the front room, only the two of us. Mama, Kenny, and Benny are sleeping.

"I'm going to bed shortly. I'm tuckered out," he says. Daddy picks up his guitar and begins to strum Hank Williams' "A Mansion on the Hill."

"Will you sing the chorus with me, Janie?"

"Daddy, that's one of my favorites."

"I know." He winks at me. Real soft, I sing with him.

"Daddy, I want to live in a mansion one day, like the ones in *Gone with the Wind*." I remember the red staircase in Rhett and Scarlett's home, even though I was a little girl when I saw the movie with Mama. I close my eyes and imagine a big manor, one that doesn't need fieldstones to stop it from leaning or rags in the walls to stop the wind from howling.

"Gal, who are you going to marry that's got money enough for a mansion?" He gets a big kick out of my idea, tilting his head back the way he does when he's good and tickled. Why Daddy finds ideas like this funny is something I don't get.

Keeping my lips zipped, I promise myself I'll never say the word *mansion* again until I have one of my very own.

Seminole strong, I'll keep my dreams to myself.

Chapter 14

School Sentence

Janie

"It's pretty near three miles from our house to your school, but the bus don't come by our house," Daddy explains as we set out for my first day. "Somebody's gonna be there to drive you home today, but I ain't got the details worked out yet. You watch for one of the family."

"Yes, sir."

On the right is a red brick schoolhouse, two stories with a shake roof. It's got a long, narrow wing built onto it.

"Let's go, gal." Daddy leads the way to the office. I read the announcements on the bulletin board while he signs some forms.

"First two classes are English and social studies," says an office lady who has dingy brown hair and eyes. I wonder if some lipstick might perk up her pale face. "You'll have Mr. Brown for both of those courses."

"You talking about Mr. Moody Brown?" Daddy's face gets a soft frown, the space between his eyebrows trying to disappear.

"Yes, Mr. DelChamp," the pale lady says. "After Mr. Brown's class, Janie will go to Mrs. Shepard's class for math and science."

Daddy looks stern until Buster trots in.

"Buster is here to show you to your class, Jane," the lady says. I look back at Daddy, and he winks at me.

Buster takes my arm and pulls me into the hallway. Painted yellow walls have student artwork hanging on them, mostly horses, tractors, trees, flowers, and dogs. I haven't seen nary a house or even a building. The odor of Pine Sol reeks from the walls, and the worn wooden floor creaks. Every time I put my foot forward, it reminds me of something I have to take care of. Kenny. Creak. Benny. Creak. Mama. Creak.

I am not weak. I will not creak.

♩♫

Buster turns to look at me from his desk on the front row. Mr. Moody Brown yanks on his ear.

"Buford, I appreciate your concern for your cousin; however, young man, I will let you know if she needs you. You shall not look at her every whipstitch. If you do not understand, we shall have a meeting: you, me, and a paddle."

Buford. His real name tickles me. No wonder Buster goes by a nickname. I glue my eyes to my books, but now and then I think about sneaking a look at the teacher. He's wearing a red-and-blue plaid bowtie, a white shirt, and thick glasses with black rims. His neck and face look real pink, pretty near red, next to his white collar, like his tie is choking him. I keep waiting for him to run out of air and turn blue.

The bell signals it's time for phys-ed, and Buster's the first one out the door. I race to catch up with him.

"Buford."

"Don't get started with that mess, Janie." And without skipping a beat, Buster changes the subject. "Hey, on Wednesdays we have music class. Our teacher plays music with us once in a while."

"A music teacher?"

"Yep. Her ole man, Matthew Bailey, used to coach football in Wylie until he got crippled up in a bad car wreck. Now he's in a wheelchair. I reckon she ain't got nothing else to do but sing with us."

"Does her husband come with her?"

"Sometimes." Buster lets out an exaggerated sigh. "Janie, point is, I told Mrs. Bailey you sing near about as good as me."

"Near about?"

"Got you good, huh?"

"No, *Buford*." I break into a run with a wild coyote cousin chasing after me.

♫♪

After lunch, Mrs. Bailey wheels a black Baldwin piano into our classroom.

"I hear we have a new student," she says, smoothing her blonde hair. It's swept up on the back of her neck all pretty like Doris Day's. She points at me. "Young lady, would you join me?"

"Up front?" I know I sound stupid.

"Please."

"Let's begin with 'America the Beautiful.'"

O beautiful for spacious skies, For amber waves of grain.

Singing makes me forget I'm the new girl, in front of kids who would make fun of me if they knew about our leaning house. Mrs. Bailey's alto voice harmonizes with my soprano melody.

"Our voices blend together splendidly, Janie. Don't you think so, class?"

For a second, one person claps, and then the whole room goes wild with applause. One boy in the back hoots and hollers. I feel a big grin exploding on my face. But one thing I know is this: no matter how good I sing, these kids can't ever find out where I live.

♪♫

The last school bus drives by, and only the teachers' cars are left in the parking lot.

"Well, bitin' bass, Janie. Rose ain't out here. I'd walk you home, but it's a pretty far piece," Buster says.

"Somebody'll be here. Don't worry. You go on."

"I'll wait with you."

"Janie!" a woman's voice yells out.

"There's Rose," Buster says, pointing towards the parking lot. "I'll see you tomorrow," he says, breaking into a run.

In Ma's car, Rose drives my way. I climb in and put my books on the rusty floorboard.

"How was your first day, Janie?"

"I sang with Mrs. Bailey, our music teacher, at the front of the class. Do you know her, Rose?"

"I think so. But if she's who I think she is, she doesn't sing nearly as pretty as you." Rose keeps her eyes on the road.

"Hey, Rose . . . how do you like being married to Uncle Percy?"

Her smile disappears. "It sure feels good to have somebody for keeps. And now I'm your aunt. Did you know I thank God for a niece like you?"

"You do?"

"I do."

Great day in Green Cove! I've never thanked God for anything. And I forget to keep my promise to Him about praying. Looking out the window and up at the clouds, I wonder where He lives.

"Janie? Maybe me and you could sing together some Friday night. Pick a song, okay?"

We pull up to the leaning house, and the twins run out to the front porch, waving and pushing each other.

"Okay, I'll think of a real good song, Rose. Right now I have to play with my brothers." I rush to check on Mama, but Kenny stops me at the foot of the steps.

"Mama losted another little baby," he tells Rose.

"I'm real sorry about your mama and the baby, Kenny, real sorry," Rose says. She leans over and hugs his waist. Benny runs through the yard.

"Stop in the name of the law!" he yells out, chasing an imaginary bank robber, using his fingers like he has a gun. I walk up the steps and discover something good. If I look at how bad the house leans hard enough, I barely notice the way the steps creak.

♪♫

"When you diagram a sentence, start by identifying its subject," Mr. Moody Brown says. His chalk scrapes the blackboard. "Remember, the subject will be a noun. Now class, who can tell me what a noun is?"

Nouns. Dinner. Mama. Twins. Mop. Floor. Eyes. Mine won't stay open.

Mr. Moody Brown stands over me, wearing a red bow tie a shade or two darker than his face. The kids sitting in front of me have turned around in their desks, looking at me and sniggering. But Buster doesn't laugh, not even a smirk.

"Jane DelChamp, are you aware of the rule, no sleeping allowed in school?" Mr. Moody Brown clenches his jaws real hard. I can picture his front teeth crumbling, flying out of his mouth, and jamming into my face, like the Pinter boy's teeth that got stuck in the wall of Junior's Dance Hall. I nod my head, too ashamed to say nary a word.

"Answer me. Yes or no."

"Yes, sir." *If I get in trouble at school, I'll be in trouble all over again when I get home.*

"Perhaps standing in the corner will help you to remain awake." He waves his hand, and I walk to a back corner. I hear some kids laughing at me.

"The lil' singer ain't gonna get away with sleeping!" Buster yells out for the whole class to hear.

I'm really in big trouble now, my own cousin making fun of me. Everybody else will, too.

"Buford, the front corner. Right now!" shouts Mr. Moody Brown. Buster jumps up and runs to his assigned spot and pokes his neck backward and forward like a woodpecker striking a tree. The class busts apart with giggling, and he shakes his hind-end around. But when Mr. Moody Brown picks up the paddle, quiet drops over the room.

"One! Two! Three!" The teacher drives hard strikes onto Buster's rear end. Nobody's laughing now.

Buster's taken the blame for me before. When I was eight years old, I broke Daddy's brand new rod and reel. Daddy wouldn't let me touch it. When he was busy working under his car, I went out to the back porch, picked up his fishing gear, and started pretending I was catching a big bass. I tossed out the line, and it grabbed a bush in the yard, tangling up the wire. Daddy got ready to go fishing when he got done with the car. His face went as red as a stripe on as a barbershop pole when he found his gear.

"Who's gone and tore up my rod and reel?" Daddy hollered, taking off his belt.

"I did," Buster claimed.

"You?" Daddy cut his eyes at me, like he knew the truth.

"Yes, sir. Me. I ain't got no right," Buster lies.

My breath stopped. I didn't have the guts to tell the truth. Daddy handed his belt to Ma. She switched my cousin. He never yelped or cried. *No wonder Buster runs from me.*

♪♫

When phys-ed time gets here, Buster won't look up. Walking all by himself, he stares at the ground, his hands balled into the pockets of his thin jacket. He must be pretty near freezing because I'm wearing my new coat plus a sweater on underneath it, and I am shivering.

"Buster, could you help me with this equipment?" Mrs. Long, the phys-ed teacher yells out.

"Yes, ma'am." Buster hurries over to Mrs. Long's side.

"Janie?" calls a voice from behind me. A skinny girl, who has long stringy brown hair, stands behind me. Her face looks funny because her eyes are way too close together. Then she smiles and looks a whole lot better.

"Hi. What's your name?" I try to smile at her.

"Zelda. You don't remember me, Janie?" Her smile starts to fade. "Back from first grade?"

"No kidding? Zelda!" She didn't say nary a word back then. "Mrs. Johnson's class."

"Yeah." Zelda's pretty smile doesn't cover up her pitiful clothes. She's got on a mustard-colored shirtwaist dress with a red sweater. It's too small, and the sleeves barely cover her elbows.

"Great day in Green Cove, Zelda. We sure have grown." I think of what Zelda's house might look like, and judging on what she's wearing, it can't be good.

"Yep, we're big girls now, ain't we, Janie? Teenagers. You must have little brothers and sisters?"

"Yeah, brothers."

"I have five. I'm the oldest. You ain't the only girl who Mr. Brown's put in the corner for sleeping." A cold wind whips Zelda's dress pretty hard. She hugs herself.

"Really?" I hope none of her sisters have to wear Zelda's hand-me-downs.

"Yeah. Me and a couple of other girls have got in trouble with Mr. Brown before."

From out of nowhere, a rock hits Zelda's back. Some kids from our class huddle a few feet away from us, laughing. Any one of them could have thrown it. I wait for Zelda to cry or flinch. She closes her eyes and stays quiet.

"Why are they picking on you, Zelda?"

She shrugs her shoulders. "They do that sometimes."

"Didn't the rock hurt you?"

"A little . . . mostly hurt my feelings." Her voice cracks.

The brisk winds rustle the oak tree leaves. House wrens, perched in their branches, sing their sweet, choppy song. Zelda tugs at her sleeves, but they won't reach her wrists. I unbutton my coat.

"Zelda, why don't you wear this until we go back inside? You look downright cold to me."

"You sure about that, Janie?"

"I'm sure." *I am?* She reaches for my coat.

"You wear my sweater. Then you'll have two."

Wearing Zelda's raggedy sweater is a good way to get a rock in my back, too.

"All right." I take my sweater off real quick and put Zelda's on underneath it. Her tight red sweater disappears under my navy blue one.

Zelda smiles again. The coat has stopped her from shaking, and my coat helps her blend in with the rest of us.

"Janie, you just made a friend for keeps."

I hope it hasn't cost me a coat.

♪♫

Rose

"Buster! You want to ride?" I call to him, but he shakes his head and runs from me. "Have you seen Janie?" I call. He keeps on, not looking back.

A sign near the new wing of the school says *office.* Maybe Janie is waiting for me there. Standing behind a wooden counter, a bald man with a pockmarked face ogles my bosom, and his eyes travel down my body and get fixed on my flat belly.

"Hey. I'm here to pick up Janie DelChamp, but she ain't outside."

"Young *lady*," he says, just a gritting his teeth, "could you wait for her in the car? We'll send her out."

Two secretaries, their faces wrenched with smirks, stare at me, too. "You know she *had* to get married," the older woman says, right to my face.

"Why else would Percy Ebbing marry *her?*" the younger woman hints. Their laughter taints the air.

I've got a good notion to smack them, like Momma slapped me. My blood burns, a boiling up into my cheeks. Heat pops out all over me, covering my face with beads of sweat. My fists curl up so hard my knuckles hurt. I hold my head up high and walk out. Janie runs through the parking lot, waving at me and smiling. Every time I look into her sea blue eyes, I hope me and Percy have a girl like her.

♪♫

Buster

"Read the note aloud, Buster," Ma says.

"Dear Mrs. Ebbing: Buford received three swats with the paddle today due to his misbehavior. Please discuss with him the consequences of disrupting class. Thank you. Moody Brown."

"Tarnation, Buster!" Ma shakes her finger near about my left eye.

"Ma, I'm sorry. I'll get Percy's old belt, so you can go on and whip me." My rear still stings from this morning.

"Buster, you ain't been in trouble in a long time. Now you're ready to bring me a belt. It don't make sense. Son, I suspect this has something to do with Janie. What went on today?"

"Ma, it ain't her fault. She fell asleep when Mr. Brown was diagramming sentences. Please don't tell Uncle Willard."

"Well, I'm gonna have to tell. That young'uns got too much weight sitting on her shoulders. I'll talk to Willard, and she ain't about to get in trouble. Just how did this 'disrupting' happen?"

"Mr. Brown sent her to the corner . . . the class was hootin'. Ma, I . . ."

"You acted plumb crazy to get the blame. Right?"

"Yes, ma'am."

"Let's head over to Bessie's house," Ma says.

♪♫

Janie sits on the front porch, watching Kenny and Benny arm wrestling. Her hair sticks out in near about every direction, and her face is tore up by a frown.

"Boys, you want a piggyback ride?" I holler. Kenny and Benny like to have run each other over trying to get to me.

"Ma's face says she's mad," Janie says.

"It'll be all right, Janie."

"Buster, you saved me today, but you didn't have to. I was the one who fell asleep."

"Bitin' bass, Janie. I've had a whole lot worse than three licks." Janie perks right up.

"No kidding? How many?"

"It weren't exactly licks, Janie."

"What was it, then?" She leans toward me, and I take a step back. "Come on, Janie! I ain't got to tell you everything."

"Why not, Buster?"

Last time Janie saw me cry, Pistol was near about dead. Most anybody would cry over their dog, but I don't want her to see me squalling again. "It was Maggie. She was drunk. She beat me all over with an extension cord."

Janie's mouth drops open, and her face goes plumb gray. "*Maggie* beat you? Why?"

"She was mad at Ma and took it out on me, I reckon."

"Were you at her house?"

"Naw. I was outside at mine. She came out of the house with a cord and switched me till Percy heard me screaming."

"I'm sorry, Buster." Janie's eyes are full of tears.

"Janie, promise you ain't never going to bring it up, to me or nobody. All right?"

"I won't, Buster."

"First one to tag Ma's car is the winner." I elbow Janie in her side, catching her off guard. She tumbles down the porch steps. I slap the passenger door and run on back to help her up.

♪♫

Janie

"Willard, it don't matter that we just got here," Mama wails, waking me up from a good sleep. "I can't stay in this house another cotton pickin' minute. We're way on the other end of town from Ma. If I need to, I'll leave you and the young'uns and go live there."

"I'll fix it," Daddy says.

"That cabbage field out back stinks, and this house is about to fall on its side. Birds are nesting in the gap in the fireplace."

"I said I'll fix it, Bessie," Daddy says. "Did I ever tell you 'I'll fix it' before and not do it?"

Mama hushes.

♪♫

Mama's still quiet at breakfast. Daddy hands me a sealed-up envelope with Mr. Moody Brown's name on it.

"Janie, your teacher owns this here house and a whole lot of other things in Bradford County. Did you know that?"

"No, sir."

"He runs a potato business. I reckon that's how come he teaches, so he can be off work in the summer. And this here letter's about his business affairs. It ain't about school," Daddy says. "Ma told us about you sleeping in class yesterday."

"Daddy, I didn't mean . . ."

"I suppose you couldn't help it, gal. From here on out, Ma'll be here mornings, and Rose'll carry you home from school. She'll help you fix supper."

I lean over and kiss him on the cheek. When I pull back, he winks at me. The strong smell of coffee rises from Daddy's cup. I put on my coat, ready for another one of Mr. Moody Brown's sentences.

Chapter 15

Crazy Heart

Rose

Driving down the dirt roads to Momma and Papa's house, the car radio belts out Hank Williams' "Crazy Heart." The sound cuts out, and I smack the dash. Hank's voice ain't enough, though, to stop me from a thinking about how Momma threw me out. My blisters have near about healed, but my heart ain't anywhere close to it.

I park alongside the old house, near the back porch where Homer is a slicing oranges. Ruth squeezes their juice into empty milk bottles, and the sweet citrus smell fills the air. Tinkering with Mama's old wringer, Joe and Lonnie don't bother looking up. Kathryn sings "London Bridge Is Falling Down" in the backyard, with Betsy, Grace, Mark, and Mickey. Papa shimmies hisself out from under his car. He's a greasy mess.

"Hey, Rosie!" calls Betsy. Roger, Mark, Grace, Mickey, and Kathryn wave to me. I hurry their way, my arms spread wide.

"Percy's gone and sent you back, huh?" My brother Joe ain't a smiling, so I guess he thinks so.

"No, it ain't nothing like that." I stop and clamp my arms down to my sides. "I just wanted to come see y'all."

Momma walks out the kitchen door and crosses her arms. Joe, Homer, and Ruth form a line with her, like they're building a wall around theirselves. *Sometimes I hate Momma.* But I always love her.

"I wanted to come see y'all and invite you to church."

Momma glares at me. Papa, who's leaning against the porch, hangs his head. She don't move but keeps on staring. I take a deep breath like I'm ready to sing a solo. "I got good news. I went to Thankful Country Church and gave my heart to Jesus."

"I wanna go!" Roger says.

"Take me, too, Rosie," says Grace.

"Rose, I'm gonna walk you to your car now," Papa says. I follow him six or seven steps until we're at the driver's door. Papa talks low, almost a whisper.

"It ain't right for a girl in your fix to act so happy. Don't come around here smiling. It ain't right for your little brothers and sisters, thinking they can do what you done and things'll turn out good.

"But Papa . . ."

"Next time, I'm expecting you to act like somebody who's full of shame. You hear?"

I yank the handle of the car door, hop into the driver's seat, and roll the window down. Papa's already turned his back. "How about me taking Grace and Roger to church?" I holler.

"It just ain't fittin' yet. Give it time, Rosie," Papa says. I start the car, put it in neutral, and pump the brake. I stick my head out the window.

"I love you, Momma!" She keeps a walking like she ain't heard me. At least she ain't slapping me.

♪♫

Sister Daisy opens her door, wearing a pink bib apron with red stains on it. The smell of spaghetti sauce hits me, making my stomach feel a little queasy.

"Rose, how good to see you. What brings you out this way?"

"I went over to see my family."

"Your mother and father?" She closes the door behind me.

"Yes, ma'am. I wanted to invite them to church."

"I see." Sister Daisy points to the couch. "I was delighted to witness your baptism." She sits down next to me.

"Something real special happened when I went under the water."

"Tell me about it." Sister Daisy reaches for my hand.

"I felt like a river was a flowing through me. My shame got washed away." Some tears break loose.

"Rose, that's wonderful. But I suspect the visit with your family was upsetting." Sister Daisy takes a white Kleenex from a box on an end table and hands it to me.

"They don't want me. Papa told me not to come back around." I hug my stomach, almost like I'm trying to stop my baby from feeling sad like me.

"Oh, dear." Sister Daisy's brown eyes get watery. She opens her Bible and starts to flip through its pages. "Romans Eight, verse one says there is no condemnation, Rose, to those of us who have given our hearts to Jesus."

"No condemnation?" I'm way too embarrassed to tell Sister Daisy about how I don't understand.

"Right. No judgment, no reason to feel guilty, Rose. Listen to verse two. For the law of the Spirit of life in Christ Jesus hath made me free from the law of sin and death."

"Does that mean *I'm* free?"

"Yes, you are free. You are walking after the Spirit."

"Walking where, Sister Daisy?"

"Seeking the Spirit of the Lord."

"I'm doing my best."

"Rose, I love you." She wraps her arms around me, and I feel safer than ever before.

♪♫

Ma-Ki

Bessie, mourning day after day, rips skin clean off my nerves. Still staring into space this morning and squalling, she is.

"I've lost three babies, Ma."

"You got three left, Bessie. Don't go forgetting them. Every last one of them needs a mother."

"Ma, you don't know what it's like." She rolls over, hiding her face from me.

"We all got our sorrows. Two of them babies never came to full bloom. Spirits never got planted. But Tommy died in this family's meadow, a perfect blossom. A beauty like him can live only so long. Bessie, rouse yourself. Put your life into them three who still breathe."

"Ma, I'm tired. Give me some peace."

Times like this, I miss my own mother, her way of accepting bad and appreciating good. Most of all, her wisdom. After Bessie's twins were born, I sent for my sisters, but no word come back. Been wondering since if they're dead or gone way into the Seminole camp, too far back to hunt down.

Twins, *thunder and lightning.* Awful bad luck hit Bessie quick when them boys were born. I ain't told my young'uns about how the Seminoles separated twin boys, weren't allowed to stay together. One had to go to another family or be killed soon as he was birthed. Who could we find to raise one of them twins? And I reckon it's too late now. Bessie's heart has done gone crazy. Secrets of our dying breed, times like this, they spear through me.

I got to get Bessie strong enough to stand against a raging storm.

The cypress chifforobe that once belonged to my mother stands tall and wide in my bedroom. Long ago my *táàte,* my pa, gathered wood for it. Mother, my *wáàche,* touched its smooth cypress doors with her own hands. I run my hand over it, recollecting how Burl oiled and shined it.

"Ma?" Rose stands at my open door. "Is everything all right? I thought you were at Bessie's."

"Yep, but I had Willard bring me home." Comes a time when people want to be left alone. "Come on in."

Rose perches on my bed. "I went to see Momma and Papa."

"How did that go?"

"They don't want me around, Ma."

"Well, I do, Rose. Y'all can stay as long as you want, even after the baby comes. I got a lot to teach you. Percy ain't good with money. Not ready for marriage and he ain't fixin' to change overnight. But I seen him look at you with a light in his eyes, so don't give up."

"I've seen that light, too." She smooths her hand across the sawtooth quilt I made with my sisters. I sit down, across from her. "Ma, I want to be a good wife to Percy. These past few days, I've been changed."

"You're a good girl, Rose, and you got a right to be happy."

"Ma, I feel so pure and light. My sins are forgiven."

Sins. I done had a bad day, and now Percy's young wife wants to change my way of thinking about her God.

"Uh huh."

"Ma, I have a river of peace running through me."

I got to stop this, now. "Rose, the only spirits I know are the ones my granny, mother, and pa taught me. I believe *Hisakitamisi,* the Master of Breath, lives beyond the sky." I point to the ceiling.

"Yes, ma'am." Rose leans back, steadying herself.

"Some people say *Hisakitamis* has a son named Jesus. They say Jesus let people kill him to prove his love."

"Oh, yes, ma'am!" She's halfway off the bed.

"I don't know Jesus, Rose. Don't expect I ever will. I been believing some things too long to change."

She backs herself onto my bed, getting away from my index finger. It ain't unusual for people to act like I'm gonna poke them in the eye.

"Yes, ma'am."

"I knowed people who wanted me to 'get saved.' I reckon I already am saved, making it this far in life. But I'm happy for you, Rose."

"Okay, Ma." Rose's lip trembles.

"I think you'll make Percy a right good wife. Just don't go stirring up trouble here about religion, and everything'll be all right."

"Yes, ma'am. Good night, Ma."

"Good night, Rose." I hear her climbing the stairs with hurry in her step, and the door to Percy's room opens.

"What else you fixing to want from me, Rose?" Percy hollers, his voice trailing into my room. "You think you can drag me to church like I'm an old, sorry bull? No!"

"Percy, I ain't trying to force you!"

Love blooms from two enemy tribes.

♫

Rose

"Aw, honey. I didn't mean it last night. I was hurting. Drive my car to church," Percy says.

"I'd rather walk!"

"Look. I ain't goin' anywhere this morning."

"No."

"Rosie, I ain't letting my wife walk when she don't have to. Remember them blisters of yours?" Percy crosses our bedroom and stands behind me. He wraps his arms around my waist and kisses my neck. That's one surefire way of making me forget about church.

"You sure you want me to drive the car, Percy?"

"Yep, darlin', I do."

♫

More than two dozen cars sit in the parking lot of the Thankful Country Church. Women hurry by with their young'uns, and some have their husbands with them, too. Old couples hobble along together, but I ain't seen anybody alone. *Dear Lord, help me fit in here.*

"Rose!" Sister Daisy waves to me from the church yard.

"We've been waiting for you," she says. "Rose, I'd like you to meet Sister Thelma Green." Thelma's brown hair is salted with gray. Like her name, she's wearing a green car coat, a green dress, and green shoes. She smiles at me, strong and wide.

"Nice to meet you, Rose," Thelma says. "Sister Daisy has said some really nice things about you." She holds out her hand for me to shake.

Once we get inside, I slip into a back pew. Sister Daisy and Thelma ain't noticed I'm not behind them anymore. Thelma looks back over her shoulder and motions for me to sit with her, but I shake my head and smile.

From the piano, Sister Daisy asks the congregation to stand and leads a song, "Just a Closer Walk with Thee."

I am weak, but Thou art strong,

Jesus, keep me from all wrong.

"Our new sister in the Lord, Rose Ebbing," Brother Little calls from the pulpit. I didn't notice the whole congregation had sit down. I'm the only one in the church standing up besides the preacher, and everybody turns to look at me. My face stings, my knees start a wobbling, and my jaw drops open. I sit down quick.

"Rose is a wonderful musician. Come join me, Rose," Sister Daisy calls from the piano.

Sister Daisy! Why are you doing this to me?

People start clapping, and I've got a good notion to run out the door, but I walk to the platform. *My sins are forgiven.* Brother Little hands me a guitar, and Sister Daisy starts playing "Somebody Touched Me." I close my eyes, strum the guitar, and sing with her.

"Amen!" shouts someone in the crowd.

I can feel that river of peace, just a rushing through me.

"Rosie, why don't you hurry up with your cleaning?" Percy hobbles into the kitchen, smiling at me. "Help me go for a walk. I got to get my strength back."

I hurry up with the last couple of pans. The smell of fried chicken and biscuits is still in the air. I grab a fresh towel, a wiping down the front of my skirt where the dishwater splashed.

"Percy, I'm real proud to be part of your family." We ease down the front steps, and I wave to Buster and Pistol.

"Me, too, baby. Glad you're one of us." He turns to Buster. "We're walking part ways to the fishing hole. Think you can beat us?"

Buster charges ahead, Pistol barking by his side. Buster throws his softball to Percy and barely misses him.

"Boy, I ain't ready for that yet."

"You ain't ever going to be ready for me, Percy," Buster says. He and Pistol run to the pond, but me and Percy turn back around.

"Walking's rougher than I thought," Percy whispers. I hold my arm tight around his waist, climbing back up the stairs.

"How are you going to work like this, Percy?"

"Light duty, Rosie."

"What does that mean?"

"I ain't sure. But will you bring my guitar out to the porch?"

"Sure will." I race to our room, grabbing Percy's flattop Gibson.

"Thank you, honey." He strums a couple of chords and smiles, "I can't go back to work without serenading my bride." Then he starts singing Tennessee Ernie Ford's "Shotgun Boogie." Singing about a boy being chased with a shotgun, Percy winks at me. He gives me another big smile when he winds up the song.

"I wasn't figuring on getting married, Rosie, but I'd rather be married to you than anybody, even the first lady of country music, Kitty Wells." He puts the guitar on the floor and props it against the wall. Percy pats his knee. I walk over, put my arm around his neck, and real careful sit on the edge of his chair.

"Percy, I ain't a honky tonk angel anymore."

"I know it, baby." He kisses the back of my neck. "You're a married woman."

I ain't had a day sweeter than this one. My heart beats a little faster, a letting me know how happy it is.

Chapter 16

Movin' On

Janie

Great day in Green Cove. I could've walked with Buster to his house if I'd have known nobody would show up to carry me home. Hoping Rose will pick me up along the way, I trudge on toward the leaning house. The winter sun beats down. Singing ought to help make this walk go by faster. *You are my sunshine. . . .*

I take off my new coat, fold it over my arm, and wipe the bubbles of sweat off the top of my upper lip. *Eh a ha! Eh a ha! Jolie Blonde my tea feet crinoline. . . .*

A big, mean-looking dog runs toward me, about to bark his head off, until an old lady runs out her front door and calls her back. I break into a sprint, knowing I'll be home in a couple of minutes.

I hope Mama is all right.

♪♫

Rose

Pain rips through my woman parts and all the way down my legs. I downshift Ma's car, but working the clutch makes the cramps worse. I pull off the road, put the gears in neutral, and turn off the motor. Am I losing my baby the same way Bessie did? *Dear God, no. Please let this young'un be all right.*

I pull my green skirt around, check for blood, but I'm dry and clean. Maybe I can make it to the school to pick Janie up. Another pang clutches me. I lay myself down across the front seat. I draw my legs up, hug my stomach, and bundle my coat under my head.

I try to fight the blackness, but it ain't no use. *Lord, please keep my baby safe.*

♪♫

Janie

What's happened to Mama now? She won't stay home without nary a car, even though the doctor won't let her drive. Daddy's been catching a ride to work with his friend. Now his truck is gone instead of where he left it. Something is wrong.

I race up the porch steps, open the front door, and the front room is empty. Running through the house, I look for proof we live here. Out on the back porch sit some of our things: an old dresser drawer, some lamps, an end table, and Mama's best dishes. Taped to the wheelbarrow is a note. I snatch it up and read Mama's handwriting: *Take these things to the dump if you can't use them.*

I walk back inside like I am in a slow-motion movie. The wood floors are a little damp, a sure sign Mama has cleaned a house and moved on. Then my heart jumps, giving me a scare all its own. The fieldstones are still in the house. The one in the front room has a note on it, again in Mama's handwriting: *These stones will stop this house from leaning one day.* I check the front windowsill and see the key to the house sitting in it. I feel sick, real sick. Mama and Daddy have moved without me. I walk out to the front porch and sit down on the steps, trying to breathe. My heart chokes.

Bad trouble like this makes me think about promises I've made, the ones I haven't kept. I never said those prayers every night like I gave my word to God. *I wonder if He'll listen to me now.*

I push the wheelbarrow with Mama's dishes in it real slow and careful. I tucked my coat around them for padding, trying to make sure they don't chip. Pretty near half a mile from the leaning house, a car looking like Aunt Maggie's Buick heads in my direction. "Hey!" I jump up and wave my arms in the air. "Help!" Aunt Maggie pulls off the side of the road. A cigarette hangs from her lips, and her car smells like sour mash, like blueberries that rotted in the sun. At least there's a good song on her radio, Hank Snow and the Rainbow Ranch boys sing "I'm Movin' On."

"What is wrong with you?" She takes a big puff from her cigarette.

"Mama and Daddy packed and moved without me." *Don't choke*, I tell myself. "They're gone . . . I don't know where."

"What? Now that beats all I've ever heard." She throws her cigarette on the ground. "What's in the wheelbarrow?"

"Mama forgot her dishes."

Aunt Maggie motions for me. "Get in. I'll take you over to Ma's." She hops out of the car and pops her trunk. I help her arrange the dishes. "I ain't got room for this." She points to the wheelbarrow. "Willard'll need to get it with his truck."

I get in the front seat, next to her, nodding. I don't care about an old wheelbarrow.

"Maggie, do you know where Rose is?"

"Nope." She takes a sip from a bottle of coke tucked in between her knees.

I close my eyes and think about Zelda. Mama's always told me there's somebody who is worse off than me. Zelda had on her mustard dress again today. Every time she wears it, she looks sick, like somebody who just got out of quarantine for tuberculosis.

Aunt Maggie stomps her brake pedal. "Would you look at that?" She points to Daddy's truck. He's hauling our kitchen table into a house.

"Are we moving to this house?"

"Yep, looks that way," Maggie says, pulling into the yard. "Bessie!" she hollers. "You and Willard forget something? About a hundred pounds of your load?"

Mama looks at me. Her lips tremble and her eyebrows arch like two rainbows.

"Janie, I was going to send for you," she says.

Looking at Mama hurts my heart. I bite my lip, get out of the Buick, and take a good look at the outside of the house. Smaller than the last place and trimmed in white, it sits real high up off the ground. It stands straight. No leaning. No big cracks to let the wind howl.

I don't have to worry now about what the kids at school will say if they see where I live. But something makes me feel worse. Deep down, in a scary place in my heart, I wonder if Mama and Daddy planned to bring me with them. I remember the notes Mama wrote and think about one she might have written to pin on me.

This girl will sing to you and take good care of your young'uns.

♫

Rose

The smell of meatloaf, creamed corn, and turnips drifts up from the back seat, reminding me I'm in Ma's car. I'm supposed to be picking up Janie. I've got to take Bessie and them this food me and Ma cooked.

I try to force my eyes open, but they aim to stay clamped shut. There's a melody a coming from somewhere, words I ain't understanding even a wee bit. Light floods in, chasing the darkness away. The singing stops, but a river surges through me, a burbling my name. It's like I'm being baptized all over again.

Rose. Rose. I AM with you.

♫

Janie

The late afternoon air comes up through the floor, circling my legs and traveling up my rear end. Pine knots have given way to the strain of people walking across them. This house has holes in its bottom.

"Woah!" Kenny yells out. He squats down over the floor with a piece of honey bun in his hand. After he pinches off a piece, he reaches for a hole and drops some of his goody into it.

A muffled "Bawk! Bawk!" comes from under the house.

Kenny claps. Benny stomps. I look through two holes so close together, they look like one big hole. Below it, three chickens walking around on the ground under our floorboards. Great day in Green Cove, these two boys are going to get in big trouble.

"Be careful, boys," I tell them. "Those chickens could bite your fingers off. You hear?"

Outside, a horn honks as a truck from Badcock Furniture pulls to the front of our house. Daddy helps the delivery man haul in a General Electric "Black Daylite" television in an oak cabinet.

"Mama, Mama!" I run to Mama's side. "Daddy's bought us a television!" She jumps out of bed and walks into the front room.

"Ah, Willard," she says, cupping her hand over her mouth.

"You're still my girl, Bessie. Always will be," Daddy says. "Where do you want me to put it?"

"Right there," Mama says, pointing to a spot across from the fireplace in the front room. Daddy turns the television on and dials the knob. A man who sounds like Little Jimmy Dickens is singing "Echo of Your Footsteps." His cowboy hat is pretty near big as he is, so I figure it's got to be Little Jimmy.

I wonder if Mama will like watching television as much as she likes dancing.

♪♫

Rose

"Hooooooonkkkkkk!" The horn blasts loud and long. This car ain't moving, so it must be aimed at somebody else.

My eyelids flicker a bit, then open halfway. The pain, so bad I had to stop driving, is gone. The best singing I've ever heard must have been a dream, smack dab in the middle of me a hurting. I open the car door, swing my legs out onto the grass, and stand up.

Dear God, don't let this baby die. I run my hand over my belly, feeling a wee bit of swell. We're all right. Yes, we are.

Janie

I run out to greet Rose. She smiles at me but looks pale. Her eyes have dark circles under them.

"Rose, where were you after school?" I get right to the point.

"I had a little bit of trouble on my way to the school, Janie. I'm sorry." She's trying to balance an orange bowl in one hand and an aluminum baking pan in another.

I reach for the bowl. "Did you have some kind of trouble?"

"It's all right now, Janie," she whispers.

I've got a lot of secrets to figure out.

Chapter 17

Down in the Valley

Janie

"Bessie, we're ready for you," Daddy yells out. But Mama doesn't stir. A good-looking young man with black wavy hair is fussing with Sergeant Joe Friday on "Dragnet," and he's got Mama's full attention.

On the front porch, Aunt Dora warbles out "Tennessee Waltz." Rose sings backup and plays the guitar. A tall, brown-headed man named Buzzy picks the banjo, joining her on the chorus. When the moonlight hits him just right, it shows the pocked marks on Buzzy's face. Uncle Percy strums his mandolin. Pickup trucks and cars are parked along our front and side yards.

"Wind 'er up, Dora," Daddy says when he sees me step onto the porch. She keeps singing, and he points his index finger in the air and makes a circle with it. Dora shuffles around and goes real, great day in Green Cove, *real flat* on a G note, and slaps her hands onto her hips.

Daddy stands up and walks to the edge of the porch. "Everybody who don't know it," Daddy yells out, "this is my girl Janie. Janie, how about 'Salty Dog?'"

He takes a seat in a ladderback chair with a rush bottom, playing guitar while I stand next to him. I sing the melody, and Daddy sings harmony.

Onions and pickles laying in a bed.

One rolled over and the other one said,

'Honey let me be your salty dog!'

"What do y'all think of this little gal?" Daddy yells to the crowd.

"Janie! Janie!" people shout, jumping to their feet. Hands clap. Teeth, fingers, and mouths whistle. Fists drum the hoods of cars. I curtsy but jump a little when I feel a hand on my shoulder. Mama is standing behind me.

"You ready to sing, Bessie?" Daddy wants to know. Mama nods her head and walks to the edge of the porch. Her hair falls in knots from a silver comb. She's got on old bedroom slippers with their toes cut out, and her sapphire blue dress shows wrinkles.

"Yep. All I want's the harmonica," Mama says. She looks around at Uncle Percy, and he whips one from his pocket.

Roses love sunshine, violets love dew

Angels in heaven, know I love you.

Like a house wren, crying for a fledgling that's been snatched by a hawk, Mama croons.

Down in the valley the valley so low

Hang your head over, hear the wind blow.

Mama's voice, so perfect and high, rises through the night wind and touches the stars. With every note, they twinkle a little brighter.

Build me a castle, forty feet high,

So I can see him, as he rides by.

Mama leans her head to one side and wraps her right arm around the front of her waist. The crowd is quiet, like if someone breathes too loud, they'll break her spell.

Will you be mine, dear? Will you be mine . . . ?

Send me a letter, if you'll be mine.

Mama sings the last notes. The night rests, not even a cricket chirping. Nobody makes a sound. The quiet lasts a few seconds, and then the crowd goes crazy.

"Bessie! Bessie! Miz Ebbing!" voices yell out, fists shake in the air, and hands pass a hat jangling with coins. Mama curtsies and walks back inside of the house. Through the window, I can see her outline. She bends over, picks up one of the twins, and sits in a rocker in front of the television.

"Beautiful! More, Bessie," call some of the folks outside. "Sing us another one!" But she stays inside, not moving from the chair.

Daddy and Buzzy pick up fiddles from an old pine coffee table, and Percy puts his harmonica to his lips. When Daddy begins to sing the first lines of "Jolie Blonde," one of the couples snuggle up to each other and waltz around the front yard.

"Janie!" yells out Buster, who's perched on the hood of Ma's car. I climb up next to him. "Betcha there's a ruckus coming any minute."

"A ruckus? Over what?"

"Dora sings that song, *Down in the Valley.* She wants Buzzy to think she's got the best voice in the world." Buster lies down on the hood, hoots, and slaps his ribs.

"You mean Aunt Dora's sweet on Buzzy?"

"Been that way since I can remember. He's over yonder, waiting."

Buzzy leans upside the cab of his truck, smoking a cigarette.

"For her?"

Dora stomps out of our house, slamming the door. She stops at the top step, pats her long hair, and runs her hands down her thighs.

"Huh! All this time I figured Dora was way too mean to like somebody." I laugh, almost loud enough for other people to hear me.

"Nope, just too mean for somebody to like her."

Aunt Dora strolls over to Buzzy's truck, softly singing. "Will you be mine, dear? Will you be mine?"

♩♫

Looking around for a place to put the clean dishes, I wonder why nobody built wall cupboards in this house. There's nary a spot for Mama's good dishes. When I got them here, I packed them good in some newspaper and put them into a brown box.

Back when we lived in Green Cove, Mama chipped one of the plates. She called Daddy into the kitchen. "Willard, look a here." She held the plate up, running her finger along the cracked deep blue rim. "I busted it. Can you fish that chip out of the dishwater? Maybe we can glue it back together." Slow tears ran down Mama's cheek, and she held up her arm and wiped them into the top of her sleeve.

"Back away, Bessie." Daddy worked on emptying the water, slow and easy and took the dishes out. He didn't say nary a word but walked over to Mama, who was sitting at the table. "This here should do it."

That evening, Daddy glued the missing pieces into Mama's plate while she sat in the front room with Tommy. By the time he got done, it was hard to see the break. I walked to the table to look over his shoulder.

"Daddy, why don't you and Mama buy another plate to match?"

"It ain't that easy. This here is a pattern called Geneva. It's made by a company that is all the way in England, and nobody around here sells them."

"Then where did you buy them?"

"We didn't. They came from the house where Ma worked. Back when she was a maid." Daddy looks up from the plate he's been eyeballing. "You know who I am talking about?"

I nod. All I know about the place where Ma worked is that Mama's daddy lived there. Mama doesn't know him, never has. Mama's babies and her dishes. *She keeps losing things.*

A sound like a bunch of hammers pounds our front door. Nobody but Buster knocks like that. I run through the house to meet him.

"Ma sent me to get Bessie. You gonna come with us?"

"I reckon. Buster, where are we going?" I hope Mama won't get mad at me for waking her up.

The sun hits Buster's freckles, and for a minute, he looks like Howdy Doody. When he laughs hard, the sides of his mouth pretty near touch the corners of his eyes.

Chapter 18

Hakla! Hica! See! Hear!

Janie

"Young'uns, stay outside," Ma says, pointing her finger at us. We stay put on her front porch, and I look through the screen door. Ma nods at her daughters and sticks her index finger out. "I'll meet you in my bedroom."

"Hey, Janie," Buster whispers from behind me. He scrunches his lips to one side of his face. "This is gonna be real good." He tugs at my arm. "Walk quiet and keep your kisser shut." Buster leads me to a grassy spot right outside Ma's bedroom window. "Climb aboard." He squats down, and I crawl up his back. When I get my knees locked onto his shoulder blades, I wigwam my hands across the top of his head.

Through the window, I can see Ma standing in front of her closed bedroom door. And I hear Mama hollering. "I sing that old song all the time, Dora!"

"Yeah, when I ain't around!" Aunt Dora yells out. She fluffs Ma's bed pillows and leans back against the headboard. "Bessie, what in tarnation came over you last night?"

"Dora, you act like you wrote 'Down in the Valley.' What's eating at you?" Aunt Maggie asks. She leans forward in a straight-backed chair in the corner of the room, not far from Buster and me.

I tug on a lock of his hair, making sure he notices Aunt Maggie siding with Mama. He tips to the left. A hunk of my calf gets wrenched, me trying to hold onto his shoulder. I grab a bigger hunk of his hair and lean over to the right.

"Maggie, you think I'm stupid? Maybe you done forgot how Bessie treats her own sisters," Aunt Dora yells out, jumping up from the bed and strutting toward Mama.

"Sit down," Ma commands, shaking her finger at Dora. "We're fixing to get things straightened out. Don't go hurting somebody you love just because you're jealous."

"Get this straight, Dora," Mama squawks. "I started singing that song before you were born."

"Bessie, don't pretend you don't know about me and Buzzy!" Dora shouts. She paces back and forth from one end of the footboard and back. I get dizzy watching her. I hold on tighter to Buster's head.

"Dora, what do you want with old Buzzy, anyway?" Mama hollers. "He's married and got a bunch of young'uns."

"He loves me!" Dora shouts. "*Me, Dora, the unlovable.* Besides, Buzzy's got Seminole in him!" She shoves her face into Mama's. "Not everybody's gonna catch ahold of a Willard, a man who will love her and take care of her. Some of us gotta steal one away. Right, Bessie? *Steal.*"

"Dora, this ain't good for anybody's nerves," Lily says.

"Bessie didn't steal anybody's man, and all y'all know it," Ma says.

"Ma, I don't care about Buzzy," Aunt Maggie says. "But while we're all here, what I got to know is what happened way back. When we were little."

"Ain't no use talking about that, Maggie," Mama says.

"Easy for you to say, Bessie. You're the oldest, and you could've helped us," Aunt Maggie hollers. She jumps out of her chair and shakes her fist at Mama. Buster yanks on my shirt.

"Is Maggie slugging anybody yet?"

"No, I'll tell you when she does," I whisper.

"I was still a young'un, too!" Mama yells out, pointing to her chest.

"Who was it, Ma? Bessie, who was it?" Aunt Maggie screams.

"It's for Bessie and me to know," Ma says.

"Why, Ma?" Aunt Maggie growls. "That old man, black hair with silver running through it, big belly, stinking breath! He tied a rope around us. All three of us were screaming!"

"He ain't that old." Mama squalls hard, wiping tears from her face with the bottom of her flowered shirtwaist dress.

"Ain't? You mean he's still alive?" Aunt Dora yells out. Her head turns and juts forward like a rotating fan. "Who is it? Ma? Bessie?"

Ma shakes her head. "I won't let none of my young'uns end up in jail. If I tell you who done you harm, who killed Burl, you'll get yourselves locked up."

"Secrets, Ma!" Aunt Maggie interrupts. "They're killing me!" She screams, pounding the bed with her fist. Aunt Lily wraps her arms around Aunt Maggie's waist, putting her cheek against her sister's back.

"Burl's already dead! Ain't nothing we can do about it. Won't help to dig it back up. Rich people get away with killing and hurting little girls. You understand?" Ma wails, her tiny hands covering her face.

"I remember the old man saying 'Christian charity' over and over," cries Aunt Dora. She dabs her cheeks with Ma's bedspread. "What church was he from, Ma?"

"I don't recollect. He brought us hay and canned goods."

"We had a farm. Why did we need food?" Aunt Maggie wants to know.

"Burl had been laid up with a broke ankle," Ma says. "We were hungry. The bad man asked if you girls would help him haul the food to the barn."

"I remember. Daddy couldn't stand up straight," Aunt Maggie bawls.

"Buster," I whisper. "Aunt Maggie's crying!"

"Let me see!" I lean to the right real hard, so Buster can peep around me and through the window.

"It's *my* fault! *Not* Bessie's. You hear? I didn't know he'd throw a rope around you and plunder your private parts!" Wringing her hands, Ma walks in a circle.

"I never been the same!" Aunt Maggie yells out. "What about you, Bessie?"

Mama doesn't answer. She lies face down across Ma's bed, her forearms wrapped around the back of her head.

"When I brung you back inside, your daddy, part lame, went over there. He took a pistol but said he'd use it only if he needed to protect hisself. But he was gunned down first," Ma says.

Buster raps his knuckle against my right calf.

"Ma, trust us with his name. Please?" Aunt Lily pleads.

"What difference does it make to you, Lily?" Aunt Dora yells out. "You weren't there!"

"She was too young to help!" shouts Ma. "Quit blaming your sisters! You gonna blame Percy cause he was safe in my womb?"

"Ma! I'll kill that old man one day!" Aunt Maggie hollers.

Buster nudges my elbow.

"I ain't gonna let you, Maggie," Ma sobs. "One of us'd kill him. Maybe even Percy. It's better not to know who he is."

"Ma, you and Bessie are cursed," Aunt Maggie yells out.

"Maybe I am, but Bessie ain't. I'm the one who let you go out to the barn with him!" Ma wails.

I slide down from Buster's shoulders, kneel down, and cup my hands. Using them for a step, Buster hoists himself up, holding onto the window's ledge. I turn my back, lean up against the wall and lock my hands around his thighs, trying to support him.

"I wish I could change places with my young'uns," Ma says.

"We're going to be all right, Ma," says Aunt Lily.

It gets quiet for a few seconds, and then Aunt Maggie starts to screeching. "Buster, is that you, boy?"

Buster topples to the ground. My head thuds against the grass, and Buster steps on my arm. Before we can get up, Aunt Maggie is standing above us.

"Ma told y'all to play outside!" she hollers. Aunt Dora runs up, her face red and sweaty.

"That's what we're doing, playing outside," Buster says. He hops to his feet, wraps his hand around my arm, and pulls me up.

Aunt Maggie raises her fists, clobbering Buster's head and shoulders.

"Oww! Bitin' bass! Help!"

Mama runs up, takes off her moccasin, and slaps Maggie in the face with it. "Leave the boy alone, Maggie!"

Maggie grabs Mama by the hair, and Ma opens her bedroom window and shoves the screen out of its frame and onto the ground. She crooks her head.

"Hakla! Hica!" Ma yells out. Mama drops her shoe, and Aunt Maggie turns from Buster. Her eyes are red, and tears are pouring down her cheeks. "Hakla! Hica!" Ma repeats. Great day in Green Cove. I wish I know what those words mean and why everybody gets still when Ma says it.

Mama reaches out and puts her arms around me. Aunt Maggie runs toward her car. Everybody else stays still, like deer trying to outsmart a hunter.

"*Listen*, daughters: *look* for tomorrow! See it in your mind. Send your hurt away on the wind. Recollecting it don't do a thing but steal peace right out of your life. Bessie, when that murderer dies, you can tell your sisters who it was. Keep quiet 'til then. Can you?"

"I'll do my best, Ma." Mama draws me even closer to her. Tears fall down her cheeks.

"Dora," Ma says, "you deserve a man who ain't married, but I ain't fixing to stop you and Buzzy. You'll do what you want. But know this: he don't love you or his wife, only hisself." It gets quiet again. "Buster, come on in here," Ma says. "You want so bad to hear grown-ups talking, so you'll sit yourself inside all weekend. Bessie, I'm counting on you to talk to Janie."

"Yeah, Ma." Mama turns to me and strokes my hair. "But first we need a ride home."

"I'll take y'all, Bessie," Aunt Dora says. She tucks her arm through Mama's.

"Bessie," Aunt Dora says, "you can sing that song anytime you want to, anywhere you want to. You sing it real pretty. You sure do."

Mama turns to Dora. They hug like two people in love, but they cry like two people who lost something precious.

♪♫

Mama walks inside and goes straight to her bedroom. I tiptoe in, hoping she's all right.

"Mama, can I bring you something?"

"Yeah, honey. Some Maalox and a glass of water. And bring me my bottle of nerve pills, too." She sits up in bed to take the medicine. Mama lets out a big sigh.

"Mama, am I in big trouble?" Daddy took the twins to the fishing hole, and I want to get things settled before he gets back, just Mama and me. She looks at me and pats the bed. "Come here, Janie." I ease onto the bed. "Let's take a nap." She still doesn't answer me. I try to sleep, but too many questions run through my head. Trouble. Getting a switching. The bad man who murdered my granddaddy, but he's not *really* my grandaddy. The barn and what happened there. *Secrets galore.*

"Mama, what words did Ma say today when she knocked the screen out of the window?"

"Hakla. Hica."

"What does that mean?

"Hakla means 'hear,' and hica means 'see.'"

"It made everybody stop what they were doing. How come?"

"It's Seminole words. Ma's always learnt us how anger makes people go deaf and blind. She's worked hard to stop us from being mad. Always when she saw pain festering, she warned us. Don't get too mad to see things, too mad to hear things. I reckon she was right."

"But, Mama, you aren't mad."

"Just at myself, honey. Ma tries to take the blame for that awful day, but it weren't her fault. I was old enough to see trouble coming. I should a figured it out and run back to tell Ma."

Mama throws her arms around me and holds me so tight it's hard to breathe. Maybe my heart is choking again. When I'm fixing to pass out, Mama lets go and strokes my hair.

"What's the word for *hear* again?"

"*Hakla.*"

"What's the word for *see*?"

"*Hica.* Shhh."

When Mama is good and conked out, I walk to the back porch. The wind rustles through the leaves, and in my best singing voice, I follow the rhythm. With my own melody, I start to sing.

Hakla hear the truth.

Hica see the love.

Hakla hear the truth.

Hica see the love.

Chapter 19

What Have I to Fear?

Rose

"Rose! Over here!" Thelma Green calls from the steps of the Thankful Country Church. She's got on a light green skirt, a top with green and brown leaves on it, and a sweater that's a surefire perfect match.

"Hey!" I wave, a hurrying to the front of the building. Thelma finds us a spot on a pew smack dab in the middle of the church.

"Sister Daisy says she needs your help today with the music."

"Is that right?"

Sister Daisy nods in my direction. I walk on up to the front, where she's a playing "Leaning on the Arms of Jesus" on the piano. I follow her on the guitar.

Leaning on His arms, I'm trusting,

What have I to fear? I'm resting.

What have I to fear? I got a long list. It's scrawled across my heart. Maybe my baby ain't healthy. Maybe Percy don't love me. Maybe Momma and Papa ain't ever going to have anything to do with me.

"Brothers and Sisters," Brother Little begins, "today we're going to look at how Jesus responded to the woman caught in adultery."

"Jesus forgave this woman," Brother Little says. "We must forgive one another. Forgiveness means not wagging our tongues or shunning people who come to Christ. Instead, be a shoulder to lean upon, a prayer partner for someone who is weak. Help everyone you can."

Comfort blankets me, a warming my soul.

♪♫

Ma-Ki

"Maggie, tell me what you recollect." My winsome daughter sits on the edge of my porch swing, looking away from me.

"Mostly, Ma, I remember how it felt, how I burned . . . my wrists and ankles from the rope. My insides." Maggie gulps, then coughs like she ain't never gonna stop.

"I wish it would've burnt me, not you, Maggie."

"Ma, it felt like hellfire when that old man put his hands where he shouldn't have." She lifts her head toward the sky.

"You were helpless, Maggie." I lay my hand on her back, between her shoulders.

"First I heard Bessie screaming. Then me. Have you ever heard yourself screaming, Ma?"

"Yep." I breathe in deep, drinking the air.

Maggie has a way of asking questions but not wanting answers. So I keep mine to myself. But I done heard myself cry plenty, like when Bessie's pa gave me money but no ring. And the day Mother and Pa died.

But my insides screamed loudest when Burl got shot. They carried his body to me, his heart shot clean out of him. When they moved him, tiny pieces of Burl floated in the air and onto the ground, pieces I ain't never seen or touched. My husband, who had the biggest heart I ever knowed of, ended up with no heart at all. But Maggie ain't really interested in my grief. Only hers.

"I heard myself hollering, Ma. Then Dora started crying."

"How old were you, Maggie?"

"I was six, Ma. You know that."

"What did the bad man look like?"

"I don't know, Ma. Does Dora remember? Lily?"

"Dora was too young to recollect much. Lily was too little to go with you girls. She stayed with me while I cleaned house. Percy was still in me, not ready to be born. No matter what good or what bad comes to us, Maggie, we can't change one thing about what happened back yonder. But if we set about changing our todays, our tomorrows will get a little sweeter."

Maggie hunches over again and covers her eyes with the back of her hand. She sighs heavy, trying to breathe out the weight of the secrets. She tucks her feet under her bottom.

"You got the power of an eagle, Maggie, but you went and caged it. You done shut the door of your mind, trading recollection for comfort. We all do it."

She turns to me, tears falling from her amethyst eyes, humming her favorite song, "Nobody's Darling but Mine."

I sing the words, hoping she'll follow. But she ain't ready to fly.

Janie

"Buster, are you still in trouble with Ma?"

"Nope. She made me stay inside all weekend. Couldn't go no further than the porch. I was going plumb crazy till I started on my homework."

"You're doing homework? You're lying."

"Nope. I started reading *Huck Finn*."

Me and Buster are eyeball to eyeball, still as stones. Great day in Green Cove. He looks like he's telling the truth, but I've never known my cousin to read a book.

"You're really reading *Huck Finn?*"

"Yeah. Aren't you? Mr. Brown's making us, crazy girl."

How can I tell Buster I'm skimming the dumb book, hoping it will get me a passing grade? "Buster, you don't think that story is boring?"

"How can a book about floating on a river raft be boring? Shucks, what a life. Me and Pistol, we oughta try it, drifting down the St. Johns River with Chief Osceola for our guide."

"I guess."

"I reckon I like the way Huck talks, too. Makes me bust a gut laughing."

"Buster, Huck's talking makes you laugh?"

"Yeah. It don't make you giggle a little bit?"

"No, and you talk exactly like those boys, Buster."

"Huh?" Buster scratches the top of his head. "I do?"

"Yes."

Buster's face sports a new shade of red. "If I do, Janie, then you must talk like me."

"No, I don't."

"Hmm." Buster crosses his arms in front of his chest. "Come to think of it, maybe not. Why don't you sound like me and Huck?"

"I don't know. Maybe because I read a lot."

"Like what? What books make your talking so different?"

"Buster, I've read ever since I was a little girl, all kinds of stuff. Like *Pollyanna* and *Anne of Green Gables* books. *Lassie Come Home* and *Heidi.*"

"Well, I ain't fixing to read any girls' books. You can be uppity all by your lonesome." His voice shakes a little bit.

"Buster, I'm sorry."

He turns and walks away from me. I follow him, hoping if I change the subject, he will forget all about sounding like *Huck Finn*. "Hey, Buster. Did you know what Ma was talking about when she hollered those Seminole words?"

"Ma says Indian words all the time. It's pretty corny if you ask me."

Sometimes Buster doesn't get it. Now he's pretending he's real tough.

"Are you afraid of sounding dumb, Buster?"

"I ain't afraid of nothing!" Buster runs, making dirt from the road scatter into the wind.

"Buster!" He doesn't look back.

Buster

Even running full speed, I ain't able to keep Pistol from passing me. He looks back a couple times, showing his teeth. At the golden rain tree, I steady myself and slide to the ground.

"Here, boy." Pistol cozies up to me, and I throw my arm around his neck. He offers me the stick, and I throw it gentle. He fetches it and lays down next to me.

"You ain't scared of nothing, are you, Pistol?" His brown eyes look through me. He's got collie in him, no mistake, with his long nose. Strands of white, too, but mostly he's sable red. White runs through his feet, collar, and the blaze that streaks through his face. I take my comb out of my pocket and work tangles out of his coat.

"Scared of nothing, boy?" He barks this time, letting me know he ain't scared. He whines a little, not liking to be groomed. "You smell like dead fish." He licks my face. "All right, just one dead fish."

"Well, it's a good thing you ain't scared of nothing. But I'm spooked when I think of never getting out of here. We'll take off, one day." I wipe my sleeve across my face, drying up his dog slobber. "Pistol, that ole tree house has about had it. Percy built it for me when I was little." Pistol gets to barking as I climb the tree. Holding onto a stout limb, I kick the pine planks of the playhouse. They're near about rotten. Thinking about rotten . . . "Pistol, if your own mama don't want you, who does?"

Standing on his hind legs, Pistol scratches the trunk and whines. I crouch on the limb, steady myself good, and rip the roof off. It tumbles to the dirt. A couple of foundation boards are nailed tight and ain't going nowhere. I jump to the ground.

Pistol stretches out by my side, and I scratch behind his ears. "Boy, I ain't going to sound like Huck Finn much longer. I'm going to talk proper. We'll go cruising down the St. Johns River, you and me, but it'll be in a fancy boat, not some ole raft."

I pick up *Huck Finn*. I'm near about finished, and I ain't quitting. Pistol taps his front paw on my chest.

"You know what, Pistol? We're adventurers. Nothing scares us. Race you to the fishing hole!"

The water's awful chilly this time of year, but I ain't worried about it. Pistol swims up to me, and I forget about everything except how I'm freezing and how good it is to have a dog.

Chapter 20

The Holey House

Janie

"Janie, drive me up to Crowley's Drug Store," Mama says, shuffling across her bedroom floor. "Pssshaw!"

"What's wrong?" I call from the front room.

"That hole's got splinters. Done ripped my stocking. Come here." She sits on the bed and raises her leg. A big run crawls from the bottom of her heel and all the way up her ankle.

"Let's go," she says. "I need to get something for my nerves, anyway."

With me driving, we might all need something to help our nerves. Mama puts the twins between us. "Sit still," she says, holding her pocketbook up next to her window and using it like a pillow.

"Choke it, Janie, choke it!" Kenny hollers. He shakes his right leg, leans his head to the left, and uses both hands to grab a chunk of air. I love Kenny, but right now I feel like choking him.

♪♫

The store clerk rings up Mama's new pair of stockings, some Maalox, Goody Powders, and a hot water bottle. On the way out, I ask Mama if I can stop by the hardware store next door.

"Take the boys with you. I'll wait in the truck."

I hold their hands tight, keeping them close at my sides.

"May I help you, young lady?" An old man leans over a counter.

"Sir, I need supplies to make papier-mâché," I say. One of his eyebrows arches way up. He reaches behind him, taking a big, indexed book from the shelf.

"There's more than one way to make it, depending on how stiff you want it to be," he says. His face is full of wrinkles, crevices, red marks and brown splotches, looking like maps I've studied in geography class.

"Stiff, sir. Real stiff, just as strong as I can get it."

"I'll be right back." He walks to a display crowded with tin cans and bottles and comes back with a tiny brown package. "This resin glue powder will give it a lot of body, will make it strong. Do you plan to paint your project?"

"Yes, sir. I want it to look like pine."

His eyebrow perks up again, and he reaches behind him and grabs a small can of wood stain. "This should do it."

"I'll be right back with your money," I say, hurrying the boys out the door. Mama jumps when I tap on the truck window where she rests her head. She rolls down the window.

"Mama, can I have some money?"

"Will a dollar be enough?" I nod, and she slips off her right shoe and takes a bill out of it. "Bring me the change."

♪♫

As we drive into the front yard, Buster and Ma are getting out of her car. I stay outside with the boys, hoping my cousin will talk to me. "Buster, I'm sorry about what I said, you talking like Huck Finn."

"Aw, Janie. Don't worry about it. I ain't mad no more."

I don't want to stir up Buster and get him mad all over again, so I change the subject real fast. "You ever made papier-mâché?"

"Nope."

"Will you watch Kenny and Benny for me this evening?"

"Yep."

Nope. Yep. Buster lied to me. *He's still mad.*

♪♫

Into a big pot of boiling water, I add flour and powdered glue resin. I beat the stuff like crazy, trying to get the lumps out of it. It stinks like a dead varmint, rank and rotten. I sprinkle a bunch of cinnamon into it, so I won't stink up the house. I shape the newspaper into small round discs and put them on the kitchen counter. Daddy, Buster, and the twins come in from the back porch.

"What in the world are you doing, gal?" Daddy wants to know.

"It's papier-mâché, Daddy. These little round things will dry hard. Then I'll varnish them up like wood, so I can put them in the holes in this floor. I'll need to use a little more of this." I point to a concoction in the pot. "When I get them done, they'll stop the cold wind from coming through the floor."

Daddy gives me another one of his *are you crazy* looks. "Plus, the boys won't be able to feed the chickens through the holes. Mama won't get holes in her stockings, either."

Daddy looks into the pot and then back at me. "Well, I guess it ain't the first time you've had an idea about fixing a house. Get to it. We ain't got all night."

Daddy, Buster, and I fit the papier-mâché discs into the floor's holes and put more of the hot liquid over the fillers. They start to harden. "I've got something that will turn them the same color of wood." I hold out the can of stain to Daddy.

"Real good, Janie. Reckon we can get 'em all filled in a day or two. First we'll wait to see if this here notion works. I'm fixing to take Buster home now. You get the boys in bed."

Real good, Janie. Real good! Maybe we'll stay in this house long enough to know if this works.

♪♫

"This here's wood putty." Daddy shows me. "When you finish drying them dishes, you can help me." On his knees in the kitchen floor, Daddy fills in between the discs and the holes they patch. I dry the last dish and sit next to him on the floor.

"After this here dries, we'll stain it. But first we got to sand it, make it smoother." Daddy takes some sandpaper out of his carpenter's apron. Kenny runs behind us with a tiny piece of sandpaper in his hand.

"I wanna help Daddy," Kenny says. He follows us around while we stain the putty and the newsprint.

"Them spots tonight need a day or two to set. Ain't going to hold if we step on them tonight."

"Yes, sir." It looks good. The discs match the floor just perfect.

"Yep, it does. You sure done a good job, Janie. Real good idea." He squeezes my shoulder.

"That's purty, Janie," Kenny says. Benny is in the front room watching television with Mama. She doesn't notice anything, except the Jack Benny show.

♪♫

Daddy finishes his breakfast and pours himself another cup of coffee. "Janie, your mama sure ain't in any shape to sing or have people over here tonight. But we'll be going to a cane-grinding at Alvin Foster's farm tomorrow morning."

"In January?"

"Yep. They had a big crop, and it was a little late this year. There'll be singing, so don't be surprised if you end up front and center."

"Is Mama going with us?"

"Yep."

"Good." Cane-grindings mean smelling a syrupy scent of sugar. Maybe the sweetness will settle into Mama's heart, lift her out of her sadness.

Chapter 21

Grinding

Janie

I roll down the truck windows, so Mama can smell the sugar cane cooking over the wood, like cotton candy at a fair. "Mama, you sure you don't want to get out?"

"I'd rather stay right here. You go have some fun."

"Thank you, Mama. I'll bring you a plate later."

A quarter horse, tied to a pole about twelve feet long, circles a brick wall. Men wearing bib overalls and straw cowboy hats tote stalks of sugar cane to the machine squeezing juice out of the plant. The liquid goes into a whiskey barrel underneath the press.

Across from the grinder, ladies stir dough and chop cabbage in an outdoor kitchen. It has clapboard walls and a tin roof. Great day in Green Cove, I don't want to get stuck cooking. I run to where the men are working. Farm hands spread barbeque sauce on big slabs of ribs roasting above an open fire. A low fire roasts corn, sitting atop chicken wire.

Ma and Uncle Percy stand on the back porch of the Fosters' big farmhouse. Just above Ma's elbow, she wears her rattler, two little turtle shells strung together. They sing "chee chee chee" when she shakes her arm. She usually wears them on her ankles the way other Seminoles do.

"Ma, why are you putting your rattlers on your arm instead of your leg?"

"Shhh. Got a bunch of white people here, and it ain't good for an Indian granny to dance around. This way, with the rattler up here, all I have to do is get my arm to trembling," she says, pointing to her elbow.

"You don't have to wear it, do you?" Just thinking how people might say something bad about Ma shoots a flame of hurt, spearing my heart.

"I *want* to wear it, Janie. I told you a long time ago, my mother wore this thing. My pa made it for her. He strung it and put canna lily seeds inside. Makes them clatter." She ruffles her fist above her head. "Nowadays folks use a tin shaker with seeds inside them. It's easier. But this here rattler is something real special."

"Okay, Ma. That's neat." I wait a minute, hoping she isn't mad at me. "Ma, where is Buster?"

"He's home."

"Is he in trouble again?"

"Must be," Uncle Percy butts in, tuning his guitar. "He's at home reading a book."

"Ma?" I wait for her to tell me Percy is kidding. "Is he sick?"

"Buster's reading, all right, and he ain't sick."

For the first time ever, Percy's right, and Ma's wrong. If Buster's home reading a book instead of here at a cane-grinding, he's got to be sick.

♪♫

Rose

"There ain't room for you up here with the singers, Rosie. See about making yourself handy over there making them biscuits," Percy says in a real hushed voice. He's ashamed of me and doesn't want me next to him.

The women in the kitchen hardly look at my face, but they stare at my close-fitting black skirt, pink blouse, and black sweater. "We've got all the cooks we need," says a middle-aged lady with a missing front tooth. She motions for me to go.

Right outside, Dora and Lily sit in folding chairs, just a waiting for the music to start. "Rose, would you go see about Bessie?" Dora's face turns bright red, and she motions for me to go, too. Kenny sits in her lap, and Lily bounces Benny up and down. She looks at me and smiles.

"I would if I could figure out where she is."

"She's sitting in her truck." Dora points to a field with mowed grass. "Willard and Janie up and left her there."

Willard's truck is parked a ways from the chairs. "Hey, Rose!" calls my papa, from behind me. He smiles and tips his hat. I stop and turn to him. "How you getting along?" he asks. He gets close and looks deep into my eyes.

"I'm all right, Papa, but I miss you. And everybody."

"Homer and Joe's here. They're helping make the syrup, but don't go bothering 'em. A bunch a men's in there." He points to the barn. "Rosie, I been meaning to talk with you about your momma. She's been hurt bad . . ." Papa's chin jitters. "Got in trouble when she was a wee bit older'n you. You ain't the onliest one. She sees you following her own bad ways."

"I heard that, Papa, but I didn't know if it was true or not." *Explains why Momma acts so hateful to me.*

"She ain't proud of it getting herself *in trouble*, way back when. I wisht I could a told you afore now. Makes it a wee bit easier to say the truth, now that you and Emmaline ain't living under the same roof. She couldn't stand to see you in the same fix she was in. Too much like staring in a looking glass, stirring her hurts up all over again. It ain't all your fault."

"Papa . . ."

"I gotta keep some peace at home. We got other young'uns to raise."

"Papa, I didn't mean to hurt nobody." I reach out for his arm, and he lets out a wee yelp, like he's afraid of me.

"I know it. But you're gonna figure out sooner or later near about everybody hurts the ones they love most. How's that husband of yours?"

"Surefire good, Papa."

"Percy's treating you good?"

"Yes, Papa." *Forgive me, Lord, for lying.*

"Well, I got to go back, help with the syrup. Good seeing you." Papa leans over and gives me a hug. It's so light, a sheet of waxed paper that covers a sandwich, barely touching it, not enough to keep it fresh but just enough to protect it from getting wet or eaten up by bugs. He whirls around and heads toward the barn, his head turned my way. *Papa's gone again.*

Now I know what's a bothering Momma. A long time ago, I heard a little about her and Sheriff Grainger Tannen. He left these parts before my oldest brother was born, when Momma was *in trouble.* It's how the story goes, anyway. But I ain't got even a wee notion about what would make Papa marry her mean self when she had somebody else's baby inside her.

Bessie. I'm supposed to be checking on her. I hurry and find her still in Willard's truck, her head a leaning up against the passenger window.

"Hey, Bessie. How about me and you sit together a while?"

"All right," she says. "What are you smiling about?" Bessie sure ain't smiling.

"Hot biscuits and fresh syrup. I can't wait." I open the driver's door and climb in. "Are you hungry, Bessie?"

"Rose, right now it don't matter to me if I ever have another biscuit. Or anything else."

Fear wells up in me. I ain't able to look at Bessie, after having a scare with my own baby. "Bessie, I sure am sorry about what happened. Your operation, too. I think about you a lot, especially here lately."

"Uh huh."

"Bessie, I'm praying for you."

"Is that so?" Bessie looks real sad, and I want to help her like Sister Daisy helped me. "Can I say a prayer for you now?"

Bessie closes her eyes and clamps her jaw. "Listen here, Rose, I don't want to talk. Or pray."

Real slow, I get out of the truck, like if I move too fast I'll break into a bunch of little pieces. I sure could use another one of Papa's wax paper hugs.

♫♪

Janie

Horses, tossing their heads and spouting their neighs, roam around the Fosters' farm. High-falutin' girls, their noses pointing straight into the air, wear circle skirts and ride sidesaddle atop the steeds. I'd rather be right where I am, on this makeshift stage with the musicians.

Standing a little in front of me and to my left is Mrs. Bailey, my music teacher. She's got a red kerchief tied around her neck, and her bleached blonde hair falls over her shoulders. At the edge of the Fosters' porch sits her husband, in his wheelchair. He's got movie star good looks: thick shiny black hair, dark round eyes, and dimples. Over his lap and legs sits a gray wool blanket.

Percy stands at the front of the pickers. A boy I've seen at school uses a thick strap to beat on an old washboard. Ma stands with her hand above her head, her pa's rattler strapped onto her arm.

"All right, folks!" Uncle Percy hollers. "We'll be opening with Roy Rogers' 'Don't Fence Me In.'"

The crowd yells out, "Don't fence me in," when we sing the chorus. We finish the song, and a bunch of men turn from the barbeque pits and whistle like crazy. We do two more tunes by Roy Rogers, "My Chickashay Gal" and "Blue Shadows on the Trail."

I whirl around a little, pretending I'm at Junior's Dance Hall. Then I think about Ma and her rattler, and I leap up. From the back, a girl guitar player hands me a tambourine. I shake it by my side while we play "Tennessee Moon," by Cowboy Copas and "Red River Valley" by Carl T. Sprague.

"Hey, Percy!" Alvin Foster yells out. "Ain't it about time you sing 'Back in the Saddle Again?'"

"All right then. Here comes some Gene Autry for you folks," Uncle Percy yells out. When he starts to sing the *whoopi-ty-aye-oh* lines, I get chill bumps on my arms. His voice travels like a cactus blossom gliding through the wind. People gather around the bottom of the porch to sing with him.

An old, pink-faced man, with white eyebrows and white sprigs of hair sticking up from his balding head, dances at the front of the crowd. Dark brown ridges run down both sides of his mouth, the kind people get when they don't wipe the drool from their snuff. I was hungry, but nary a thought of food, not even a hot biscuit filled with honey, sounds good after looking at his face.

The ugly old man picks up one of his feet and hops a little. "Woo! Yessah! Saddle up, partner!" he yells out. He sidesteps to the left, and the people gathered behind him hurry to the right. When he hits the ground, his shirttail pulls loose from his pants, showing his paunch. The crowd backs even farther away from him, everybody except Mr. Moody Brown and a couple of the

Fosters' farmhands. Two of them lock their arms under the old man's shoulders and drag him away.

Uncle Percy brings the song to a close. I get close enough to Ma to whisper. "Ma, who is that?" I point to the drunk who's being hauled toward the parked cars.

"Shhh." She wraps her hand around my finger and guides it down by my side. I guess Ma thinks she's the only one allowed to point. "He's Old Man Brown, Moody Brown's pa. Shhh," she warns, leaning over and covering her mouth.

"It is?" My rich teacher, who wears bow ties and white shirts, has a drunk daddy who wears rumpled clothes and has tobacco drooling from his chin. Great day in Green Cove.

"Janie!" Ma grabs me by the arm. "Hush!"

"Hey, everybody!" shouts Alvin Foster. He's got his hands cupped around his mouth. "Let's eat!"

♩♫

Aunt Maggie sits in the cab of our truck with Mama. My aunt looks at me, scrunching up her nose. She puckers up her lips till they are pretty near inside-out. "This here conversation ain't for your ears, Janie," Aunt Maggie says. "You can bring that food back later or leave it here for Bessie." She points to a plate of fried chicken, honey-dripped biscuits, and coleslaw I'm carrying.

"Mama's hungry. This food is for her, not you, Aunt Maggie." This is the first time I've been so sassy with a grown-up, and I wonder if I am fixing to feel a switch across my behind. Aunt Maggie gets out of our truck, staggers around, and yells out words I'm not allowed to repeat. I get in behind the wheel and put the food on the seat between Mama and me.

"This is really good, Mama, I promise."

Mama pinches off a little piece of biscuit and tucks it in her mouth real careful, like it's a hot fire poker. Something clangs against the driver's door of the truck. Aunt Maggie's back, smelling like whiskey's been dumped on her face. Mr. Moody Brown stands about three yards behind her. He looks right at Mama and me, but I can't read what his face says. About another three yards behind my teacher sits the crazy old man, slumped onto a ripped-up black vinyl upholstered seat that's been taken out of a car. His snores sound like an old horse, so loud they reach the truck.

"One day I'll stop doing favors for you and your young'uns, Bessie. You hear?" Aunt Maggie says. She shakes her finger just like Ma and stomps off. From the other side of the truck, Daddy, Uncle Percy, and Ma trot toward us. Aunt Maggie stumbles back our way, swinging a baseball bat.

"Janie, go check on them brothers of yours. Now," Daddy says, real calm. Aunt Maggie and Uncle Percy holler loud enough for me to hear, and I turn around. My uncle has Aunt Maggie's head in a hammerlock. The baseball bat is lying on the ground next to Mr. Brown. He hasn't budged. Daddy waves for me to keep moving, and I know better than to turn back and head their way. If Buster was here, I know we could figure out what everybody's fighting about.

Chapter 22

Ee-te Yo-ga-hé: Fire!

Buster

Them buttered biscuits with ham Rose left for me are going a lot faster than I expected. Mmmm. Pistol stands at the back door, looking in. He hoofs in through the back door. If Ma finds out he's been in here, both of us'll be sleeping outside. He looks up, deep into my eyes, and whines. I break off another piece. He chomps it, and we eat another one. And another.

It ain't even 10:30, and we've already gobbled down lunch. Beings I'm so full, I head to the porch swing and stretch out with my book. Ma thought I had done gone and lost my mind when I told her I wanted to stay home to read and to try to catch some speckled perch.

"You in trouble at school again, ain't you, son?"

"No, ma'am. I checked out a book at the library. It's real good."

"Tarnation. Does this book have a name?"

"Yes, ma'am. *Treasure Island.*"

"Your teacher's making you read it?"

"No, ma'am. That was *Huck Finn*, and I'm done with it. I might read it again, though, someday."

"Must be good, son, if you want to stay home from the cane-grinding."

"It don't even compare, Ma. What do they have over at the Fosters? Same old horses, food, and singing. *Treasure Island*'s got pirates, swashbucklin', and buried treasure. Even Long John Silver."

"I heard tell of him. Swashbucklin'?"

"Yes, ma'am."

"You and that dog behave, Buster."

Except for letting Pistol in the house, I ain't worried about behaving. "Come on, boy," I call to him. "Let's drive on down to the fishing hole."

The wind kicks, colder by the pond than at the house. Me and Pistol climb back in the car and head for the barn. The wood bunk ain't got a mattress, but it's all right because I'm tough. Pistol jumps up with me and lays at my feet. Looks like them speckled perch'll have to wait. Outside, the wind's just a howling, but I ain't scared. I open *Treasure Island* and scale the palisade.

Ma-Ki

The smell of roasted maize haunts the air. Burning strong against the dusk, the arms of the fire, Ee-te Yo-ga-hé, wave to me. I make good on the invite, walk over to the crackling blaze of red, yellow, and blue. The bellow of its flames and the charred smell call up memories of the Green Corn Dance I seen when I was a young'un.

Taking the rattler from my arm, I tie it around my ankle like Mother done. The drums beat strong, pushing me closer to the flames. I go gentle, near as I can get. I leap up, and the *shik-shik* of canna seeds makes Pa feel so close to me. *Touch me, Pa. Spread your spirit over me. Mother, help me teach my young'uns what it means to be part of this earth.*

Ee-te Yo-ga-he! Burn away the hurt of Maggie and her meanness. She ain't ever gonna know real love, hanging onto things men's hands have made. Running off every good one who wants to give her a part of hisself. I lean forward, flutter my arms. With bird's wings, I rise back up, shielding chicks who ain't yet learned to fly.

"Soar, Maggie!" I told her years ago. She come to me after she missed her first moon. "Marry him, like he wants. You got someone who loves you,"

"We'll see, Ma. If Walter really loves me, he'll live right here in Bradford County," she said.

"Let him take you back to his life if that's what he's aiming to do."

"Ma, how can you say such a thing? A Seminole woman is followed by her man."

"You're white, too, Maggie. Like Walter."

"I won't be ruled by a white man, Ma."

"Your daddy was a white man. A good one."

"I ain't getting married, and I don't want this baby." She stood pointing at her stomach, her finger a hunting knife. "I'd rip it right out if I could!"

"You ain't gonna do anything crazy! I'll raise that baby. It'll be mine." I had grabbed her arm, twisting it hard behind her.

"Fine, Ma," she said. Quiet, she got. "But I ain't fixing to live under a white man's thumb."

"Maggie, only one white man hurt you, long ago. Look for tomorrow, not back at what you can't change."

"I don't want to be touched when I don't want to be, Ma! No married life for me."

"Things don't stay the same, Maggie. Remember that little doll I made you. You named it Bettie."

"I lost it. Still don't know how, Ma."

"Girl, I wanted to make you one just like it, but you wouldn't have it. That lost doll or no doll, instead of taking comfort with another one just like it."

Maggie had jumped up, her fists pounding on the sky. "Maybe it would have looked just like it, but it ain't the doll who went everywhere with me after the bad man. It couldn't have never been the doll that slept with me every night after that. You don't understand, Ma. I want the real thing! The one that stayed with me that same night after the bad man got ahold of me."

My girl let loose with her mad ways that day. Red-faced. Ready to fight.

Ee-te Yo-ga-hé. I ain't never told my young'uns how I was touched the first time. I was a fifteen-year-old young girl cleaning and cooking for a wealthy family in Jacksonville. *Wealthy*, not *rich*, they taught me. I boarded in their attic, and footsteps creaked on the landing late one night. I turned to see who was there. It was Dothan, with his crow black hair, brown eyes speckled with goldenrod, and lips like full-bloom sundew.

Till then, he ain't never said a thing to me but "thank you" when I put his clean clothes away. He walked close, and with nary a word, his lips touched mine. His long fingers and firm grip captured me, making me afraid to run. Giving in could mean losing my work and my room. Scariest of all, I wanted him. He seen it. But I hoped he'd love me the right way, out in the open. Not sneaking around. Not unmarried, but that's how things done went, not married. A secret love.

Bessie got big in me, and Dothan's family turned me out. He sent money regularly, but that was all he did for me. His claim of loving me vexed my young mind. I yearned for him, but he didn't come. He was done lying.

Ee-te Yo-ga-hé. Twirling and whirling, guided by the drums.

Recollecting the men in our village swallowing the black drink, purging the poison of the past year. Venom's stored in me now, but I ain't got nothing to clean me. Women ain't never been allowed to take the potion. I'm the only Seminole around here, my brothers gone west and my sisters gone down south.

Both my sisters up and married Black Seminoles. They went deeper into swamp living, far as they could get from judgment. Not wanting any part of white ways, even though they got white in them. Like me. Our place in this world sways with the wind, a rickety bridge. It pushes me from Seminole to white at a whim. It snaps, landing me back on the other side. My sisters landed in Black worlds, a dangerous spot. Targets of white folks, aiming for us because we're full of blood they hate.

I try not to be full of hate, man's strongest poison. Season after season, I go along not celebrating Green Corn like other Seminoles, but it's how we cull bitter venom from our spirits. It ain't right to keep it in.

Just a piece from the fire, palmettos grow wild. When I was a young'un, I watched women cut their arms. I slow, stop, and step away from the *ee-te yo-ga-hé.* Grabbing a palmetto frond, I bend and snap it off. I dance back to the flames. I close my eyes, willing my sorrow to leave, but it stays.

Ee-te Yo-ga-hé. Bessie's got me wore out by her notions, pure opposite of Maggie. Holding onto the leaf of the palm, I stand tall and slither my body from head to toe. One step at a time, slinking until the sound of the rattlers melt into the rhythm of the drums.

My oldest girl holds on to young'uns who done gone and left this world. She forgets she's got some left alive. Why in tarnation she throws away the best of what she owns is something I ain't figured out. I bend over, keep my back, shoulders, and head even. I butt my head against the air, herding Bessie into the time being. Hoping if I nudge her along, she'll start looking ahead instead of back.

"I'm Seminole, Ma," Bessie told me when I tried to stop her from throwing away her good dishes and settee. "I ain't attached to things."

That girl's fixing to put Willard in the poorhouse directly. Goes out and buys her any whipstitch of a thing she wants. He loves her. Always reaching for her, his eyes glistening when she sings, and taking care of them young'uns when she can't.

Ee-te Yo-ga-he. My girls pretend to understand Seminole ways, but they ain't got any idea what it means to be part of the earth. And I'm to blame. We live in a white world, better to have them fit in than to teach them things that'll set them apart.

Ee-te Yo-ga-he. I stand up straight, leap and twirl, but I ain't able to push Bessie and her young'uns out of my mind. I ain't told her how dangerous twin boys are. Thunder and lightning. Maybe they ain't got enough Seminole in them to matter. If them boys grow up mean, they may kill what's left of her. Bessie needs to brace herself, but I ain't able to help her if she ain't mustering her own strength.

Ee-te Yo-ga-he. I got to force this corruption from my spirit. I slice the frond against my arm. Blood spurts out and trickles down me. I try to catch its scent. I leap and turn, chasing the poison. The smell of the cane syrup coaxes me to rest. I take in a deep breath of sweetness. The fire's done gone out of me, but the poison, so strong, it stays.

Ee-te Yo-ga-he. Rose's face flashes in front of me. "Ma, I have a river of peace running through me." And forty feet away, Maggie hollers and cusses. Hakla. Hica. *Master of Breath, my family makes war. But I got to have some peace.*

Janie

At the side of the Fosters' outdoor kitchen, Rose stands all alone. Her eyes are all red, and her lips are swollen up, like she's been crying. I run up to her.

"Rosie, what's wrong?"

"Nothing, Janie. I'll be all right. You sounded real good singing." She tries to smile at me.

"I don't get why you didn't sing with us today. Or even play the guitar."

Tears gush down Rose's cheeks. I wanted her to know I missed her. Trouble is, I've said the wrong thing. *Again.* "Daddy sent me to find the twins. Aunt Dora and Aunt Lily have them somewhere."

"Over by the horses." Rose cocks her head to the left. "Janie, what's made Maggie so mad today?"

I don't have any idea why Aunt Maggie's so mad, and I can't figure out why she is hanging out with Mr. Moody Brown. I don't why she doesn't care one little bit about Buster. "I can't figure it out, Rose."

Rose puts her arm around me. "Let's go find them twins."

♪♫

Aunt Dora sits on a ladderback chair with a rush seat over by the barn. She has Kenny across her lap. He sleeps, his long curls almost covering his eyes. Benny has nestled himself into the crook of Aunt Lily's arm.

"It's about time to head on home. Dark'll be here in a few minutes," Aunt Dora says.

"Y'all feel like walking to Bessie and Willard's truck with us?" Rose points to the field where the truck is parked. "There's been some trouble."

"Uh. I ain't surprised," Aunt Dora moans. Aunt Lily shakes her head.

"Rose?" I put my arm around her waist. She smells good, like roses growing up on tall trellises outside big, fancy houses. My lips touch her cheekbone, and Rose wraps her arm around my shoulder.

"I'll be seeing you, Janie," Rose says. "I love you." She doesn't have nary a trace of a smile.

"I love you, too, Rose. I'm glad you're my aunt." I wave and follow my aunts to Daddy's truck, breathing deep to capture the smell of sugared smoke.

The sun seems to be saying its day is done, feathering the sky with shades of indigo, crimson, tangerine, and pink. In the distance, the drums still beat. Not too far from a blazing fire is Ma, dancing all by herself. She turns and turns, one arm partially circling her waist and the other arm talking to the heavens.

Chapter 23

A Rose in Bloom

Rose

"Rose, let's start with a song in the key of C," Sister Daisy says. She picks up a songbook and sits it upright on the piano. "Do you know where middle C is?"

"No, ma'am." *I can't read a lick of music.* Sister Daisy sits next to me on her piano stool, leans my way a wee bit, and strikes an ivory plank. "That sounds like C, all right." I give her my best smile, and she moves her index finger up the keys.

"C, D, E, F, G, A, B, and C again. Rose, I picked 'Where the Soul Never Dies,' so we can focus on the key of C today." She runs through a verse and a chorus, a singing as she plays.

"I ain't never heard it before. It's real pretty."

"All right, Rose, you want to try the next verse? Start by playing one note at a time, the top one. It's the melody, F, A, G, F, A," she says, pointing at the page of the hymnal.

I was a hoping the piano would come real easy, like the guitar. Maybe I learned it easy because I'm so crazy in love with Percy. I spot middle C and press it, moving my index finger up the keys, one at a time, C, D, E, F, and stop there.

"Very good, Rose. Now look up at the music, and play the top notes of the treble clef. Remember?" She looks at me with her round face and soft brown eyes.

"Sister Daisy. I play by ear."

The smile leaves her face, and her mouth falls open a wee bit. "What? As well as you play? Here, let me teach you some chords on the piano." She sits on my right. "Here's C, F, G." Sister Daisy plays one chord at a time as she says what they are. She moves her hand up the keyboard. "Now you follow suit."

"Yes, ma'am." I pick out the notes Sister Daisy used.

"Right. You know the chords when you hear them, right, Rose?" I nod my head.

"Let me play it, only the chords." I watch Sister Daisy and listen real close. "You call out the chords, Rose, as you hear them."

I say which chord it is when Sister Daisy strikes it. She gets her smile back and sings the first verse and the chorus one more time. She points to the second verse. "Here we go, Rose. Sing with me."

A rose is blooming there for me . . .

Where the soul of man never dies.

"A rose! You must have picked that one special for me."

"I thought you might like it. You know, Rose, the Lord has wonderful songs in his arsenal."

Arsenal? What's an arsenal? "Well, the piano is surefire different from the guitar."

"Yes, but you'll be a wonderful pianist in no time. You have so much talent."

I look away. It ain't easy to believe people, even Sister Daisy, when they say nice things about me.

"Honey, are you concerned about not being able to learn the piano?"

"No, Sister Daisy." I stop, take a breath. *Go on, Rose. If you can't tell Sister Daisy, who can you tell?* "It's other things that's a bothering me."

"Like what?" Sister Daisy's eyes look into mine, asking me to trust her more.

"Sister Daisy, have you ever felt like you don't fit in nowhere?" I take a deep breath.

She reaches for my arm and pats it. "Yes, Rose, I have. It happens often in the ministry. But let's talk about you. You've had so many changes in your life recently. Where are you trying to find your place? At home? Or maybe at church?"

"At home. We went to a cane-grinding, and Percy . . . he didn't want me a singing with him, or even playing the guitar. So, I went to help the women working in the kitchen, but they didn't want me in there, either. Sister Daisy, there was a whole farm full of people, and nobody wanted to be around me. Not even Ma-Ki Ebbing's daughters." *I have a house, but I'm a wondering if I have a home.*

"Sweetheart, I'm so sorry." Sister Daisy touches my shoulder. "As well as you sing and play, I'm a little surprised you weren't involved in the music. I can understand why being excluded would hurt. You know, sometimes when people start believing in Jesus, they experience quite a bit of rejection from others." Sometimes Sister Daisy gets a deep wrinkle between her eyebrows. Since we've been talking, it looks like it might have sunk in for good. I can't stop looking at it. "Were there any women from our church in the kitchen, Rose?"

"Maybe one, but I ain't sure. Women around town staring at my stomach and looking for signs of the baby. I ain't seen any bump yet, so I guess they ain't either. Sister Daisy . . ." There it goes. Instead a river of peace running through me, I got a river of tears a running down my face.

"What's the matter, honey?" Sister Daisy puts her arm around me and pulls me closer to her.

"Papa was there. So was my brother Joe." My voice shakes.

"Oh my. Did you have a chance to speak with them?" Sister Daisy takes a deep breath.

"Papa called for me to stop when he saw me."

"How did it go?"

"He hugged me a wee bit." Sister Daisy claps her hands in the air, all excited about that hug.

"He told me Momma was *in trouble* when they got married."

"Rose, I'm sorry." Sister Daisy leans closer. "Maybe that's why she reacted so strongly when she learned you are carrying a child."

"That's what Papa said. I stirred up her old hurts. You know, after I talked to Papa, at first I felt glad I had hurt Momma. She's been so mean to me. But I love her. Sister Daisy, I don't try to hurt nobody, but I'm surefire good at it."

"Your mother may be having a difficult time forgiving herself. Rose, it sounds to me as though you are the one who has been hurt." Sister Daisy hands me a Kleenex from a box on the coffee table.

"Yes, ma'am."

"Rose, in time, people will stop talking about you. But first, they'll have to find someone else to talk about. In the meantime, forgiveness helps us get through our circumstances. Try to forgive. It cleans up the heart, the way a good vacuum cleaner picks up dust and dirt."

I laugh, thinking about a vacuum cleaner just a sucking out the grudges I hold. "Have you ever been gossiped about, Sister Daisy?"

"Land sakes, yes. It only takes one or two people in a church who are disgruntled to cause an entire congregation to become angry."

"You're the last person who should be hurt, always helping everybody else."

"Thank you, Rose. I have the Lord to help me and a wonderful husband. During difficult times, I pick up my shield of faith to protect myself from Satan's weapons."

"I sure would like to see that." I stand, hoping she'll take me to it.

"See what, honey?"

"Your shield."

"Goodness, Rose. I don't explain things too well sometimes. My shield of faith is in here." She points to the Bible sitting on an end table, opens it, and flips through its pages. "It's in Ephesians Six, Rose, verse sixteen. 'Above all, taking the shield of faith, wherewith ye shall be able to quench all the fiery darts of the wicked.'"

"It ain't a real shield?" My face feels surefire hot, a knowing I've sounded like a dumb schoolgirl.

"It's real, Rose. It's stronger than any protection our eyes can see. It's our faith in the Lord that protects us from being hurt by people's thoughtless words and actions. When you have time, I recommend you read the entire chapter. It talks about the armor of God and how it helps us to overcome trials."

"I will, Sister Daisy."

"I want to teach you a new song." Sister Daisy returns to the piano. "'I'm on the Battlefield for My Lord.' You'll like it."

Deep inside, I start marching like a soldier, my head a nodding to the beat. The big cuckoo clock on the wall busts out, too, and a little fake bird pops out. Cuckoo! Cuckoo! It's noon.

"Oh, I've got to go to Bessie's," I say over the bird's squalls. I grab my pocketbook, and Sister Daisy follows me out to the front porch.

"Rose, 'Where the Soul Never Dies' mentions a rose that is blooming. It's what you're doing, Rose, blooming in front of my very eyes."

"How's that, Sister Daisy?"

"You're becoming a young lady. When we met, you were a scared girl. You've gained confidence, and it looks beautiful on you." She holds out her arms for me, and I reach back for her hug.

"I'll be back Monday for another lesson. I hope we go back to having our porch music tonight. I miss it. Maybe you could come?"

"Maybe sometime we can, Rose. You enjoy yourself."

Sister Daisy smiles, and I turn to go. I walk down the steps, knowing I'm a rosebud in bloom.

♪♫

Opening Bessie's front door, I hold my right arm forward a wee bit, holding my invisible shield of faith. I need something to stop them fiery darts that Bessie throws at me.

"Rose, is that you?" Bessie calls from her bed.

"Yes, it's me."

"I don't need you today. Go home." Bessie's propped up in her bed, watching the television at its footboard. The chime and xylophone and cheers from an audience fill her room.

"You watching a game show, Bessie?"

"What do you care, Rose?"

Lord, please show me how in the world to forgive somebody who ain't sorry. Somebody who keeps on being mean. "Can I get you something to eat, Bessie?"

"You think you're something, don't you, like some bigshot nurse? I don't got any use for *your* help. I know why my brother married you. You want to rub it in about that baby of yours. I done lost two of mine and can't have anymore." She throws both arms in the air. "Get out!"

I step back, a hoping Bessie won't see how I'm a wee bit scared of her. I gulp and take a big ole breath to make me good and strong. "Bessie, I want to help you."

"Get out!" Her fiery darts rush at me. In slow motion, I walk toward the front door, a hoping Bessie will change her mind. I can still hear her a screaming as I open the car door. I rest my head on the steering wheel, trying to figure out what to do next. I don't know how I can help Bessie when I ain't been through her kind of sadness. But I've had plenty of my own sorrow.

I ain't going to take my hurt out on Bessie. When I had them terrible pains on the side of the road, I learned that fear of losing a baby strikes deeper than any other hurt. I ain't told anybody what Bessie's like when I am alone with her. I'm afraid if I do, those pains'll come back. I could lose my baby.

Lord, help me use my shield of faith. Those eyes of Bessie's look dead, but her mean, sharp tongue is surefire alive.

Chapter 24

The Beat of Passion

Sister Daisy

Have you ever been gossiped about, Sister Daisy? Rose's innocent question piques my early memories of Jeremiah and how he led me to Jesus. The day after my walk to the chapel's altar, I thought about calling the local phone number the minister had scrawled across his business card. As much as I wanted to know more about Jesus and His grace, I could not bring myself to use the pay phone in the dormitory hallway. Such disgrace. Women dared not call men.

I take a seat at the parsonage piano and begin to play "Somewhere Over the Rainbow." I can hear Judy Garland's voice, and I begin to harmonize with her as I remember the day after my first meeting with Jeremiah.

Mid-morning, I received a message from the housemother. Wallace had called to let me know about a schedule change at West Point. He could not make our standing Saturday night date. At first, I was flooded with relief but couldn't explain why. Then, as the other girls in the dorm began to help one another prepare for their dates, loneliness was at my heels. I was surprised when a visitor for me was announced.

"Jeremiah Little?" my housemother said, expressing her confusion about my gentleman caller.

"Wallace's cousin," I informed her. I jumped from the sofa, all too eager, and I knew. *It was more than Jesus.* I wanted the package, the preacher and his Lord. I slowed myself down and walked into the receiving area. Jeremiah, even more humble and handsome than the night before, greeted me with a smile. His Fedora in hand, Jeremiah playfully perched it on his head, tipped it in my direction, and removed it.

Under the watchful eyes of my dormitory sisters and our housemother, we sat outside under the trees, with autumn at its peak. Gold and crimson leaves fell as we spoke, the wind carrying some of them to our feet. Jeremiah sat across from me, and often, he would stand behind his bench, with one foot on top of it. We discussed Jesus and how his ministry had elevated the position of women in His time. The Lord has a plan for each of our lives, the young minister told me, and he quoted a passage found in the book of Jeremiah. I realized how Wallace's role in my life had been accomplished. He had connected me to my heartmate, and my fiancé was soon to be history.

"Speaking of plans, when are you and Wallace getting married?" Jeremiah had inquired. His smile was gone, but his eyes, even on a day when the sun barely peeked through the clouds, were bigger and bluer than the previous night.

"Well, Jeremiah, Wallace cancelled our date this evening. To be honest, I'm not in love with him. We've been a match of convenience. His family and mine are on the same social registers. He's West Point, and I'm Sarah Lawrence. We're both doing what's expected of us." I told Jeremiah this without an ounce of regret for being honest.

"Daisy," Jeremiah said, leaning closer to me, "Wallace's mother and mine are sisters. One of them married well, but the other chose a modest path. I will not be able to offer the affluent life as Wallace does."

"Does this mean, Jeremiah, that you are making me an offer?" How I silently scolded myself for being so desirous. But World War II raged throughout Europe and Japan, and war brides were common. I thought about Jeremiah's sermon from last night and how he had mentioned his combat experience.

"Yes, Daisy, it does." He laughed heartily, and I could feel myself blush. "I've been praying for a wife. When I saw you walk into the chapel last night, my heart told me that you are the one. I can't explain how, but I felt something new, something undeniably divine. So, Daisy . . . when you graduate, I'd love to marry you. And if you are in favor of this arrangement, I will court you with enthusiasm and then propose marriage properly."

"Oh, Jeremiah." It was all I could manage to say. My heart danced, and the rhythm of authentic love paraded across the decorum of my upbringing. I reached for Jeremiah's hand and squeezed it.

"Daisy, would you like me to talk with Wallace on your behalf? Let him know our plans?" Jeremiah had asked before he left that beautiful evening. It is like my wonderful husband, the gentleman who anticipates my questions, who clears the way when a path is difficult to negotiate, and who lights the darkness with his smile.

What I had no way of knowing, though, was how much my change of plans would cause my classmates to reject me. My name would soon be on the lips of every girl in the dormitory, with derisive giggling occurring when I entered and left a room. I didn't realize how personally insulted I would feel each Saturday night when Wallace came calling for a different girl.

Immediately after graduation the next spring, my former fiancé left for Germany. Months later, he was listed as missing in action. It took years before his status was updated to killed in action. Back at Sarah Lawrence, I didn't think about the possibility of Wallace dying, the guilt I might feel, and the sadness that would settle on the shoulders of Jeremiah.

I launch into Benny Goodman's "The Glory of Love." The piano keys seem to celebrate the selection, and the pedals beneath my feet become an instrument on their own, marching to the beat of passion.

Father God, forgive me for sulking about life in this small, country town. Please help Rose face gossip and disapproval with strength and grace. You've equipped us both with Your strength. And please, dear Jesus, help Jeremiah make a difference in this town. Amen.

Chapter 25

On the Battlefield

March 1953

Janie

"Janie, you're always the first girl picked for kickball. Half the girls are already on teams," Zelda says. "Something ain't right today."

"I can't figure it out, either. I wish this school had a gym. Then the girls could have P.E. separate from the boys."

"At least it ain't so cold today."

"Trouble is, Zelda, the boys always get picked as team captains, and they don't choose girls until all the boys are lined up."

Two girls our age walk by, their faces twisted in knots, looking at me and Zelda. "You think she ever combs her hair?" one of them giggles and points to Zelda.

"Yep! I comb it, but it's stringy. It's clean, too!" Zelda yells out. She's got some courage and guts. "Not like your greasy head. You could fry a chicken on top of yours." Those two girls dart away, and Zelda laughs.

"You're helping me get spunkier, Janie."

Before I can answer Zelda, Mean Gene Pinter yells out, "You!" He points at us.

"Me?" I thump my chest.

"Yeah, you, Buster's girlfriend," Gene sniggers. He keeps it up until he's holding his sides, belly laughing. Most everybody follows along with him. Buster, who was picked for Edwin Foster's team right away, turns pretty near brick red all over his face, neck, and arms.

"I'm not Buster's girlfriend. I'm his cousin." I stay put, not about to join Gene's team. Those Pinter boys are always causing trouble.

"Me and Janie are cousins," Buster yells out.

"Kissing cousins?" Mean Gene shouts.

"Gene!" our P.E. teacher yells and shakes her head.

Faster than a hound dog chasing after a squirrel, Buster dashes up to Gene's back and yanks his shirt collar real hard. Gene smashes to the ground, and Buster pins Gene's chest with his right knee and plants his palms on Gene's shoulders. My cousin's rear end sticks straight up.

"Buster!" Mrs. Long calls. She picks up the silver whistle dangling from a chain around her neck, blows on it, and runs to the fighting boys.

"Come on, Gene, and kiss me! Pucker up! Is that what you want?" Buster yells out. Everybody but me, even Zelda, starts laughing.

"Get up right now, boys!" Mr. Moody Brown yells out, running our way. Buster and Gene ignore the teachers, rolling around on the ground with Buster on top, then on bottom, then back on top. Mr. Brown grabs Gene by his leather belt, picking him off Buster.

"Buford Ebbing!" Gene yells out, "your whore of a mama don't want you, and that crazy old lady raising you ain't your mother! Your family ain't nothing but a bunch of swamp Indians!"

Great day in Green Cove. Here we go again. Swamp Indians, just like the fight at Junior's Dance Hall.

Buster tackles Gene, knocking him back to the ground. Straddling the boy, Buster wallops his face, head, and chest with both fists. Mr. Moody Brown gets on the ground, too, and tugs Buster's arm, but my cousin jerks away from the teacher's grip.

"Enough, enough, Buster! Get up!" Mrs. Long yells out.

"Janie," Zelda says. She slips her arm through mine and holds on real tight. I start to choke. "Are you all right?"

Whore. Swamp Indian. Names that have stuck to us like we've been tarred and feathered. Tags that cause Mama to squall and Maggie to yell and cuss and beat on Buster and make Percy drink and fight. Words that smother our spirits and choke our hearts. *I can't breathe.* I bend over, trying to get air, trying to make my throat stop making a weird noise, but it doesn't work.

"Janie, Janie!" some of the girls call.

"Quick, somebody bring me your lunch bag!" Mrs. Long blares. She walks in front of me and stops. "Breathe calmly, Janie. Nice and easy." She takes a lunch sack from one of my classmates. "Thank you." Mrs. Long dumps a sandwich and an apple on the ground and puts the brown sack in front of my face. "Breathe into this."

A bunch of girls huddle around me, and Zelda holds tight to my arm. Mrs. Long holds a bag up over my mouth and nose, and I breathe. I breathe some more. I don't know where Buster is, but I can't stop worrying about him.

"Buster's all right, Janie," Mrs. Long says, like she can read my mind. "Mr. Brown and the principal broke up the fight. They went to his office," Mrs. Long says. She looks at me, raising both her eyebrows. "All you have to do is keep breathing into this bag, and you'll be fine, too."

I look back at her, trying to figure out how the fumes of ham, bread, mustard, and apple can help me breathe again, but somehow, it works just right.

♪♫

Rose

"Rose," Percy says, "I talked to Willard, and Bessie's still in bad shape, not up to singing tonight." He's a combing his hair in our mirror.

"I know. Maybe we could go over, just us, and sing her favorite songs. It might cheer her up." I straighten up the clothes in our closet.

"That's what I thought, too, Rosie, but Willard says she needs her rest." Percy came from work this evening and headed straight for the shower and put on his dress clothes.

"You sure look nice in your white shirt and dress pants, like a respectable husband and all." I flash him my best smile. Not long ago I'd grin at him, and he'd tell me I was his onliest girl. Now he don't even see me when he looks at me. I got a notion I ain't his onliest girl anymore, a feeling that stabs my heart like a knife in the hand of a butcher.

"I'll be back before too long. Save me a plate, all right?" He reaches for the doorknob.

"Can I go with you? I'll ask Ma to get Dora or Lily to do the dishes."

"Rose, this here is business. I gotta meet with a man, and it's not fitting for a female to be there. Now give your husband a kiss."

Percy gives me a quick rooster peck on my lips. I follow him down the stairs, watch him race to the car, and put his plate of food in the Frigidaire. I run my hand across my belly, feeling a swell. Percy must have noticed it, too, but he ain't said anything. Maybe he's got a notion I'm fat.

It gets real lonesome here at night when Percy ain't around. I walk into the front room, where Dora and Lily sit on the settee listening to *Dragnet* on the radio. Lily, with her black hair swept away from her tiny face and up into her silver comb, works her crochet needle. Dora's brown curls fall around her square cheeks while she fiddles with the strings on an old guitar. Neither one of them look up or say hey.

On my way up the stairs, I hum "I'm on the Battlefield for My Lord." My Bible sits on the top of my dresser. After hugging it against my chest, I try to find the verse about the shield of faith. Just a flipping from page to page, I try to remember what Sister Daisy showed me.

Closing the Bible hard, I let it fall back open. Deuteronomy Twenty-Three is at the top of the right page, and I look for its first verse. Down near the bottom of the left column, I find it. "He that is wounded in the stones, or hath his privy member cut off, shall not enter into the congregation of the LORD." I ain't got a notion what it means, so I go on to verse two, hoping to get a hint. "A bastard shall not enter into the congregation of the LORD; even to his tenth generation shall he not enter into the congregation of the LORD."

Busting into a goosebump sweat, I read verse two over and over, then slam my Bible shut. Is my baby a bastard? I ain't sure. I jump off the bed and kneel.

Dear Lord, I did a real bad thing. The baby's mama and daddy did wrong, not him. Please don't let him take the blame. I'll take it all. I'm begging You. Amen.

I wonder why in the world Sister Daisy ain't told me about this bastard thing before now. Standing up, I feel a little weak. Something flutters deep inside my belly, like butterfly wings against my insides. I hear that song again, the same melody the day I thought I was losing my baby. The bedroom gets bright, like candles burning on an old lady's birthday cake. The song fades, and so does the light.

My baby moved. It's strong and alive. I am going to love it so much that no church can turn it away. I stretch myself out on the bed, just a hugging the Bible to my breast.

♪♫

Percy throws the bedroom door open, and from clear across the room I smell him, whiskey, like stinking sour apples. He stumbles toward our bed and falls into it.

"Percy, move over." I nudge him, but he's already a snoring. I wiggle out from under him. His smell makes me want to hurl, so I walk down to the front room, turn on the light, and look at the clock. It's near about three in the morning. The Lord brought Percy home safe, but I'm so mad I want to kill him.

♪♫

Daylight shines in through the windows of the front room. Ma sits across from me, a patting her hand against the chair. She taps her foot, like she's keeping time with a song.

"Rose, sleep in your own room."

I sit up, a hoping she ain't getting a notion to throw me out.

"I reckon, girl, you done figured out why Percy ain't ready for marriage. Don't be afraid of talking to him direct. He ain't a little boy anymore, and I can't make him behave. Neither can you, but you're gonna have to try."

"I don't know how, Ma."

"The more you put up with, the more he's gonna put you through. Don't ever let a man chase you out of your own bed, girl. If you leave it, there'll be another woman warming it when you go back. Understand?"

I nod my head and stare at the floor, ashamed because Percy's a cheating.

"Keep your business between you and Percy. It's ugly." She shakes her head. "Is he still sleeping?" Ma points to the ceiling, so I go back to check on him.

My husband is sprawled out across the bed, still a wearing his pants and T-shirt. His belt and white shirt are laying on the floor. I pick up the leather strap and hang it in the chifforobe. To see if the shirt needs to be washed, I hold it up to my nose. It smells like women's perfume. *Percy's cheated.* I throw it on the bed, but Percy don't stir.

Dear God, I am a standing here with my eyes shut but with my soul wide open, asking You for help. Wake Percy up, Lord. Please.

Chapter 26

Lehomahte: Peacemaker

Buster

"I hate that creepy Gene Pinter, Ma! I hate them all, 'specially Maggie!" I pull up an old chair from the yard to the porch, something to beat on.

"I ain't blaming you for hating your mother, Buster. She's worked real hard to become your enemy."

"Ma, don't call her my mother. You're my mother." I give the seat of the old chair a couple of good whacks.

"I ain't got the power to change history or blood, Buster. She's the one who birthed you." Ma's eyes get darker, almost black, like she knows more about hate than I do. When she puts her hand on my shoulder, I start to shrug it off, but I ain't about to hurt her like that.

"But that's all she's done. Why couldn't she be like my father, gone and never show up around here? I ain't missed *him*, and I wouldn't miss her if she took off." Whack. Whack.

"Buster, you got a right to be mad, but know this. Hate steals the spirit, makes the heart shrivel up. It don't happen overnight. It settles in slow and easy, without you knowing it. One day you'll want to love a pretty girl, but you won't have any love to give, only bitterness. It ain't easy to hate one person and love another."

"But I love *you*, Ma. I love Percy, Janie, even Dora. I don't hate nobody but Maggie."

"Your hate is fresh. Young. Hasn't had time to set into your bones. You'll forget how to love. That done happened to Maggie before you came along." Ma crosses her arms and stares at me good.

"I don't want to be like *her*!" I jump up and stomp the floor.

"Buster, you don't have to be. See that tree out there? The red maple?" She points to a tree in the yard.

"Yes, ma'am. It don't have any leaves."

"Right, Buster. Them leaves been shed because they've lived their season. You take a lesson from that tree. Shed the old stuff, son. It kills the heart. Gets in the way for what's to come."

"Ma, I ain't a tree." I sit back down and pound the chair seat with my fists, hoping Ma will see a boy, not a tree. A boy who don't know what to do about his best friend being a *girl*, his *cousin*.

"You're a lot like that there maple, changing with the seasons. You're about to mature. Just like that tree, you're fixing to need full sun and good moisture, free to shoot up strong and tall. You ain't gonna be able to grow if you're standing in the shadow of hate."

I roll my eyes and pound harder on the chair. "I don't want to go hurting Janie's feelings, but I got to stop doing near about everything with her. Those kids at school are talking bad about us." Ma gives me that look of hers, the one that says *I'm the head and you're the tail.*

"You done had enough punishment for one day, Buster, getting whooped by the principal. But don't make faces when I talk." Her hands on her hips, Ma might be little, but she's fierce.

"Yes, ma'am." I ain't going to win against Ma. Ever.

"Red maples grow up real fast when they get a lot of water. You're gonna shed some tears, and so will Janie. But it ain't only the water that makes people grow. It's the hurt, too."

"I don't get it, Ma. Hurt makes you grow?"

"Yep, and the time's come for you and Janie to make other friends. For a season. May take a few winters to work this one out, but you two will get through it."

"Okay, Ma." When she's got her mind made up, I can't tell her any different. It's better to go on and pretend I believe her.

"Buster, if I gave you two little trees to plant, would you put them right next to each other?"

"No, ma'am. I'd give them some space."

"To grow, right?" Ma looks at me and smiles a little bit, her dark eyes glittering. I don't answer. I don't want her to be right.

"You want me to talk this over with Janie?"

I nod my head, and Ma walks back inside. I slam my fists hard on the old chair until my knuckles hurt. I wish I could be one of them Seminole warriors Ma's told me about. They're all gone, though, dead and buried by the rivers and lakes across Florida.

I don't want to be dead. I want to fight.

Ma-Ki

Comes a time when I gotta put myself between Bessie and her young'un. Ain't no need to ask if her and Janie talked over what happened yesterday in the schoolyard. Bessie's trapped her own self in woe. She don't see nobody else's troubles.

"You want me to come with you, Ma?" Rose wants to help.

I been sitting in the car, studying the situation, but it's time to get out. I ain't ever knowed Janie real good, mostly kept myself closed up around her. She's been asking about Bessie's daddy since she was little. Buster's, too.

"No, Rose. Go on home. Willard or Janie will take me back." I open the car door. Rose reaches into the back seat and hands me bundles of palmetto leaves we picked this morning. She's a good one, Rose. Not one question about why I wanted them.

Before I can knock on Bessie's screen door, Janie opens it for me.

"Hi, Ma. Come on in," she says. "What's all that stuff?"

"We're gonna make a basket, me and you."

"Ma, she don't want to make no basket," Bessie says. She's laying on the bed in the front room, watching the big tube.

"Mama, please?" My granddaughter likes to stay busy.

I put my hands on my hips, signaling I done made up my mind. "This'll take all Janie's attention, Bessie. Can you watch those boys while we work?"

"I reckon, Ma."

"Good. Front porch or back, Janie?"

"Back," she says. I hand her the stems, and we walk through the house.

"You got this place in good shape, clean and polished." The way Bessie used to do. Out on the back porch, I notice Janie's shoulders slumping bad.

"Ma, I'll get you a better chair from the kitchen."

"This'll be all right, girl. You're gonna be doing most of the hard work." I sit in a rush seat chair, looking like it's about to fall through. Janie sits across from me on a wooden bench.

"Will this be like the basket you have in your chifforobe, Ma?"

"Close to it. We won't be doing a lid today, though." I smile, but Janie's lips don't budge. "First thing to know about basket making is how to find good stems. When you pick them, make sure they're at least two feet long. See?" I hold one up, showing her how long it is. "Bring me a knife, and I'll show you how to trim them."

Janie hurries into the kitchen, coming back with a butcher knife.

"We're gonna split them things. Look here at the end of this palmetto stem. See how it's shaped like a *D*? Start at the little end of it and slice it into halves." I work with my knife to show her. "If one side starts to get thicker than the other one, put your thumb on the bigger side, right where it's splitting. Bend it sharp."

"Okay."

"Janie, you and Buster split a little yesterday. Didn't you?"

"Ma . . ."

"That's why I'm here. It's gotta be worked out."

"Yes, ma'am."

"Now when we get them leaves severed, we'll go back through them, slicing again." Janie takes to carving palmetto like she's born to make baskets. Her long, skinny fingers remind me of my sisters' hands. They braided fast, made strong hampers. "You're doing good, real good."

"Thanks, Ma. This is fun. What's Buster up to today?"

"He's got his nose stuck in another book. I don't know what in tarnation's gotten into my boy. I hear him reading to Pistol sometimes. Girl, you're smiling at this. Ain't you?"

"Yes, ma'am, thinking about Buster reading instead of fighting. Ma, what happened to Mean Gene? Is he in big trouble?"

"He's gonna be kept out of school a while. Both them boys got a paddling from the principal for fighting."

"It was real scary."

"Janie, you know Buster thinks the world of you. You two ain't grown, and you ain't kids no more. You'll both be courting before long. That's when tension's gonna ease up. But the age you are right now—young'uns at school liable to say things about a boy and girl who's together a whole lot."

"But, Ma, we're cousins!"

"And plenty of cousins got married not too long ago. It don't get you off the hook. What them boys and girls at school ain't figured out is that you two are more like brother and sister than cousins."

"Maybe that's it."

"Here." I point to a splint. "We'll make some weavers, splints to weave into them ribs. Bring me a bucket of water, Janie."

"Yes, ma'am."

My granddaughter hops down the stairs, grabs a bucket from the yard, and takes a hose to it. She walks up the porch stairs with it and sits it at my feet. I coil them fronds into the pail. "Keep them wet until it's time to use them, Janie. This way they'll stay easy to bend." The young'un works like a frenzy, barely looking up. "What you think so far, Janie?"

"This is fun, Ma. I've always liked making and fixing things."

"I done seen it, your skill, the way you done the floor of this house."

"Ma, fixing things up won't be fun without Buster helping me."

"Janie, spend time with your girlfriends and the womenfolk. Buster's gonna need to be around other boys. It's part of growing up."

"What next, Ma?" She's whipstitch fast, already got all the stems split.

"They look real good. It's time to weave the basket."

"Wow." Her face goes into a full gale smile, like a wind blowed through and put a happy spell on her.

"Listen, life ain't easy on you. Taking care of Bessie, them brothers of yours, and now Buster shunning you." The smile on Janie's face rolls off as fast as it came. Tears grip onto her eyelashes.

"Shunning me?"

"He wouldn't come over here today. I wanted the three of us to talk it over. He ain't ready to talk to you, he says."

Janie pulls her knees up to her chest, buries her face in her lap. Poor girl sobs so loud that Willard climbs out from under the truck to see what's wrong.

"We're having a talk about her and Buster," I tell him.

"You're still daddy's gal," Willard says, his face covered in grease. "Going to be fine. Right, Janie?" He lights up a cigarette.

"Yes, Daddy," Janie sobs.

"Okay, now." Willard walks up the back steps and into the house. He winks at us, but she don't see him.

"Janie, let's weave the basket," I say. "Take those things we split up and build something strong with it." She looks up and wipes her tears away with her forearms.

"You know, some things that look real bad work out good. Has your mama ever told you how I got my house?"

"No, ma'am. How?"

"Before I had your mama, I was a maid, worked in Jacksonville for well-to-do people. Not rich, but *wealthy*. Bessie's father, Dothan Theodore Austin, was downright handsome. He was kind to me, but he didn't want no part of marrying a Seminole. He sent money, though, plenty enough to take care of Bessie.

"Dothan put me, Bessie, my ma and pa in a high and dry house. Before that, we lived right near the swamp, our house up on stilts. I did the cooking at a boarding house, and my sweet mother looked after Bessie. When I married Burl Ebbing, your mother was just a little girl."

I take four splints and cross them in the middle. "These here are the ribs. Keep them shiny parts face down. Watch how I go over and under to make the rows."

"Yes, ma'am." Janie studies my hands, the ribs, how they work together. I can tell she's done forgot about Buster.

"Dothan's money dropped way off after I married, only sent a little bit."

"But you had enough money after you were married. Right, Ma?"

"Enough. No extras. Folks around here didn't like Burl being with a Seminole. Him and his family had a store. Business dropped off real bad after he married me. At first, we liked to have starved."

"Because you're Seminole, Ma?"

"That's how I recollect it. After Burl got killed, my young'uns and me had to work the fields until Dothan learned that Burl died. Then Dothan came down to Starke and bought us the house and land. Years ago, we had different crops. We only got a couple of acres of strawberries now, but when my young'uns were growing up, we had a lot more. It's a hard way to make a living, picking strawberries. We hired help. But before Dothan bought us a place, folks hired us to pick."

"Like *Strawberry Girl*."

"Like what?"

"*Strawberry Girl*. It's a book."

"You and Buster and them books." I smile at Janie, and she smiles back, her eyes, too.

"Here." I point to the basket. "We gotta have an odd number of ribs for this basket to come out right." I pick a place where there's a gap and stick a palmetto stoke into the weave.

"Dothan never married me, a disgrace in the white man's world. But he ended up providing for *all* my young'uns. Your granddaddy was a good man, Janie."

"I tried to get Mama to tell me about him, but she cried every time I asked her."

"Bessie don't like to remember. She was shamed, too, him and me not marrying."

"I thought about asking you, Ma. But I figured I'd get in trouble for it."

"You did right. It ain't good to ask grown-ups such things."

"Ma, there's a lot more I want to know."

"About what?"

"Maggie."

"Janie, I'll talk to you about your mama, and I'll talk to Buster about his. But it ain't good to talk about Bessie to him or Maggie to you. This family is wove together tight, like the bottom of this basket." I hold it up, the bottom finished, for her to see. "Pieces got to be in just the right place. Answering your questions about Buster's mother could cause things to unravel."

"Aren't they unraveling now? With Buster and me?"

"No. May seem like it, though. Recollect what I told you. Sometimes hurtful things work out good. Don't fret. Count on the strong Seminole blood running through your veins, girl. You're full of power."

"Ma, it's hard for me to imagine Mama being a little girl. It hurts me to think she didn't have a good daddy, like mine."

"She had Burl. He loved her like his own."

"But Mama didn't have a father for very long. Burl Ebbing got shot and killed. It's not fair. Nobody even knows who did it."

"I know who done it, Janie." I set the basket in her lap. "Bend them ribs up, real easy. Keep the shiny side out." I watch her tug at the stems.

"Ma, why isn't Burl's murderer in jail? Why do you keep it a secret, who it is?"

"This family might come apart real quick if the truth gets out. There's some crooks in this world, crooks with money." Janie's eyes get real big. "This basket is gonna be shallow, but we'll make a tall one before long."

"We will?"

"Yep. Just a bit more to go, and it'll be time to weave the rim."

I hear shuffling across the kitchen floor. Bessie barely picks up her feet, muddling to the back door.

"Bessie. You feeling better?"

"No, Ma. I came to ask Janie what she's fixing for supper."

"Sandwiches, the ones you're gonna fix, Bessie. We're about to finish up for today." Bessie waits at the door.

"Give it at least three days to cure, Janie, more if it rains."

"Ma, thank you."

"Go see if your daddy's got done with the truck so you can drive me home."

Janie runs out to the yard, hollering for Willard. Leaving the basket on the bench, I take the bucket down the back steps and empty it. The sun's beginning to set, and Willard's making a phony Indian call, like I've heard in cowboy movies. He chases little Thunder and Lightning from one side of the yard to the other. Right now he can catch them, but I ain't sure what's fixing happen when them boys get big enough to cause a storm.

Chapter 27

Wondering

Rose

Sitting at the kitchen table, I skip through the pages of the Bible, looking for the word *bastard* again.

"What's there to eat?" Percy stands at the doorway. I want to keep our business to ourselves, like Ma said, so I give him the cold plate of food from yesterday. He's a gulping it down like a starving young'un from one of those foreign countries I learned about in school.

"Percy, does the food I cooked you taste good?"

"You know it's good, Rosie, for a hungry, hard-working man like me."

"Then take me to town."

"What for?"

I stare at Percy the same way Ma stares at people, hard and serious. He looks back at his food and holds high his empty tea glass. After I fill it up, I walk to the front porch. I sit down on the swing, humming the tune of Webb Pierce's "Wondering." Percy walks out, wearing dungarees and a plaid flannel shirt. He nods toward the car, and I hurry and hop inside.

"Where you wanna go, Rose?"

"Canova's Drug Store." We don't talk along the way. Downtown sidewalks are busy, mostly people I don't know, but there's a few girls I went to school with. Percy finds a parking space, and I bounce from the car and head inside. He follows me, his hands stuffed into his pockets. Just a watching him out of the corner of my eye, I see him swallow hard. I stop at the perfume counter and wait for him.

"Which one of them do you like best, Percy?" I take the lid off one bottle after another, a looking at the price tags. I take a whiff of Tabu and Blue Grass, but I slow down to a stop, like a jewelry box ballerina that needs a wind-up, when I smell the Shalimar. I hold the bottle under Percy's nose. "You smelled this one before, Percy?"

"That smells all right," he says.

"Just all right? I was figuring you would like it real good. I smelled it all over your shirt this morning. Who does this one remind you of?"

"Rose," Percy says, in a hushed way. "Keep your voice down. Remember I'm your husband."

"Well, the woman you married, me-Rose, wants better than all right, Percy. This here's a real pretty bottle." I set the bottle of Shalimar down and pick up a bottle of Evening in Paris. This one doesn't cost near as much, and I surefire don't want to smell like the floozy he's been laying around with.

"What do you think of this one, Percy?" He nods his head. I walk to the girl behind the counter, hoping Percy has money with him. While he pays, I hurry back to the car. Percy slams the door real hard.

"What's going on in your cockamamie brain, Rose? You ain't supposed to put me on the spot! What if I didn't have the money? The whole town would know."

"How much money did you spend last night, Percy?"

"That ain't none of your business. I work, so the money is my business, Rose."

"Your business and the woman you spent money on last night?" I look him straight in the eye, direct like Ma taught me.

"I ain't sure what you want from me, Rose." He pounds the steering wheel. "We're married now. You wanted it, and you got it, holy matrimony! That baby of yours will have my name. You didn't have to go off and give it away, like some girls do."

He starts up the car, and we start a heading for home, and a miracle happens. The song "Wondering" comes on the radio. I turn it up as loud as it can go. When Webb starts a singing the chorus, I sing real loud. "I pray every night to the good Lord above . . ." Percy don't say a word until we pull up in Ma's yard.

"Now listen to me good. Get ready to love your baby enough for both of us. And you better wear that ole perfume you tricked me into buying. Maybe you'll smell so good I'll fall in love with you one day 'cause I sure don't love you now!"

Percy's words blow fire across my heart, and for a minute, I want to die, the same way I felt when I had to tell Momma and Papa I'm *in trouble*. I lean over, a hiding from everybody in the house, the top of my head touching the glove compartment. Then I remember I'm Percy Ebbing's wife, not his cheap girlfriend. I sit up, holding my head high. I ain't got a notion who he was with last night, but I'll figure it out. And even if Percy ain't going to love his own young'un, this baby will be safe.

♪♫

Janie

Ma watches the roads real close, like I'm about to run over something. She braces herself, holding onto the door handle real tight.

"Making the basket was a whole lot of fun, Ma."

"Yep. Made me recollect times I made them with my sisters, back when I was only a young'un." She tucks a few stray hairs into the silver comb on the back of her head.

"How long has it been since you saw them, Ma?"

"Before you were born. Way before." She turns to look out her window.

"Do you miss them?" I hold the steering wheel tight, so I can pretend not to notice if Ma gets mad at me.

"Yep, I do. It's why I don't like to recollect them too much." From the corner of my eye, I see Ma dab at her eyes with her sleeve. She's got her eyes closed. She doesn't have nary a thing more to say about her sisters.

"Janie, if you'll sing 'Philadelphia Lawyer,' it'll keep me from turning sorrowful."

I learned this song a long time ago, before Tommy died. Mama and Ma used to sing it together. Halfway through the song, Ma stops me.

"Janie, you sing prettier all the time." She pats my thigh.

"But not like Mama." I shrug my shoulders, figuring I'll never sing as good as her.

"You got your own style. Be proud of it."

"Ma," I say, breathing in real deep and hoping to learn a little bit more about my grandmother. "Have you ever known a Philadelphia lawyer?"

"Can't say I have."

"Been to Nevada like the song talks about?" I turn my head to the right, trying to catch her eye.

"Nope." She shakes her head.

"Just wondering why you like 'Philadelphia Lawyer' so much." I suck in a big gulp of air.

"Janie, sometimes it's them words having nothing to do with us that help the most. It helps us escape our own selves."

I pull into the front yard of Ma's house, and Ma puts her hand on my shoulder. "Look at me, girl." I turn, and Ma looks deep into my eyes. "Near about everybody in this here family thinks we have it hard, but it ain't only us. Everybody in this world has problems. Think about them words to 'Philadelphia Lawyer.' The pretty young maid in the song, her two-timing her husband is somebody else's trouble, not mine. Helps me forget my own troubles for a minute or two. All right?"

"All right, Ma." She talks to me like I'm a grownup and always has. When I was little, she didn't say much to me. She skipped right over the baby talk and started with serious business.

Ma gets out of the car, but I wait a minute, watching Buster throw a stick for Pistol to fetch. When he sees me driving up, he heads out toward the fishing hole, not even bothering to wave at me. Great day in Green Cove.

"Come on inside. I got some ham I'm gonna send back with you to make sandwiches with." I follow Ma to the kitchen, where Rose is washing dishes.

"Hey, Janie. How did the basketmaking go?" Rose asked. "It was fun, Rose."

"Speaking of fun, you want to go to church with me tomorrow?"

I don't want to get anywhere near God. I asked Him to get Mama well, but He lets her lie in bed all day. Trouble is, I promised Him over and over I'd say my prayers, and I still haven't done it.

"I guess so, Rose." Maybe she'll see I don't want to go and tell me it's all right if I don't.

"Good. I'll pick you up at nine thirty," she says. A big smile spreads across her face.

Dear God, you're probably mad at me, but please don't strike me down when I walk into the church tomorrow. Mama needs me.

Chapter 28
I Must Tell Jesus

Rose

Sitting with me on a middle pew, Janie looks straight ahead, just about to bite her bottom lip off.

"I usually go up and help Sister Daisy with the music," I explain, leaning toward her. "But I'll sit here with you."

"Go on up, Rose. I'll be all right." Janie nods towards the podium.

I watch her from the platform while we sing "I Must Tell Jesus." *I cannot bear these burdens alone.* I try to picture me and Jesus talking, sitting on Ma's settee, me a telling Him about Percy. How Percy cheats on me, the mean things he says, the way he lays out all night, I want to tell Jesus because I'm way too ashamed to tell nobody else.

Janie jumps up from the pew and darts out the church door. Sister Daisy nods at me to follow Janie. When I get out to the car, she's bent way over the hood, her head resting on it. Her arms wrap around her face, and I ain't able to see nothing but her shoulders a shaking. I ease up a wee bit closer and put my hand on her back.

"Janie, honey, what's the matter?"

"I've got to get Mama to this church." She's just a sobbing.

"We'll surefire invite her, sweetheart. You think she'll come?"

"I don't know, Rose. Mama's sad and nervous. Nothing I do helps. She lies in bed all day."

"I ain't sure how to help Bessie, except to pray for her."

"Rose, I promised the Lord I would pray, but I don't. At night when I was supposed to be praying, I went to sleep because I was so worn out. That sounds like an excuse. Doesn't it?"

"Janie," I say, a bending way over so my face can be near hers, "all the work you do . . . the Lord knows you're give out."

"I broke my promise to God, and now Mama keeps getting worse."

I ain't got a notion what to say next, especially with Bessie acting like the devil every time I go over to help her. Sister Daisy walks into the parking lot, but she stays a ways back.

"Janie, how about if Sister Daisy comes over here and talks with us?"

"No! No, Rosie, please, no." She starts crying all over again.

"The Lord is a waiting for you to talk to Him. He's not mad at you. You want to pray with me? Dear Lord, we come to You . . ."

"No! I'll pray, Rose. It's time for me to pray," cries Janie.

"Dear God," Janie says, "I'm sorry I broke my promise to you about praying. Sir, will you make Mama feel better? Tell me what to do, and I'll do it. Amen." Janie lifts up her head, her chin still a quivering and tears plopping from her blue eyes.

"That was a really good prayer, Janie."

"Rose, I'm scared Mama's going to die! We've got to get her saved!" Janie pleads. Sister Daisy walks closer.

"Janie," Sister Daisy says, "would you like us to go with you to your house right now? We can pray with your mama."

"Yes, ma'am. You said we can go right now?"

"Give me one minute," Sister Daisy says. While Daisy hurries into the church, me and Janie get in the car to let the engine warm up. She's back in a quick minute. "Thank you for waiting. I had to let Jeremiah know." As we drive down the road, I'm a wondering if Bessie will let us into her house.

Willard sits on the front porch, a playing his guitar and watching the boys. Janie jumps out of the car and walks straight up to him. I can hear her as I am a getting out of the driver's seat.

"Daddy, will you stay out here with the twins for a while? I've brought some help for Mama."

"Help?" Willard says. He looks at Sister Daisy and then me.

"Yes, sir. This is women's business. Daddy, is that all right with you?" Janie surefire knows how to take charge. Her voice is loud and deep, like a big drum.

"Well, I reckon it'll be all right. Now don't go making your mama mad or get her crying," Willard says.

Janie leads Daisy and me to Bessie's bedroom door. "Mama, I brought you a visitor, Sister Daisy. She's the preacher's wife from the Thankful Country Church, and she's come to help you get over being sad. Rose is here, too."

I've seen Bessie look real bad, but not downright pitiful like this. Her Indian skin has turned pale gray. She's got long red scratches all over her arms, and I got a notion she's clawed them.

Janie walks to Bessie's side, starts a patting the pillows and then tugging on Bessie to help her sit up. Sister Daisy eases over to the other side of the bed and takes Bessie's hand.

"Miss Bessie, the Spirit is telling me this: the music has gone out of your life." Bessie looks into Sister Daisy's eyes and nods. "The Lord sent us to help you get your music back. Would you like that?"

"I sure would," Bessie says. Her voice cracks and tears drip down her face. She crosses her arms and puts her hands around her elbows, holding herself tight. I surefire hope Willard don't see Bessie like this, after we promised him we weren't a going to upset her. Janie looks at me, biting her lip again.

"Rose," Janie says. "Daddy's guitar is in the front room. Would you and Sister Daisy sing about telling your troubles to Jesus?" Quick, I fetch the guitar. Me, Sister Daisy, and Janie gather around the bed and sing the first few lines together.

I must tell Jesus all of my troubles . . .

Like she's woke from a bad dream, Bessie sits up a wee bit more and opens her eyes wide. She motions for Janie to sit on the bed and reaches for her daughter's hand.

I must tell Jesus all of my troubles . . .

"I need to get rid of these problems. I got to get out of the dark. Help me!" Bessie hollers. She holds her arms out, bended at her elbows, and her fists balled up.

"Can I lead you in prayer, Bessie?" pleads Sister Daisy. Bessie nods, slides off the bed, and kneels beside it.

"Heavenly Father," Sister Daisy prays, "we thank You for Bessie and the opportunity to pray with her. We ask You to heal her. Father, please write love on the tablet of her heart and give her the strength to leave this bedroom. In the name of Jesus, I ask you to let Bessie hear music and see the sunshine once more." Bessie sobs so hard her head, chest, and arms start a shaking.

"Bessie, the Lord will take your sorrow and replace it with joy. Do you want that?" Sister Daisy keeps on.

"Yep. Yep," sobs Bessie.

"Bessie," Sister Daisy says, a kneeling by the bedside, "repeat this prayer after me. Dear Lord, I ask You to forgive my sins. Come live in my heart, Jesus, and fill me with Your Spirit of joy. I place my hope in You, Jesus. Amen."

Bessie says the prayer with Sister Daisy and gets down a kneeling, crying, and praying out loud. Janie stands at the foot of her bed, her eyes dryer than a pot of water that's boiled all day. A loud car pulls up, something in it just a knocking. It's Ma and Buster. He waits in the car, but Ma walks on into the front room, carrying food. Willard's right behind her.

Sister Daisy and Bessie keep on a praying, not knowing Ma and Willard are a standing at the doorway. I've got a good notion to run out of here and go back home before Ma starts pointing or Willard starts laughing.

"Help me, Lord, please help me!" Bessie cries out.

"Father, we thank You for saving Bessie's soul and giving her eternal life," Sister Daisy says.

Ma shakes her head and walks the food into the kitchen. Willard stays put. Softly, I start to sing "Somebody Touched Me." Janie joins right in, and so do Bessie and Sister Daisy. I hear the front door slam behind Willard. Sister Daisy takes Bessie's hand and helps her up.

"We have a church service tonight," Sister Daisy says. "Please come."

"Rose, will you take me?" Bessie looks at me, and I don't see even a wee bit of hate left in them eyes of hers.

"I will, Bessie."

Ma walks back to the door of Bessie's bedroom. "I'll send Buster over to pick you up, Bessie. He'll take anybody who wants to go," Ma says, looking at me. "What time you need to leave?"

"Church starts at seven o'clock on Sunday nights," Sister Daisy says.

"Buster'll be here around six thirty," Ma says. Then she looks at me. "Church may do the boy some good." I can't figure Ma out. She don't like it when I try to tell her about Jesus. Now here she is a making sure everybody's got a ride to church. "You take care of Bessie, Rose. I'll talk to Percy."

Sister Daisy squeezes Bessie's shoulder and looks at me. "Tonight, when we sing, Rose, you stay in the pew with Bessie. She'll need you right by her side."

"I surefire will." I wonder what in the world Ma is fixing to say to Percy. I don't know a soul who's man enough to go up against Ma-Ki Ebbing.

Chapter 29

The Saw

Buster

I wrap up a chunk of meatloaf in a napkin and push myself away from the table.

"Boy, make sure you leave some food for Rose," Percy says, his mouth plumb full of mashed potatoes. It ain't like me to finish eating before Percy, but I ain't got much appetite since that commotion with Gene Pinter.

"This is for Pistol."

"You might better cut it in half. If Ma sees you taking Pistol . . ."

"She just got back from Bessie's and shut herself up in her room."

"Besides sneaking food to your dog, what you up to this afternoon?" Percy puts another piece of meatloaf on his plate.

"Maybe fish a little. Then I'm going to read more of *Gulliver's Travels*."

"What's got into you? Them books." Percy shakes his head. I hope he don't open his mouth while he's got food in it, or it'll fly all over this kitchen.

"I get away from here when I read them books, Percy. They make me think about sailing around the world, maybe joining the navy."

"Don't say I'd blame you. I wanted to do the same thing when I was your age."

"Well, why didn't you?"

"Take a look around here, Buster. All these women folk, Ma, and your aunts. Who'd they get to help them if I left?"

"I reckon you're right. But in two and a half years, I'm enlisting."

"You remember when you were a little boy, you wanted to learn how to play the saw? I thought maybe I'd learn you today. It'll take your mind off the Pinter mess."

"That would be nifty, Percy." I stand up, wanting to get this meat to Pistol before somebody catches me.

"Think about a song you want to learn. You know it's them slow, sad songs . . . they sound best on the saw."

"Be right back." I go to the back porch, where Pistol's waiting for me. He downs it in one bite, and I hurry back inside.

"Wash the grease off your hands before you handle that saw," Percy hollers from the kitchen. *Just what I need, Percy bossing me around like Ma and Dora.* Sometimes Lily, too. I wash my hands at the kitchen sink, full of dirty dishes waiting for Rose.

Out on the front porch, Percy sits on a stool with a big bow, a little box of resin, and a handsaw. He holds the bow up. "First thing, boy, is you got to have a hearty bow. This one here belongs to a cello. It'll give you more control over the saw. Don't use a fiddle bow, or you may end up with fewer fingers." Percy gets tickled at his own joke, but it sends a spooky thought through me.

"I ain't about to lose any fingers, Percy. It would keep me from joining the navy. And I figure if you can play that thing without losing any, so can I."

"Atta boy! Now, what you want to play?"

"Haven't had a chance to think about it. Let's do 'Blues Stay Away from Me.' That's a good one."

"You learn to play this saw, Buster, and you'll make everybody spill some tears. I wouldn't use a saw longer than three feet. Don't use one too short, though. You can get lower tones if the saw's long." Percy takes the saw and curves it.

"You keep hold of the end of it, Percy?"

"Yep, and press the handle between your knees." He strokes the bow against the blade, going up the scale. "I rosined up this thing pretty good while I was waiting for you. Here we go. This thing needs to be a big *S*." He hands the bow and the saw to me.

"What now?"

"Grab the top of the saw with your left hand. Face your knuckles away from you."

"Like this?"

"That's right. Use your thumb to bend the top in the opposite direction."

I bend it away from me, seeing the *S*.

"Good. Now hold the bow at a right angle. Draw it across the side, you know, where there ain't no teeth."

I pluck at the saw with the bow, getting different notes.

"You're doing it, boy." He starts to sing. "Blues . . . don't know why . . . you keep on haunting me." Percy closes his eyes, taps his foot, and sways his shoulders.

"No!"

Percy's eyes fly open, and he halfway jumps off the stool.

"What's the matter?" he hollers.

"Uh, I hit a sour note."

"Boy, I done thought you lost a thumb. So what if your note's off? You're just learning."

I keep playing, not worrying about my mistakes. Percy keeps his eyes open, watching me and guiding me through the melody while he makes up his own words.

"Hitched . . . what came over me . . ."

Rose drives up in the front yard, but I keep playing. "Hey, Rose," I call. Percy doesn't look at her and keeps on singing like she ain't here.

"Fears that I won't get free . . ."

Rose doesn't pay him any mind either. "Hey, Buster," she says. "You're sounding pretty good. I surefire didn't know you could make a saw sing."

"Percy is teaching me." He stops singing.

"That's awful nice, Percy," she says. "Maybe it'll help you get rid of the blues. They hit you so hard."

Percy doesn't answer Rose. He leans back, closes his eyes, and starts to sing again.

"I want the lover who used to be . . ."

I put the bow down and let go of the saw end real slow.

"Percy Ebbing," Rose hollers, "I got a good notion to grab the saw and take a go at your neck with it!" Her arms fly around like crazy, but it doesn't stop my uncle.

"Put me out of my misery," he sings and starts to howl like a dying dog.

Rose takes her worn-out black pocketbook and slaps it up the side of Percy's head. Percy shakes himself the way Pistol does after he's been for a swim in the fishing hole. Rose takes off into the house, wailing. Percy gets up off the stool and walks to the porch rail. He grabs hold of it, leans over, and laughs louder.

"Boy, did you learn anything today? I sure did."

Chapter 30

Come on Into My Kitchen

Rose

The minute I think I'm winning the war against sin, Old Slew-foot slips in, and my old mean self comes out. What would Bessie think if she had seen me a clobbering Percy? Here I am a praying with her one minute and beating on her brother the next.

"Rose, you done with them dishes yet?" Ma calls from her bedroom.

Done with dishes? I wonder if Ma has seen the whopper of a mess Dora and Lily left for me. Every pot and pan's dirty and every glass, too. I had to drink my tea from a Mason jar. Pieces of sausage and egg are stuck to plates. Percy and his sisters ain't cleaned up after their breakfast or lunch. Some of these pots need to soak. I leave them and find Ma sitting at her Singer.

"You done already, Rose?" Ma ain't bothering to look up from the sewing machine.

"Almost. Just the pots and pans to do."

"Come on back when you're done."

I nod my head, still tore up on the inside about how bad Percy's a treating me. He ain't been the same since I started getting thick in my waist. When he married me, I thought I got a prize. Now I know I didn't get *him*, except for his name.

Living with Percy is like being with Momma. She's supposed to love me, but love ain't mean. Love don't hit. Love don't throw somebody out. Love wraps its arms around you when you have gone and messed up. It soothes when your heart is just a hurting. And love shows you how to keep walking when your feet ain't able to take another step.

Scrubbing the last pot, I think about how I hope if I'm a good enough Christian, a good enough wife, a good enough daughter-in-law, things will get easier. I ain't had enough nerve to ask Sister Daisy about my baby being a bastard. I dry the last pan and put it on the stove. I want to be by myself, but I better go see what Ma wants. I walk back to her room. This time she looks up at me.

"Rose, them clothes you're wearing done got too small. I meant to finish some things for you near about two weeks ago, but I been busy helping Bessie with her troubles." Ma takes a maternity top she's got folded over her arm and lays it on the bed, smoothing it out. It's a pretty white cotton with a solid black collar.

"This'll go with near about everything," she says, patting the white top. "But this other one's special, like what me and my sisters wore. I still got one for when I go someplace nice. This material, I been saving a good long time." Ma holds up the blouse. "These here are sawtooth patches. I sewed a beaded necklace with them same colors its neckline." The patches are gold, turquoise, and purple, sewn up against a solid white.

I pick up the white top with the black collar and hug it to me. "I ain't never had anything so pretty, and look at that necklace! Thank you, Ma!" I leave the other top on the bed, almost afraid to touch it.

"My mother taught me how to sew them things onto a blouse. I'm slow now, but when I was a girl, I went real fast. Did a lot of them," Ma says with a smile. "I'm fixing to make you some skirts, too."

"Ma, this top is surefire gorgeous." I put one top down and run my fingers over the one with the beads. I wish I could say fancy things to match the way I feel about Ma and what she's done for me. Ma ain't the hugging type, but I reach out for her anyway. She hugs me back good and hard, a surprising me so much I jump a little.

While me and Ma are a hugging, notes from Percy's harmonica drift through the house. I strut out to the porch to show him my pretty new clothes. Percy sits on the porch rail. He ducks when he sees me a coming, probably because I tried to beat the meanness out of him earlier this afternoon. I stop myself quick and slow down, so he won't think I'm running out to hit him again.

"What's that?" he asks, looking at the blouses in my arms.

"Ma made me some maternity tops. Ain't they pretty? Now I can look all proper. I love you, Percy, even when I'm mad at you." I smile real big, hoping it'll remind him of me, the way I was, before he got me *in trouble.*

"Well, Rosie, you sure got a crazy way of showing love, hitting me with your pocketbook. If Hitler had that old thing, he coulda won the war."

"I'm sorry, Percy. You forgive me?"

"Hmmm. I reckon anybody who doesn't know about the baby will know now with them maternity tops. The whole town'll be talking about you, Rose."

"Percy, you sound like my momma. People are already talking. And if the whole cotton pickin' town is going to talk, I can't do nothing to stop them. And you didn't answer my question about forgiving me. After all, I forgive you about laying out almost all night with some floozy."

Ma's warning comes to my mind: *the more you put up with, the more he's going to put you through.* If Ma says not to let him get away with cheating, then I'll do my best to stop him. Eying Percy's guitar propped up against the post, I reach over and pick it up.

"This is one of my momma's favorites." I start strumming the tune to Robert Johnson's "Come on Into My Kitchen." I change the words a little bit and sing. "When a good girl gets *in trouble . . .*"

I pick up my foot, not a missing a beat of playing or singing, and jam it up against the picket under my husband's rear end. I park my shoe right between his legs and finish the chorus, but I leave my loafer where it is.

"You afraid they going to talk about *you*, Percy?"

"I ain't afraid of nothing, and don't you forget it. Sit down a minute so I can talk to you."

I ease my foot to the floor, backing onto the porch swing and sit down.

"Ma tells me," Percy says, "you'll be riding back to church with Bessie tonight. If that don't beat all, spending all day and all night at the church house. You got a husband to take care of, Rose."

"Percy, I can't stop you from cheating on me, just like you ain't going to stop me from a going to church tonight."

"You don't make no sense, Rosie. One minute you're talking about Jesus, and the next you haul off and hit me. You're carrying on like Emmaline, and I ain't putting up with it, you acting like your momma. And I sure wish I hadn't ever gone into that kitchen of yours." Percy hops over the rail and lands on the ground. He don't look back but gets in his car and drives off. He's right. One minute I talk about Jesus, and the next minute I act mean like Momma.

Them gumballs that like to dance in my gut are a cake just a baking. Take flour, baking powder, and salt. They don't get big and hot by theirselves. They need some Crisco and a hot oven. Momma and Percy, they pour their fiery meanness onto me. My hurt pops up big and full, just a rising.

There ain't enough room for it all in the pan, so it spills onto the stove and makes a big ole mess. Sister Daisy showed me in the Bible how the Lord's people are the salt of the earth. I need more Jesus, so I can be good salt and not spill my guts where they don't belong.

Lord, please forgive me. One minute I'm mad and the next minute I'm happy. I told Ma I've got a river of peace running through me, but lately it feels like the river is about to dry up.

♩♪♩

Janie

"Mama, is there anything I can do to help you get ready for church tonight?" She's been out of bed all afternoon and humming. I have my mama back.

"Janie, do you want to keep company with them brothers of yours this evening or go with me and Rose?" Mama walks from her bedroom and into the front room, and I can see her in good daylight. Mama looks scary pale, especially with those scarlet scratch marks on her arms.

"I'll take care of the boys, Mama, so you won't have to worry about them one little bit."

Mama brushes her hair, making it flow down her shoulders in black, shiny waves. She smiles at me, her eyes looking into mine. "Come here."

I join Mama on the settee, and she hugs me close to her breast. Stroking my hair, she hums, "Somebody Touched Me." I press my head against her and wrap my arm around her waist, tucking my hand between her and the couch. I know I'm too old to be hugging Mama this way, but she's been gone a long time. Her body's been in that bed, but her mind has been real far away.

The sound of Daddy's footsteps lets us know he's near. He motions for me from the hallway. "I'll be right back, Mama."

"Okay." Mama starts brushing her hair again, and I follow Daddy to the kitchen.

"Daddy, is everything all right?" I whisper. There's a look on his face I don't quite get, his mouth in a straight line and his wide eyes narrowed somehow.

"I reckon, gal. But I ain't never been too trusting of people who go around talking about the Lord all the time." Daddy talks in a hushed voice, too.

"Sir?"

"Ain't every Christian bad. But if somebody's pure evil, you can count on one thing. He'll call himself a Christian."

"I didn't know, Daddy." I gulp. Maybe I've done the wrong thing, getting Mama saved.

"I shouldn't have to say a thing like this to you," he says, "but I'm afraid your mama's going to get herself hurt. That's all."

"You think Rose'll hurt her?"

"No. It won't be Rose. But I'm jumpin' the gun. I shouldn't."

"I made a mistake, didn't I, Daddy? Getting somebody here to pray for Mama?"

"No, honey. You did just right. But if somebody ain't treating her right, tell me as quick as it happens. Don't wait."

"Yes, sir. Is that why Ma was shaking her head today when Mama was praying?"

"I ain't had a chance to talk to Ma, but I think you got it right. If there's anybody who don't trust Christians, it's Ma."

"I never heard her talk about it."

"Well, Ma don't mind saying what she thinks, but she sure can keep things hushed up. For now, she wants to save Bessie from what's tormenting her. What's important here is that your mama's feeling better." Daddy gives me a wink.

"Daddy, what's bothering Mama so bad?"

Daddy turns toward the truck and calls back over his shoulder, "I got to go pick up a carton of cigarettes. I won't be gone long, Janie."

"Yes, sir." I watch Daddy walk across the yard. He rubs the back of his neck. I bet he knows exactly what's been driving Mama crazy. Ma knows it, too. She told me plenty yesterday, but trouble is, she must have left a whole lot out.

Chapter 31

He Set Me Free

Buster

Well, bitin' bass, Ma's calling me, and I can hear her near about halfway to the fishing hole. Pistol turns and runs back toward the house. Now I can't get away with saying I ain't heard it. I trudge back to find Ma sitting on the side porch.

"Ma'am?"

"Buster," she says and leans toward me, "I told Bessie and Janie you'd go to church with them tonight."

"What?" I holler. Ma raises up off her chair, putting her face in mine.

"What do you mean, Buster, saying, 'What' to me? You're going." Pistol sits down at my feet, whimpering a little.

"Ma? You don't believe in church. Why do you want me to go?"

"Do you recollect what I told you about letting bitterness growing in you?"

I roll my eyes, waiting for Ma to whack me, but she doesn't.

"When Rose first came here, she was a mess. I done seen how much church helped her."

"Well, you should've seen her today, Ma, clunking Percy on the head with her pocketbook." All right, I can't stop myself from laughing, even if it means Ma is going to whack me.

"I seen it from the front room, Buster. You know, it ain't like he didn't have it coming to him."

"No . . . no." I can't get the word *ma'am* out of my mouth. Ma starts laughing with me, looking younger than I've seen her look in a long time. And I may as well face it: I'll be at church tonight. When Ma says I'm gonna do something, there ain't any way out of it.

♫

Rose

Bessie sits out on the porch swing this warm evening, and she's wearing a fancy yellow-flowered dress. It ain't nearly as pretty, though, as the smile on her face. Me and Buster get out of the car, and I look around for Janie but I don't see her or them boys anywhere. Bessie stands up to greet us.

"Bessie, you look so pretty. I'm glad you are coming with us. Where is Janie?"

"Her and the boys rode out to the dump with Willard," Bessie says.

"Well, it was good to have Janie along this morning."

"She's a real good girl. Rose, I got to clear the air right now. I was mean when I said there was only one reason Percy married you." Bessie turns to me with a hint of tears in her eyes. "My heart's been tore up, but that ain't any excuse for me saying hateful things."

"You sure are sweet, Bessie. I've been praying for you." We hop into the car and start our drive to church. "You've been a going through a lot, Bessie."

"I was so down in the dumps, and your light was shining real bright. You have a baby coming, and I was jealous." Bessie's voice, usually as smooth as melted butter, cracks.

A lump, like a Tootsie Roll sucker that's come off its stick, is a popping up way in the back of my throat. The Lord has answered my prayer about saving Bessie. Now all I want to do is say the right thing. "You know, I thought about what it would be like to lose my baby, and somehow I knew you were hurting bad."

I check the rear-view mirror. Buster's got his eyes slammed shut, probably just a thinking about me smacking Percy in the head with my pocketbook. I got a notion that before too long, Bessie will see me slip up, too. Then she'll know I ain't no saint.

"Thank you, Rose," Bessie says. She smiles at me. "Hey, what a pretty top. Did Ma make it for you?"

"Yes, she did. Ain't it pretty?"

"Yep. I'd recognize Ma's handiwork anywhere. It looks mighty good on you."

"Thank you, Bessie." I look in the mirror again and see Buster pulling an old blanket up over his face. "Buster, are you all right back there?"

"Just hunky dory."

We pull up to the church, so early I thought we'd be the onliest ones here, but the parking lot is jammed with cars.

"Pssshaw!" Bessie yells, scaring me good. "I forgot to take my medicine, and it's a big old horse pill. Rose, I need some water."

"Bessie, Sister Daisy won't mind a bit. I'll get a glass from her at the parsonage." I point to it. "Want to go with me?"

"Nope. I'll wait here."

"Okay. Buster, want to go inside?"

"Nope, not me, either."

I head for the church parsonage, trying not to laugh at Buster. I ain't never known him to be so quiet, except when he's trying to catch a fish. I stop smiling at the top of the porch steps, when I hear some men a hollering.

"I didn't say turn her out! I said sit her down," comes the booming voice of Deacon Chester Stokes.

"We've prayed for help with the music," Brother Little says. "She's a good girl who loves the Lord. We can't hold it against her, what happened before she became a Christian. Think about it. She's a new creature in Christ Jesus."

With one foot on the top step and the other on the Littles' porch, I freeze. They're talking about *me*. Through the front door, I see five men from the church sitting around the kitchen table.

"It ain't no example to be setting for our young folks. You got no business parading her around up there on the platform!" Miles Sinclair's gruff voice is easy to recognize.

"Brother Miles, let's consider . . ." pleads Brother Little.

"Preacher, everybody in the whole church can tell she's in the family way. You may think we're dumb farmers, but we can put two and two together!" hollers Deacon Stokes.

I lift my left foot onto the porch. I got a good notion to open the Littles' front door and bless them all out. But I can't. All of a sudden, I know what Janie meant about her heart choking. I ain't up to facing these mean people, people who say they love everybody.

I clutch my stomach and try to picture Jesus and think about how His people should be the salt of the earth, but it don't work. Heat is a stirring up inside me. Standing here all by myself, I got a bastard inside me. Doomed. I've got Bessie outside, and I ain't totally sure God wants her either because she's a bastard, too. I turn around real fast, aiming to run back to the car, but the toe of my shoe hits the edge of a big clay pot.

"Owwwwwwwwww!" I yell, hurting inside and out. I start a limping down the stairs when Brother and Sister Little run out. Tears sting my eyes as Sister Daisy grabs me around my waist. Bessie stands a few feet away, watching us.

"Oh dear, Rose, you shouldn't have heard such mean-spirited talk," Sister Daisy says. "Bless your heart."

"Shouldn't have heard what?" Bessie wants to know.

"Sister Bessie, some people had gathered here, saying unkind things about Rose," Sister Daisy admits.

"Yes," Brother Little says, "but we held our ground. Rose is a new creature in Christ. He doesn't hold her previous sins against her, and neither will we."

I want to believe Sister Daisy and Brother Little, but I'm afraid of what I read in Deuteronomy. My baby won't be welcome in the house of the Lord. I hold my breath, a hoping it will stop me from bawling.

"Sins? Rose has always been a good girl, taking care of me when I was way down in the dumps."

From behind me, I hear my preacher's voice. "Ma'am, we haven't met yet. I'm Jeremiah Little."

"Bessie DelChamp," my sister-in-law says, her hands balled up and pressed against her hips.

"We're so happy to have you with us, Mrs. DelChamp," he says. Brother and Sister Little ease me down to the steps. He turns towards Bessie. "Sister Daisy and I understand that all good people make mistakes. I've made a lot of them. And we're delighted to have both of you in our congregation. Please bear with me. I'll be showing those men out." Brother Little walks up the steps and into the house.

"Bessie, thank you for coming. We'll get this situation under control." Sister Daisy turns to me. "Rose, you're like family to us. We love you."

A door slams, and the men at the kitchen table follow Brother Little out the back door of the parsonage. I watch them a walking into the church. They don't look my way, but I ain't about to stop staring at them. These church men ain't even a wee bit nice.

"Bessie, Rose, it would mean so much if you would come inside. We'll talk this over," Sister Daisy coaxes. She takes my hand, a helping me up from the step. My big toe throbs like somebody's taken a steel meat tenderizer to it.

"Have a seat, ladies." She motions us into her living room and hurries to her kitchen. The preacher walks in through the back door and stands in the living room. He has his hands weaved together, a twiddling his thumbs real fast.

Sister Daisy comes back to the living room with a glass of iced tea for me and Bessie. Bessie reaches into her pocketbook for her medicine. I look into Bessie's eyes, waiting for her to slide back into sorrow. But there's something about her I ain't able to read. "I saw Buster in your car," Sister Daisy says. "Is he still there?"

"Oh my," Brother Little shouts. "Why don't I take him on over to the church and let you ladies talk?"

"What a fine idea, Jeremiah," Sister Daisy says. "Ladies, the situation you encountered tonight troubles me. There are some people who simply do not understand that God is love. One of the most important commandments Jesus gave is to love our neighbors. Clearly, some individuals are unaware of these concepts."

"It ain't your fault, Sister Daisy. Or Brother Little's." Bessie ain't never looked as strong as she does this minute, sitting up straight, shoulders back, and her chin up.

"It's not the entire church who thinks this way, only a handful of people," Sister Daisy says.

"Well, all my life, I ain't been welcome at some places. See, my daddy never married my ma," Bessie says. "She's half Seminole. Ain't a likely match for a respected white man. But no matter how upright my father was, he saw fit to love on Ma, his family's maid."

"I didn't know, Bessie. I'm so sorry you and your mother have endured such heartache," Sister Daisy says.

"Not having a daddy has warped me . . . all my life, and I gotta know one thing. Are me and Rose *really* welcome here?"

"Yes, Bessie, you are. Will you give us another chance?"

"If Rose will, I will." Bessie waves her hand at me.

"Surefire will," I say. But I don't mean it, not even a wee bit. I got a good notion to send for Buster, go home, and never come back.

"Bessie, I wish I could undo what these men said, but I cannot. Your first day as a Christian, and you've already witnessed how badly God's people can behave."

"Hmph! I've seen Christians done acting a whole lot worse than this, Sister Daisy. It's why my family don't have much to do with them."

"I see. What can I do to make up for it?" Sister Daisy wants to make things right.

"Ain't no need in trying. Today when Jesus came into my heart, I learned He ain't nothing like the sneaky people who hurt people and say they belong to Him. I came to the Lord to get stronger, not weaker. And stronger I am! He touched me today, and I ain't letting those sorry excuses for men turn me or Rose out of here."

"You're right, Bessie, stronger not weaker." Sister Daisy goes to the piano and turns to a song called "He Set Me Free." She starts singing, and Bessie joins in. When they're finished with the first verse and chorus, Sister Daisy gets up from the piano.

"Rose, we can't let anything turn us around," she says, "no matter what people think."

"What about my baby, Sister Daisy? I read how bastards ain't allowed in the house of the Lord, down to the tenth generation."

I ain't never seen Sister Daisy cry, but my question does it good. Tears well up in her eyes, and she puts her arm around my shoulder.

"Oh, honey, I think you're talking about a verse in Deuteronomy. It was written back under the Law, and God's people don't have to obey those rules anymore. Jesus came to set us free, just like the song says. God's people had to obey those rules before Jesus came." She squeezes my hand again, so hard that I think the blood's going to spurt out of it.

"Rose, you helped me when I was flat on my back. I can't let you get in the same kind of shape I was in," Bessie says.

"Take up your shield of faith, Rose," Sister Daisy says. "It will stop the fiery darts coming your way."

Brother Little walks in the back door of the parsonage. Part of his shirttail has come out of the front of his pants, his hair falls onto his forehead, and sweat pops out from under his arms and onto his suit jacket. He grabs a napkin and wipes his brow.

"What an evening," he says.

"I'd like to start a little differently tonight. Rose, Bessie, and I are opening the service with a song, if you don't mind," she says.

"Tonight?"

"Yes, Jeremiah, we'll be coming through the front door, singing."

"If you're ready to take the heat, I'm in the fire with you," Brother Little says. "I hope the church doesn't split apart." He shakes his head, causing more hair to fall from its place.

"Where's Buster?" I lost track of him.

"He is sitting in the back pew, clutching its arm. The boy's knuckles are pure white." Brother Little laughs real loud.

"Why don't you take him to the front, dear? No point in him sitting alone."

"Be happy to." He takes another napkin off the kitchen table and dries his face again.

"Jeremiah, will you have a guitar for us at the front steps of the church?" Sister Daisy hands Bessie and me a songbook to share, telling us the page for "He Set Me Free." Me, Bessie, and Sister Daisy step out the front door of the parsonage.

"This way," points the preacher's wife. I stand tall, picturing my shield of faith covering me and my baby. We walk to the front steps of the church, where Brother Little has propped a guitar up against a column. I strap it around me.

Bessie stands between me and Sister Daisy. "Once like a bird in prison, I dwelt . . ." she starts the song. Me and Sister Daisy chime in, walking through the front door and up the aisle. People turn around in their pews, some with their eyebrows raised high and their mouths a hanging open. Deacon Sinclair hangs his head, and Deacon Stokes squishes his eyes. Bessie holds her head high, a looking straight at the hymnal in front of her. I look at her forearms, and they ain't got a trace of the bloody scratches I saw this morning. Not even a wee bit pink.

Thank you, Lord. You've fixed her, inside and out.

Buster's sitting way down at the front, the song book open, and him a singing as we pass by. For a minute, the onliest thought I have is how happy I am to see that boy, his moon pie smile just a beaming at me.

Chapter 32

Hisakitamisi: God

Ma-Ki

Being half-white and half-Seminole turns near about every day into a tornado. My mind gets sucked into the twister, and then it gets spit out. My heart, too. The Seminole part of me, I done known it better than the white, no matter me living in the white man's world all them years.

I ain't sure I done the right thing by getting Bessie to church. Recollecting the missionaries that came to our village when I was a young'un, they took and made sure I got to school. I learned to read, write, and cipher numbers. But we were suspect of them. My grandmother told me they rounded up some older young'uns when she was a girl, said it was to educate them. But the young Seminoles slaved in the fields. Indians were the ones who done the teaching, showing the white people how to work our hot, damp soil.

I done spent months, years, trying to keep Bessie's mind from coming apart. Now Rose has dumped a bunch of religion into a weaved basket that ain't yet cured. The day Bessie got on her knees and prayed, I thought she'd get her nerves settled. But after hearing what Buster said about them men at the Thankful Country Church and what they had to say about Rose, it sounds like the bottom of that basket is fixing to give way. I ain't able to stop them from talking, lying, or stealing.

Hisakitamisi, Master of Breath, hear my sorrow. Watch over my Bessie.

Chapter 32

♪♫

Rose

I spread the three new skirts Ma made across the bed. One has a full skirt, purple with a drawstring at the waist and a hole in its stomach to let my baby grow. The other two skirts have open bellies, but they're straighter. Both of them have kick pleats, one made of black material and the other one an orangey shade of brown.

Kitty Wells' is a singing "Honky Tonk Angel" on Percy's record player. I slide the purple skirt over my walloping belly. No wonder Percy's out all night every weekend, me shaped like a Barlett pair. But I ain't about to let this lonesome feeling dig in too deep. My baby needs me. I reach for a hanger, but there's a knock on my door.

"Give me a minute!" I unbutton the old work shirt belonging to Percy. I put it on this morning a hoping to remind myself he'll come back home, trying to feel close to him. I hurry, throwing my patchwork blouse over my head. "Come in!"

Bessie opens the door, her big black Bible tucked under her arm. Her hair, the color of midnight, shines. Her skin does, too.

"Hi, Bessie. What are you doing over here so early on a Saturday morning?"

Bessie walks in and sits on the chair. "I woke up early this morning, feeling deep in my soul that Percy'd laid out all night. It ain't right, and I'm worried about you, Rose. I came to get you out of this here room. I'll make some sweet biscuits if you'll perk the coffee."

"Sounds real good, Bessie. Maybe Percy will come in and remember what he's missing."

In the kitchen, we bake side by side. From the back porch, the sound from Ma's ringer is a drowning out near about everything we say. But when the smell of cinnamon biscuits and coffee floats through the air, Dora and Lily forget about their wash and walk in. Ma puts some palm fronds on the back porch.

"Mmm, that smells good," Dora says.

"They're about ready to come out of the oven," Bessie says. "Help yourself, little sisters."

"I'm glad to see you in such good spirits, Bessie," Lily says. Her and Dora sit down at the table with me.

"You said it right, Lily," Bessie says. "The Spirit. It's the sweet Spirit of the living God."

"Bessie, you got a one-track mind these days," Dora says, cramming her mouth full of biscuit. "I wish you'd hush about it."

Lily shakes her head. "Well, I sure want to know how God's spirit got you up and out of your bed."

"It was real simple, Lily. I asked Jesus into my heart, and it was like happiness was pumped into me," Bessie says.

"Like a river of peace," I add, feeling like a surefire hypocrite. That river seems like it's dried into a stream sometimes. But it's still in me, helping me when Percy ain't home at night.

"Right," Bessie agrees. "Why don't y'all go to church with us tomorrow?"

"I've done heard enough," says Dora, getting up and walking toward the living room.

"Bessie, tell me more about that happiness," Lily says. "How it helped you get over the hurt."

"You know how Ma talks about being Seminole strong?" Bessie stops everything and looks at her sister. Lily nods her head. She stares into Bessie's eyes, still as a stalk of celery on a cutting board. "Everything Ma taught us, it came alive in me."

"But the old Seminoles believe in Hisakitamisi, don't they? The Master of Breath?" Lily looks a little mixed-up, a bringing her shoulders up higher and frowning a wee bit.

"Hisakitamisi. Yes. He has a son named Jesus," Bessie says.

Ma busts in from the back porch. "Done had enough religion talk for now." She grabs ahold of the biscuits on top of the stove and runs back out with them.

♪♫

Buster

The bad thing about Saturday mornings is having to mow the stinkin' yard, especially when Percy ain't around to help. At least I've got Pistol to keep me company. I'm rounding the corner from the side to the back when Ma pitches something, with a Mickey Mantle thrust.

Pistol runs around, grabbing up what Ma threw out. I throw the handle of the grass cutter down and run to make sure Pistol ain't eating something tainted. I bend down to take a good look and discover it's only a sweet roll.

"Give it here, boy," I say. I hold my hand under his mouth. He whines but drops the biscuit into my palm. It's still a little warm, ain't burned or nothing.

Porch Music | 221

Ma's been switch-hitting lately, one curve ball right after the other. I turn around and look for her while Pistol runs off, looking for more treats. I scratch the back of my head, even if it ain't itching. Maybe it'll help me understand what's come over Ma lately. I don't see her anywhere, but I hear her yelling.

"Hisakitamisi! Hisakitamisi!"

Bitin' bass, I wish Percy was here. I could ask him what God has to do with biscuits and baseball.

Chapter 33

The Charred House

Bostwick, Florida

July 1953

Janie

"Janie, come on in here," Mama yells out from the kitchen. I'm running late for school, but I run to her with my shoes in hand. "Sit down, honey."

I pull out the dinette chair, sit down with her and Daddy, and start putting on my socks.

"Your mama and me, we've been talking," Daddy says. "Hercules needs me over in Bostwick."

"You mean we're moving again?" *Oh no. Oh no.*

"I reckon we are," Daddy says and nods.

I look at Mama. She's given up most of her television programs to go to church and prayer meetings, and I wonder what will happen if Daddy yanks her away from the Thankful Country Church. I like having Mama happy.

"What about church, Mama?"

"Brother Little says there's a good church in Palatka, near about ten miles from Bostwick. I'm ready to move. How about you, Janie?"

"Me too." I liked living in Bostwick, back a few years ago, when I was a lot littler. Mama and Daddy never *asked* me about moving before. Great day in Green Cove, I hope this time they'll remember to take me with them.

♪♫

Daddy wakes me up real early, still dark. I smell the dark, strong coffee steaming out of his cup. "Janie, you want to ride over to Bostwick with me this morning?"

"You want me to miss school again, Daddy?"

"Today's Saturday, gal."

"Oh, yeah." I sit up on the bed. "I'll get the boys up."

"Your mama's taking them with her to Ma's today. It's just you and me, Janie." I wonder if Daddy can see me smiling in the dark.

♪♫

Daddy knocks on a kitchen wall smudged with dirt and ash. When we drove up outside, I got excited because this house is so big. But when we walked in, I started to dread moving here because this place has had a fire. It'll take a whole lot more than rags or papier-mâché to fix this place.

"What happened to start the fire, Daddy?" I run my hand up and down one of the studs.

"Short circuit in the electricity, Mr. Manning told me. There ain't many houses here in this little town. This is the only one vacant, except for a one-bedroom shack." He breaks away more of the smoke-stained plaster.

"Daddy, was anybody hurt in the fire?"

"A little boy's arm got burnt, but I hear he's doing all right."

"I'm glad he's all right, Daddy." I'll have to watch out for Kenny and Benny. I imagine them running through this kitchen with their arms on fire, screaming for help, me knocking the boys down and throwing myself over them. My stomach starts to burn, choking out the fire. Mama runs in and prays for us, telling us the Lord understands pain. Trouble is, I don't understand why He lets people hurt. I don't understand Tommy dying or Mama's lost babies. Deep in my daydream, Daddy's voice brings me back to the real world.

"Janie, an electrician'll be here in a couple of days to fix this here circuitry. But they ain't going to get anybody lined up to repair the lathe and plaster."

"What is a lathe?"

"See these here thin strips of wood nailed to them studs?" Daddy grabs hold of a long piece of wood. "They support the plaster finish. Can't make this look right again unless we redo the lathe and plaster over it."

"Hmm. What's this hairy-looking stuff coming out of the wall?"

"Horsehair," Daddy says.

"Sir?"

"Yep. To stiffen the plaster. Don't see much of this stuff going into houses these days. The man who owns this house says we can have a couple of months free rent if we fix it ourselves. And we could move quicker." Daddy stops to light a Lucky Strike.

Black smut covers the studs, but the framing is solid. I run my index finger down one of the posts near the fuse box. It'll be hard being away from Buster, even if he ignores me these days.

"Do it ourselves, and we can be living here next weekend," Daddy continues. "Janie, I was thinking about how you came up with an idea about sealing that holey floor. What about me and you fixing this charred wall?"

"I'm a little scared of messing with this horsehair, Daddy. Will you do it?"

"Don't be scared. Using horsehair is an old-timey way of building houses." Daddy puts his arm around my shoulder. "I ain't giving you the whole job to do. You'll be my helper."

"Yes, sir. I'll help."

"That'll be just dandy, gal. We'll pick up supplies today and talk to the landlord. I'll let him know we'll be moving in."

"Does Mama know about the fire?"

"You know your mama. She ain't going to worry about a fire or anything else if she's living next door to Charlotte."

"Charlotte?"

Daddy's big grin shows up, spreading across his face after being on a long vacation. "Yep. Charlotte Southerland, Cherry's mother. Go on over. I betcha she's at home." Daddy points to the house next door.

I jump, wrapping my arms around Daddy's neck, and he hugs me, too. I turn and run out the back door, down the porch steps, through the back yard, and run up Cherry's back steps.

"Cherry! Cherry!" I yell out. I haven't seen her since she left Green Cove a couple of years ago, back when Hercules transferred her daddy. She's a year older than me, but I can't remember not knowing her. We've gone to school together two places, Starke and Green Cove.

Cherry runs out her door, smiling at me and hollering. Before she gets to me, she stops and straightens her legs straight, closes her feet together, and clasps her hands out in front of her chest.

"Two bits!" Cherry yells out. She steps up on her tiptoes and brings her arms into a high V position, balling her hands up into fists. "Four bits!"

Swinging her arms down in front of her and crossing them, she bends her knees. Cherry leans forward a little but looks directly at me. Her blue eyes sparkle, and her smile shows off her straight teeth, white as cotton balls. "Six bits, a dollar!" She springs up into the air, graceful, like a mockingbird taking flight.

"If it's good to see me, Janie . . ." She whips her legs down and lands on the balls of her feet, her knees bent a little bit. Her arms are straight by her sides. "Stand up and holler!"

I'm already standing up, so I start hollering. But she yells out louder. "Whoo!" like she's cheering for a quarterback running toward his goal. Great day in Green Cove, she's good at this cheering thing.

I jump into the air, ready to whoop, but I'm not sure what to do with my hands. I throw them out at my sides as I come down. I land rough, twisting my ankle a bit. I pick my foot up off the ground real fast, holding it up behind me.

"Are you okay, Janie?"

"Yep, but I hurt my ankle a little." Cherry made the jump look so easy, but it sure was a lot harder than I expected, so I decide to lie. "I hurt it doing cartwheels yesterday."

"Hey, my mom told me y'all might be moving in next door. Are you gonna?"

"Yes, I'm going to help Daddy fix the charred up wall in the kitchen."

"Oh man, that place smelled for days. And it looks like it near about but went up in smoke."

"Yeah, there's smut on everything left in the kitchen. Hey, Cherry, have you ever hurt your ankle doing a cheer?" Mine's throbbing real good now.

Cherry stares at my foot. "It's swelling up. Mama will put some ice on it. Come on inside."

I hop inside, noticing more that Cherry has grown up. She's wearing a purple shirtwaist dress with a purple pansy scarf around her neck. Her long brown hair is in a ponytail, and her lips sparkle with pink peony lipstick.

"Hey there, Janie," Cherry's mother says. "Why are you hopping?"

"She had a bad landing, Mama." I'm glad Cherry's explaining this. Next to her, I must look a little dumb, hurting myself the first time I jump a little.

"Looks like it," Mrs. Southerland says. "Cherry, maybe you ought to let Janie leave the cheering to you, the way you leave the singing to her." All three of us are laughing when we hear Daddy knock on the back door.

"Hey, Willard," she says. She motions toward the kitchen table where I sit with my foot propped up on a chair. "Come on in. Janie's gone and hurt herself a little bit. Her and Cherry were outside doing cheers."

"Cheers?" Daddy's light blue eyes go narrow, but his mouth stays wide open.

"You know, Mr. DelChamp, football cheers." Cherry jumps in the air again, and Daddy breaks into a grin.

"I came to see if Janie wanted to go to the hardware store with me. But I reckon she'll be staying put." He looks at my ankle again.

"Yes, Daddy." As he turns to walk out the door, something new happens. It's all right with me to see Daddy go. I want Cherry all to myself for a little bit, to find out what her lipstick will look like on me and to see what kind of clothes are in her closet. I wonder how fast I can grow up if I start working on it *right now.*

Chapter 34

Oh, Come, Angel Band

Starke, Florida

June 1953

Rose

"Help!" I holler as loud as I'm able, but Dora and Lily don't come. "Help!" The black night swirls all around me, my bed sheets and my body soggy. "Help!" Pain cuts through my belly and loins, all the way down my calves. I try to get up out of the bed, but pangs scorch my back. *I must be a losing my baby.* "Help me, Percy! Help me!"

Ma flings the door open and pulls on the light chain hanging from the ceiling. "Rose, this baby's ready to be born." She puts her hand on my forehead. "You're burning up, too. And Percy ain't here. Confound him." She lets out a big sigh. "Can you get up?"

I shake my head. Ma wraps her arms around my back, trying to lift me up, but I start hollering again.

"Rose, them's back pains?"

I nod my head, and a hard chill hits me. I start a shaking. Ma's eyes turn soft gray, and her chin quivers. Now I know what Ma looks like when she's scared.

"What's the matter?" Dora hollers, standing at the door of the bedroom.

"Dora, ain't you got a bit of sense? Hard labor and a raging fever. Bring some blankets. Now! And wake up Buster. We got to get Rose to the hospital."

Dora comes right back, throwing some quilts over me. The bright light overhead fades, and so does Ma's voice. *Hold on, little baby, hold on. Live, even if I die.*

♪♫

Ma-Ki

Buster swoops Rose up. "Careful carrying her down those stairs, son."

"Yes, ma'am."

I pick up my lucky quilt, gold and purple sawtooth, and follow right behind Buster. He carries Rose down the stairs and to the car. Lily holds the door open, and I help Buster lay Rose down. She's done slipped away with a fever. I put my quilt over her, pick up her feet, and slide under them.

"Let's go," I tell Buster. Lily waves, and Dora yells something from the front porch. Buster takes off fast, jerking my head back. Rose moans loud, but her eyes stay buckled shut. I seen this before, women full of poison when the baby comes. Plenty of them died, but this one's got to live. Rose loves me better than my own young'uns do.

Hisakitamisi, help me. And Mr. Jesus, you don't know me, but you know this girl. She's yours. All my watching over her ain't done one bit of good because she ain't gonna make it if you don't help her. If you are real like she says, you'll bring her through.

♩♫

Rose

A bright white light is just a shining in my eyes. Tall men, wearing pointed metal helmets on their heads and swords on their hips, make a circle around me. There's so many I ain't able to count them. Every one of them holds an iron shield up to his chest, like he's protecting hisself and me. I hear the music again, the melody I heard that day in the car, on the side of the road, when I was a trying to get some food to Bessie and Willard.

The warriors open their circle, letting me see what's in the middle of them. Men, so beautiful they could be women, are a playing musical instruments. They've got harps and cymbals, but some of the strings and woodwinds are things I ain't seen before. The men sing, but the words ain't in English, and I ain't got a notion what the song is about. The smell of fresh roses floats up, and I hear something bubbling.

A waterfall of red splashes from the top of a mountain and down into a brook, just a sparkling like rubies. It's the blood of Jesus. *It's the River of Life.*

♩♫

Ma-Ki

"Doctor, everything was fairly well when we went to bed. Then near about two o'clock this morning, I heard Rose hollering." The empty emergency room is stark white, the color of Rose's skin when we brung her down to the car.

"Anything else you can tell me?" He fidgets with his stethoscope.

"Well, she was plumb wet from head to toe and burning with fever." I spit out the words fast, hoping the doctor will hurry back to tend Rose.

"We're doing everything we can, Mrs. Ebbing. She may be toxic." He leans my way, close enough for me to tell he's got sleep in his eyes. "Look, it may be a long night. The nurse is in with her now, but we'll brew some coffee soon."

He done read my mind, but I can live without coffee. Don't know that I can live without Rose. "Doctor, you got to save her and the baby."

"I'll do my best. In the meantime, we've got a phone if you want to call someone." Dr. Kelly turns quick, pointing to a phone on the waiting room wall. I walk to it and call the operator.

"Can you connect me to a preacher's house?"

"I can try, ma'am," says the woman at the other end of the line. I hear her stifling a yawn. "Who is the party?"

"Party?" I think she's got her cords crossed.

"The name of the preacher," she says.

"Brother Little at the Thankful Country Church."

"Just one moment, ma'am."

I wait.

"Hello?" says a man's voice, sounding more awake than the doctor and the switchboard woman.

"Is this Brother Little?"

"Yes, it is. May I ask who is calling?"

"Ma-Ki Ebbing. I'm at the hospital with Rose. She ain't conscious."

"Oh my. We've been up most of the night. Neither one of us could sleep. We'll be right there, Mrs. Ebbing." I hear him slam the phone down.

Blue vinyl chairs with big arms line the waiting room. Buster's sleeping across one of them. I sit down and wrap my arms around me, like I'm cold. I got my robe and a nightgown on. Tarnation.

"Ma!" Dora and Lily bust through the front door. "How is she?" Dora hollers.

"Still asleep."

"We brought you a dress, Ma," Lily tells me. "But it was Dora who remembered it, not me."

"You're good girls." Sometimes I know I ain't loved them daughters good enough. My heart turned cold when they were just young'uns.

"Ma, you want me to find Percy?" Dora stands up, ready to look for him.

My kids ain't never seen me cry, only Rose. I bend over, put my head in my lap, and circle my face with my arms. Them two girls of mine, they're squalling at my feet.

Rose

I AM with you, Rose. Trust in Me.

I look for Jesus, but all I can see is light. A hand touches my belly, and the pain is back, a ripping through my back and belly. I open my eyes and see hot bright bulbs.

"It should be any minute now, Rose," Dr. Kelly says.

"You're all right," says a gray-haired lady in a nurse's uniform. "You hold on, young lady."

I ain't sure what she wants me to hold onto. A pain hits me so hard, I can't scream or breathe.

"It's a girl!" Dr. Kelly shouts.

Then I hear my baby's cry, her very first song, a sounding even sweeter than the angels' singing. I reach for her.

♩♫

"Sure is a pretty little thing," Ma says, standing at the side of my hospital bed. "I been worried about you, Rose. We near about lost you." Ma's eyes still look gray, a reminding me of how scared she looked when she came to help me.

"She surefire is." My baby rests atop me, and I stroke her back. "Ma, the Lord brought us through." I got a good notion this is the time to talk about the Lord with Ma, her being so worried about me.

"I know it," she says. "The Littles are out in the waiting room. I called them."

I wish I could figure out what Ma is thinking, her calling my preacher and his wife, but her face is set firm. I take a deep breath. "Where's Percy?"

Ma reaches for my free hand, squeezing it hard. "Dora's gone to fetch him." Ma leans in a little closer and squeezes my hand tighter. "I'll send your friends in."

"Okay, Ma. Anybody else out there?"

"Lily. You want me to send her in, too?

"Yes, ma'am."

Ma leaves my side. I close my eyes until Lily comes through the door of my hospital room with Brother Little and Sister Daisy.

"Hi, sweetheart," Sister Daisy says. Her and Brother Little stand on my left side, but Lily comes around the bed and stands on my right. She's real quiet, like normal, but Sister Daisy keeps a talking. "How are you and your beautiful little girl?"

"I'm tired, Sister Daisy. You look a little tired, too."

Brother Little laughs real loud. "We couldn't sleep last night. Finally, around one o'clock this morning, we got up and started praying. When Mrs. Ebbing called, we were still deep in prayer."

"What happened, Rose?" Sister Daisy's eyebrows look like somebody's pinching them together.

"I went to bed a feeling real tired but not sick. Then the pain woke me up."

I hear Lily sniffle, and tears start a rolling down her face. I reach for her hand.

"Rose, your little girl looks like you," Sister Daisy says. "What have you decided to name her?"

"Send for Ma. Then I'll tell everybody."

"I'll be right back," Lily says. She hurries out of the room and comes back with Ma.

"You done decided for good about the baby's name?" Ma stands with her hands on her hips, a sign that things are going back to normal.

"Well, they ain't fixed the birth certificate yet. Melody," I say. "Her name is Melody. I heard a beautiful tune, some singing, right before she was born."

"Singing?" Lily shakes her head a wee bit.

"I like *Melody*, too. What about her middle name?" Ma wants to know.

"I ain't decided. Maybe I'll leave it up to Percy." I hear a knock on my door, and the nurse walks in.

"Mrs. Ebbing," she says, "I'll have to ask your visitors to come back in a bit. It's time for the baby to feed. Then the doctor wants you to take a nap."

"See you again soon, Melody," Lily says. Lily's big smile turns her from a plain-looking woman to a pretty one. She's got perfect, straight white teeth, like Percy.

"Take good care, Rose. We will continue to pray for you and Melody," Sister Daisy says. Brother Little nods. They walk out, leaving Ma and the nurse in the room with Melody and me.

Ma gets closer to my bedside. "Rose, you are my daughter," Ma says. Her lips quiver, but her eyes are strong, piercing mine. "Like I carried you, that's how I love you."

♪♩

Just when I'm a sleeping good, I hear footsteps in my room and smell Shalimar perfume. When I figure out how in the world I can love Percy *and* hate him at the same time, maybe I'll feel like opening my eyes. For now, I ain't going to look at him.

I hear him a shifting around in the chair. I roll over a little, so my back is to him. He ain't told me he loves me for near about three months, ain't held me close unless he was sleeping.

"Rose," Percy whispers. I stay still. "Rosie, honey." I hear his feet scuff along against the hospital floor, and the scent of his woman's perfume gets stronger. He touches my shoulder. "How you doing, honey?"

What I say now, he'll always remember, and me, too. *Dear Lord, help me do the right thing. Help me not to act like Momma.* I feel something whisk against my side. Real slow, I turn to see Percy a kneeling on the floor. He's wearing his white shirt, his sleeves rolled up. His arms are up on my bed, and his hands are folded.

"Percy?" I whisper. With his face buried in my sheets, Percy nods. "Have you seen her?" His head makes an up-and-down motion again, but he still ain't a lifting his face from the bedclothes. He drops down, a crouching lower.

My husband starts a bellowing, loud and low, sounding like a bass fiddle and an accordion busy a telling each other off. I look over the side of the bed, trying to figure out what in the world he's doing.

"Percy, was she all right?" Panic hits me. Maybe Melody died, and nobody ain't told me yet. "Percy! Is the baby okay?" I feel sweat a popping out of my face.

He lifts up his head, his eyes a looking almost as red as they did on our wedding day, after my brothers beat him up. He looks into my eyes, something he ain't done in a while. His shoulders start to shake, and tears gush from his eyes. I ain't never thought I'd feel sorry for Percy. I reach out, touch my hand to his cheek. He snatches my hand and kisses it, still bawling.

"Rosie, I'm so sorry." He gulps out the words like he's a drowning and coming up to yell for help. Percy lifts himself up and puts his arms around me.

"She's so beautiful, little Melody, like her mama. Rosie, will you forgive me?"

"Percy, I've been awful sick."

"Ma told me." Tears still slide down his cheeks.

"In the middle of all the pain, I had a dream, some real pretty singing. It was the most beautiful melody. I want to name her that, *Melody*."

"It's a real pretty name, Rose. Like the melody you and me make together." He smiles back at me.

"Well, we used to."

"Honey, you and me, we'll keep on making music together. I held her, the little bitty daughter of mine while you were sleeping. I done learned my lesson." More tears roll down his face. I ain't never seen a man cry this much.

"What are you saying, Percy?" I stare into his blackberry-colored eyes.

"I'll be staying home with you and . . . Melody." He chews his bottom lip. "I ain't anywhere near perfect, Rosie, but you're pretty close to it. I'm to blame."

I ain't never heard Percy say he's the blame or seen so much love in his eyes. Them gumballs in my stomach get real quiet. Surefire still. And now it ain't just a river of peace running through me. It's a song of hope, too, just a leaping up like waves caused by a windy day.

"Your cheating ways are behind you, Percy?"

"Yes, ma'am. Gone."

"I want you to go freshen up, come back with clean clothes. Get rid of that Shalimar smell and bring me my Evening in Paris."

"Sure, honey, I will. Anything else I can do?"

I nod. "Percy, if nobody told Momma and Papa about Melody, would you go let them know?"

"You can count on it." Percy squeezes my hand. "I'll be back soon as I get showered and go by to see Avery and Emmaline." He stands up.

"Is Ma out there?"

"No, she's at home. But Sister Daisy is out there. You want her to come in?"

"When you leave," I say. I've been a missing him like a violin needing a player to make it weep. For now, I want Percy all to myself.

♩♫

I watch Percy walk out my door, a knowing he's been with another woman and loving him anyhow. I close my eyes, remembering the sweetness of Melody's face. Sister Daisy walks into my room, stepping quick and smiling big.

"How long have you been here, Sister Daisy?"

She reaches out to stroke my shoulder. "I haven't gone home yet. I wanted to spend some time with you and Melody."

"I'm ready for them to bring her to me. I ain't seen her in a couple of hours."

"Well, you've been a very sick young lady. You need rest, so you can take care of her." Sister Daisy smiles at me and is a squeezing my hand.

"Right before Melody was born, I had a dream, Sister Daisy. There was an army a circling around me, had their armor on and their shields up. The Warriors opened up a showing a choir singing so beautiful, but I couldn't figure out their words."

"Sweet Rose, it sounds as though you had an encounter with the angel band." Sister Daisy's voice shakes a wee bit.

"The angel band?"

"Yes, the very angels who sing in Heaven." Sister Daisy's big smile gets even bigger.

"Why in the world would they sing to me?" I close my eyes, a hoping to see them again.

"Sometimes it happens when people are really sick. And Mrs. Ebbing tells me the doctor said you were toxic."

"But it happened one other time."

"The angels?" Sister Daisy's smile starts to fade again.

"Sister Daisy, keep this between me and you. Okay?"

"I won't tell anyone, dear."

"On the side of the road one day, I went to sleep when I was supposed to be picking up Janie. Terrible pains hit me hard. I couldn't drive, so I stopped the car. I must have fainted."

"How long ago was this?"

"The day Willard and Bessie moved and Janie didn't know nothing about it." I imagine Melody being Janie's age, a walking home from school to a house that's gone empty. How scared she would be. Real gentle, Sister Daisy takes my hand.

"It must have been frightening for you," she says. "And Janie."

I ain't able to hold back the tears. Sister Daisy picks up some tissues from the bed table and hands them to me. She strokes my hair.

"Look who's here, mother," a voice says from my doorway. It's a nurse, holding my daughter in her arms. The sight of Melody makes me forget about anything that ain't happy. Sister Daisy turns around to look at her, and I hold my arms out.

"She's perfect," Sister Daisy says.

"She surefire is." Melody suckles at my breast, and Sister Daisy sings a few lines.

Oh, come, angel band,
Come and around me stand.

I ain't never heard this song, but Melody seems to like it. She's good and hungry, and she ain't shy about getting milk. Sister Daisy keeps on a singing.

Oh, bear my longing heart to Him,
Who bled and died for me
Whose blood now cleanses from all sin,
And gives me victory.

"Sister Daisy, now I know all about victory." I look down at my baby. "Melody. She ain't been alive even a whole day, and already she's taught me what winning is."

Sister Daisy puts her hand on my shoulder. She closes her eyes, lifts her chin high, and starts humming "Angel Band." I hum with her, thinking about how good it is to love and to be loved back. We don't sound as good as the angels, but their melody will play in my heart forever.

Chapter 35

Hayopalecha: Roses

Ma-Ki

Dora hits the brake, pulls off the side of the road, and cranes her neck around at me. She ain't had hardly any sleep, and from the time she was a young'un, it's made her grouchy to go without it.

"You want to go where?"

"Aw shaw! You heard me, to the Monroes. To tell Emmaline and Avery about Melody."

"You think they care?" Dora's face turns scarlet.

"Don't matter. Doc says that infection ain't well yet. When I was a girl, I helped my ma when she went out . . ." Those tears of mine want to break lose again. I got to stop them.

"To deliver babies. I know, Ma. You saw a lot of babies die. Some get killed."

"You're right."

Dora leans way back toward the driver's window, and I figure out I got my finger right in her face. I bring my hands down into my lap. "And the doc says Rose ain't rid of that infection."

Dora bites at her lip and leans her head against her door. Her face is plumb white, now.

"If she dies, it'll kill Percy," Dora says. Her eyes stay shut. "I never did think he'd carry on about her like he did when I found him. Said he ought to be dragged and quartered."

"Nope, it sure don't sound like him. He loves her. So do I."

"Me, too," Dora says. Her face takes on the likeness of a twister, gearing up for a big storm.

"I ain't got time for you to squall again, Dora. Get me to Emmaline's."

"Yes, ma'am." She straightens herself up and starts the car. We drive down the country road to the Monroe's place, and Dora honks the horn at the edge of the front yard.

"Dora!"

"I ain't any ruder than they are."

"You're right." I lean toward Dora and honk the horn, too. Young'uns start running onto the front porch. Dora honks again, and this time Emmaline comes out, frowning. Her lips pucker like she's ate a sour lemon. I open the door and get out.

"Emmaline, good to see you."

"Ma-Ki." Her red hair's done got some grey in it.

"Rose done had her baby this morning. A girl."

"That right?" She starts running her fingers through her hair.

"She's taken a fever. Near about died." I take my fingers to my own hair, patting the bun on top of my head.

"But she didn't, right?" There go those lips puckering again. I ought a bend over and shock her something awful, smack her, my lips to hers.

"She's fighting it. She's awful proud of her baby. And in love with Jesus."

"She shoulda fell for Jesus afore she got wrapped up with Percy. Woulda kept her outta this mess." She moves her hands from her hips, crossing them in front of her.

"She ain't in a mess." There goes my finger again. "She's done got a family who loves her, even if it ain't you."

"I'll tell Avery," Emmaline says, starting to turn away.

"You coming down to the hospital?"

"That ain't one bit of your business, Ma-Ki. But don't go down there getting her hopes up."

"Emmaline, when it comes to you, there ain't no hope." I turn quick, hurrying back to the car. I hear her spitting at me, but I'm too fast for her. I open the car door and get in, and Dora starts the engine.

"Well, Ma. How did it go?"

"She ain't visiting Rose, even if she tries."

"Good."

♪♫

I pull over me a quilt my mother made. The wringer's just about wore it to a frazzle, but I ain't about to let it go. It's got turquoise waves, red arrowheads, and purple diamonds. Wrapping it around me, I settle deep into my bed. I'm wore out good, too tired to take Emmaline's foul head off like I wanted to. Avery deserves better. So does Rose.

I feel myself drifting into sleep. Pictures of caskets, Bessie's lost babies, and little Tommy float through my dreams. Buster as a baby, loving on him, and recollecting how I wouldn't let Maggie give him away like she wanted. Percy tiptoeing by my door wakes me up.

"Percy!"

"Ma," he says, "I was trying to be quiet, to let you sleep." His footsteps get closer.

"Come on in, son." I pat the bed, and Percy walks in and sits down. "What you got?" I nod at the sack in his hand.

"I went to the store. I got me a fresh white shirt and Rose a new gown," he says.

"She smelled that hussy's perfume on you, huh?" As soon as I say it, I'm sorry. Percy's mouth drops down in the corners, and he looks down at the floor.

"Yes, ma'am."

"I know you're sorry, Percy. It's plain to see. Stay sorry. You got a good wife and a pretty baby. It's time for you to be a man."

"Ma, the minute I saw Melody, something in me changed. And knowing Rosie near about died . . ."

"And she could still die. Full of infection. Our girl needs you."

"As soon as I get cleaned up, I gotta go over to Emmaline's and tell her about the baby. Rose asked me to." He starts scratching his chest, like the thought of it is giving him the wooly boogers.

"Ain't no need. I already been."

"Huh?"

"Yep. Thought it was the right thing to do. That Emmaline tried to spit on me, but I got away too quick." I can tell I ain't slept enough when I start laughing like a crazy woman. But Percy stands up and slams his fist into his other hand.

"I'm going over there!"

"No, you ain't. Rose been hurt enough. And you been heaping it on her, and you're in no position to judge nobody else."

Percy sits on the edge of my bed again, buries his face in his hands. "I'm so ashamed, Ma."

I sit up on the bed and reach for him. He puts his head on my shoulder, hugs me hard like he did when he was a hurt little boy. I reckon he ain't never outgrown not knowing his daddy or coming from a part-Seminole family. And his good looks didn't help him one bit. Girls made things easy for him. Then women did.

"Percy, you got to look forward. Don't say another word to that hussy you been laying up with. Make a clean break. She knows she's been messing with a married man. And she's married, too? Ain't she?"

He draws away from me and nods his head. "How did you know?"

"I got my ways. Now you go on. Rose'll need some lotion, her toothbrush, and all. Get it ready for her."

"I will, Ma. Thank you." Percy looks at me like he's about to cry again. I shake my head at him, wanting him to stop before he starts. He bucks up, throwing his shoulders back and straightening out his face. Rose done turned my family into the town waterworks.

Rose

Melody, perfect and beautiful, is a sleeping in my arms. Dr. Kelly says she weighed six and a half pounds when she was born. Sitting in the big brown chair in my hospital room, I turn to look out the window. It's a pretty day. The sun is a shining, and the breeze moves the leaves on the trees a wee bit.

"How are my girls?" Percy's voice sounds loud and happy. I turn back around to him, and he's a holding red roses in one hand and Ma's alligator skin satchel in his other one.

"Hey, Percy. Look who's up?" I give him my best smile and look down at Melody. Her hair is thin and dark. When the light hits it just right, you can see the red in it.

"Hey there, beautiful." Percy sets the bag down on my hospital bed, but he's still holding the roses.

"They're beautiful, Percy! Did you pick those from the yard?"

"I sure did, Rosie, but they don't look nearly as good as you. Or Melody."

"Percy, you want to hold her?"

"Yeah, but first I need to find something to put these roses in," he says. He looks around the room. "Maybe I can put them in your sink for now." Percy bends over, reaching out for Melody. He cuddles her in his arms and leans over and gives me a kiss. I get up from the chair.

"You two can sit here. I'll stretch out on the bed." I stand up, a feeling stronger than I have since Melody was born. "You sure look like a prince, Percy. How in the world did you get the Shalimar out of your shirt so fast?"

"It's brand new, Rosie. I went to the store and bought it and something for you, too. It's in the satchel. Go ahead." He nods at the satchel.

I open it up and see a brown bag with a pink ribbon tied around it. It's a pretty pink nightgown with lace a covering its yoke. Percy smiles real big.

"It's real sweet, Percy. Thank you."

"We're starting afresh, Rosie." He looks down at Melody. "Our girl's done drifted back off. A real sleepyhead." Percy laughs a wee bit.

When me and Percy first got married, I dreamed about days exactly like this one. Him looking like a prince, bringing me presents, and holding the baby in his arms. But I thought Momma and Papa would be here.

"Percy, did you go by Momma's house?"

He looks at me, and every trace of happiness leaves his face. I know he ain't got good news. Maybe he didn't have a chance to go by there. Maybe they weren't home. Percy gets up from the chair, comes around the side of my bed, and puts Melody in my arms. "You got enough room for me?"

246 / Kathy Maresca

I scoot over, and Percy climbs in, facing me. He wraps one arm around me and Melody and nuzzles his face in my neck, just a giving me goose bumps.

"Rosie, Ma had already gone and come back by the time I got home." He kisses my neck and squeezes us tighter.

"What happened?" I think about Janie, how her heart chokes. How hers must have felt like mine does right now.

"Ma says we're going to love you enough to make up for your folks."

With the three of us wrapped up like a fancy jelly roll on the bed, it's enough. I don't need what's behind me. But there's one thing that's still undone. "Percy, we still ain't given Melody a middle name. You get to pick it."

"Honey, I been thinking about this, and I like *Rose*. Melody Rose Ebbing."

♪♫

Ma-Ki

Up in Percy and Rose's bedroom, I blow out the last bit of burning sage and fan it with a turkey feather I keep in my chifforobe. I been through the house, letting the smolder chase out the bad spirits. They been hanging on these past few months. My young'uns raise a ruckus when I burn sage. Say it's one reason people call me pagan. But I ain't a pagan. I'm Seminole.

I can feel Rose's peace, strong, like a current powered by a strong undertow. Bessie done got herself a dose of calm, too. Says the Master of Breath sent Jesus here, and He's made her a stronger Seminole. I ain't heard it put that way before.

Percy and Rose pull up in the car, and I ain't finished getting this house ready for them. I hurry down the stairs and into my room, put away my feather, and go into the kitchen. I got a pail of roses for my girls, some I picked here and some Daisy Little gave me from her garden. I ain't had time to get them into vases yet. Here they sit in the same bucket I doctored Rose's feet in.

The front door squeaks open, and I ease out to the back porch. Times like this, a family needs to forge their own circle. I ain't fooling myself about who belongs in it. Percy'd do good to get his own house, but it'd wallop the spirit right out of me to see them go. The spring breeze blows swift, the scent of pine and milkweed dancing through the air. I twirl my arms and make my feet waltz. *Hisakitamisi* done brought my Rose and her Melody home.

Chapter 36

Smoke

Buster

We're starting my summer vacation right, Pistol and me. School got out a little early today. Like usual, Pistol greets me at the hard road, but he's extra excited right now. He's jumping up on me, barking, and yanking his head around toward the house. I know what he's saying: Come on!

"Okay, boy, okay." I hurry after him, thinking Rose must've come home with Melody, getting him all riled up. But Maggie's car is parked in the front yard, right by the door. This is what Buster was trying to tell me. I slow my pace, pretending we're in *The Jungle Book*. I'm Mowgli and Pistol is Akela. I halt and crouch.

"You wanna go to the fishing hole?" I whisper to my lone wolf.

He wags his tail a little faster and stays on course toward the house. Way I see the situation is, if I stay outside, I might hurt Rose's feelings. If I go in, I'll have to put up with Maggie and her big mouth. A snare waits for me. But prey can stay safe, if they recognize the danger that awaits them.

"All right, boy. We'll go on in." Maggie sits on the settee, holding Melody. I take a deep breath, wishing I could bolt. I ain't going to act chicken, but I'll protect myself from the woman who is supposed to be my mother.

"Buster," Maggie says, her cigarette hanging from her orangey-red lips. She never says *hi* or *hello*, just "Buster."

"Maggie," I say, hoping she'll see how her rude ways don't bug me. I look her in the eyes. Ma sits on the settee by her, looking at me and smoothing her hands over her skirt, over and over. "Where's Percy and Rose?"

"Rose took a nap. They should be down here, directly. Percy don't want her on the steps by herself, and she yelled for him to help her a couple minutes ago." Ma rubs her palms against her thighs pretty hard.

"Well, who needs Rose? We got the world's prettiest baby right here," Maggie says. "Sure wish I had a girl."

I lunge forward, my head stopping a couple of feet from Maggie's. I reach my arms toward her, my fingers clenched together. She ducks her head back.

"What are you doing, you crazy boy?" Maggie's mouth drops open, and her cigarette falls from her lips and onto Ma's settee.

"Hey! You come near burning the baby. Give her here, Maggie!" Ma stands up and gets in front of her daughter, between the two of us. I can't see Maggie's face now, only the backside of Ma.

With Ma mad at Maggie, I'll take a shot, too. "You're burning up the settee!" I pick the cigarette up, take a big honking drag from it, lean over, and blow out smoke in Maggie's face. I'm ready to choke when she jumps up and grabs my wrist, knocking the smoke right out of me. *But I'm a stealthy cub.* Quick, I grab her other wrist. I slip my one arm out of her grasp and clutch hers. She tries to wiggle free but ain't able. In the background, I hear Ma hollering both our names, but I stay focused on the enemy.

"You ruined my life, Buster!" Maggie screams, kicking my legs.

"Well, I ain't about to let you ruin mine!" I shove her back onto Ma's settee. "Don't touch me again. Ever!"

"Akela! Akela!" I open the front door. Dogs ain't allowed in the house, but nobody's said a thing about wolves. Pistol comes into the front room. "Come on, boy," I call. He follows me through the house and out the back door. But once we're outside, he takes the lead again. It ain't long before we're at the fishing hole. Free, free, free. Huck Finn, Jim Hawkins, Mowgli, and even Chief Osceola would be proud of me.

"No one can catch us, boy. Unless we want to get caught." I sit down by the edge of the lake and close my eyes. I feel Pistol lay down by my side. A breeze stirs around us, and the face of the new girl at school, Julia Mae Searcy, comes to mind. Maybe I'll ask her to the picture show when Rock Hudson's *Seminole* comes to town. All the girls go crazy over him. Maybe Julia will go crazy over me.

Janie

Daddy turns onto Ma's dirt road, and my stomach aches a little, knowing I'll be seeing Buster in less than five minutes. I wonder if he's still mad at me.

"I sure hope Percy ain't still running around," Mama says. We pull up to the front of Ma's house, and everybody hurries out of the truck but me.

"Come on, gal," Daddy says. "Show off your new clothes." He winks at me, his way of telling me he's real proud. He stands at the driver's door, holds out his hand, and I take it. I jump down, my crinoline swinging around my calves. Me and Daddy follow Mama and the boys inside.

Rose sits on Ma's settee, holding her little baby daughter. Percy stands next to her, leaning up against the wall. How come I never noticed how bad the wall needs painting? It's got a couple of marks from a fountain pen, smudges of dirt, and a round hole that looks like somebody put out a cigarette in it. After fixing the burnt kitchen wall with Daddy, I think I could get this one in shape in no time.

"You want to hold her, Bessie?" Rose's question grabs my attention away from the wall and back onto my new cousin.

"I sure do," Mama says. She takes the tiny newborn, cradles it smack against her bosom, and sits down in one of Ma's rockers. Her chin starts to quiver. "She's beautiful, Rose. You named her Melody?"

"Melody Rose Ebbing," Percy says. "I picked her middle name." I've never seen Uncle Percy smile the way he does right now, his face calm, like he's holding nary a feeling back. He puts his hand on Rose's shoulder and squeezes it.

"Janie, I almost didn't know it was you," Rose says. "You've surefire grown up."

"Sure has," Ma says, walking in from the kitchen. "How do you like Bostwick, Janie?"

"I like it a lot, Ma, but I miss everybody." Ma has a way of hooking people's eyes into hers, and I can't break her spell.

"Buster and Pistol are down at the fishing hole. Why don't you go tell him we got folks coming over for porch music tonight?"

"Yes, ma'am." There will be a whole lot of time to fuss over Melody later. Right now I'm fixing to find Buster.

With his back to me, Buster crouches and springs into a dash, Pistol right behind him. Then he stops real fast and reaches for Pistol. The dog sees me, barks, and runs my way. Buster follows right after him.

"Janie?" Buster cocks his head to one side and scratches his brow.

"Hey, Buster." I can't tell if he's glad to see me or not. "Hey, Pistol." I reach down to pet him, and he puts his front paws on my right hip and barks again. "Buster, Ma wanted me to tell you about company coming over tonight to sing."

"Bitin' bass. She didn't have to send you all the way out here."

He doesn't want me here. Best thing to do is head back to the house.

"Where you going, Janie?" Buster yells out. I walk faster, Pistol following at my side. Buster catches up with us. "Oh. You're scared of getting your new clothes dirty," he says. "I know how you girls are."

"Right." Something about Buster is different. Real different.

"I near about didn't recognize you, Janie. Where'd you get those new clothes?" Buster elbows me hard in the side, and I let out a deep breath. Nothing has changed between us, after all.

"Daddy bought them. I helped him fix a burnt-up wall."

"Lipstick, too?" Buster's dimples show now.

"Yes, he bought me lipstick, too." I smile at him. "Perfectly Pink. Mama picked it out. She said I'm too young for Romance Red."

"Well, Miss All Grown Up, can you run in your fancy skirt?"

"You know it." I elbow him back.

"Race you to the barn?"

I watch Buster take off, his long arms and legs dancing against the wind. I start to run after him, but instead, my foot hits an old fieldstone, and I land flat on my face. My right calf stings, and I sit up to take a look at it. My flesh is skinned good, dirt and blood mixed together. Great day in Green Cove, I'm getting clumsy. I'm just getting over my hurt ankle, and now I bust up my leg.

"Hey, Janie, are you all right?" Buster runs back in my direction. "Here you go." He reaches for my hand and helps me up. "Your knee looks pretty nasty, girl. Did you trip over the fieldstone?"

"Yes, I guess that was it."

"Stay here a second." Buster lets go of my hand and takes a few steps to the big rock. He kicks it hard, and a scowl of pain runs across his face and disappears. "I got revenge on it for you, Janie. It's hurt you for the last time."

♪♫

"Well, hurting your leg gave you a chance to slow down and visit with Melody." Buster stuffs a big bite of fried chicken into his mouth. We sit on the side of Ma's front porch, away from everybody else.

"Do you ever hold her, Buster?"

"Now and then. Oops. I ain't supposed to be talking with my mouth full." Buster picks up his napkin and covers his mouth with it.

"Since when did you care about manners, Buster?"

"I've always cared." Buster moves his napkin and smiles at me, his lips closed tight.

"You sound different, too. Not so much like Huck Finn." This time I elbow him in his shoulder.

"So, back to Aunt Bessie. How is she these days?" Buster whispers.

"Most of the time she's good. She misses going to church with Rose. She doesn't go to church as much as she did when we lived here in Starke."

"When y'all left here, she was *on fire* here with religion."

"There's still a smolder," I tell him.

"Janie?" Buster leans toward me. "Ma always says to watch out for the smoke. It clouds the way, and it ain't easy to breathe when you're in the middle of it."

Chapter 37

Love Lifted Me

March 1954
Starke, Florida

Rose

Bessie stands beside me at the piano, singing "Love Lifted Me" in her perfect way. I've been a practicing the song over and over, trying to get it perfect for Lily's wedding. Playing it for real, I ain't made even one mistake.

I was sinking deep in sin,

Far from the peaceful shore . . .

Bessie's pretty soprano voice rings through the church, making people dab at their eyes. I think back on how Lily met Nate at work, right after Melody was born. He had just moved into town and was a looking for a church. Lily told him about the Thankful Country Church, and the two of them have been coming here ever since.

Nate walks into the side door with Brother Little and Nate's brother.

The groom wears a black suit, white shirt, and a black tie. Every third beat, he steps up on his tiptoes real quick and then right back down flat on his feet.

From the waters lifted me, now safe am I.

Love lifted me! Love lifted me!

Dora, Lily's maid of honor, walks down the aisle slow, one step at a time. Ma helped her make a new dress for today, a golden shade of orange. She's a carrying a bunch of marigolds with white tips.

When nothing else could help,

Love lifted me!

Maybe Dora will get married next and move out of Ma's house. As soon as I get home, I'm a putting that on my prayer list. Lily and Percy start up the aisle toward me, and I pound "Here Comes the Bride" on the keys just like Sister Daisy taught me. I ain't able take my eyes off Lily. She's just a shining. Her smile is like the glow the sun casts over a lake.

Ma made Lily the prettiest wedding dress. It's white cotton, trimmed in silk and lace, and it goes almost all the way down to her ankles. There's a sash around her waist, the same color as Dora's flowers. Lily's got a store-bought pillbox hat with a net a hanging over her eyes and the tops of her cheeks. Ma put together Lily's flowers: dried blazing stars, marigolds, stalks of sage, and what Ma calls "Rose's red roses."

Percy bought hisself a gray jacket. He's a wearing black pants and a brand-new tie, looking fancier than the day he married me. But his heart is surefire nicer than it was back then. Percy ain't smelled like Shalimar even once since Melody was born. And he brags on me all the time, the way my figure came right back after having a baby. My husband looks away from Lily and up at me, blazing his movie star smile.

Nate looks deep into Lily's eyes while Brother Little pronounces them man and wife. The groom puts his hand on the back of Lily's neck and gives her a gentle kiss. I ain't heard even a wee bit of their vows, too busy thinking about me and Percy and how good it feels to be loved again.

Now I know why people cry at weddings. *There's something about being happy that makes us think about how sad things used to be.*

♪♫

Ma-Ki

Seeing my youngest girl get married ain't an easy thing. It's done tore Dora up something fierce. Far as I know, she ain't ever been asked. She's a little plain, but the real hitch is her sour ways. Still, she did good today, smiling and all happy for her sister.

Lily put away money a good while, and a big chunk of it went toward today's affair. She paid Thelma Green to bake a cake and gussy up its five layers. Percy, Willard, and Nate's brother tote it from our kitchen to the front room.

"Careful, careful," Bessie whispers.

About the time the house done feels like it ain't going to hold one more person, Lily and Nate cut the first piece of cake, feeding it to each other. Maggie, who ain't even here, hollers. Everybody hushes real quick.

"There ain't no such thing as love. You're only fooling yourselves!"

Aw shaw! If this house was a boat, it would tip over, everybody running onto the front and side porch. I ain't able to see a thing, so I run through the kitchen to get outside. I spot Maggie's Buick in the front yard. She sticks her head out nodding toward Ma.

"You think you're better'n me, Lily, but you'll find out different! You wait!"

"Well, I declare!" Dora screams from the porch. "You're plumb hateful, Maggie. Get out of here!" Dora waves her arms in the air and runs towards the car.

Maggie hauls off down the road, and the crowd of church people stand around with their mouths open, like they're inviting flies in. Nate's one of them. How can I tell him Maggie's like a clown, tears painted on her face, but hers are covered by makeup. Invisible. She don't show people her hurt, only her foolish ways. Lily's done turned as pale as her wedding dress. She wrings her hands and totters back and forth. Percy stands beside her.

"Folks, we ain't gonna let this ruin my sister's special day," he calls to the crowd. "Buster, will you bring our guitars? And what about the mandolin? We're going to serenade the bride."

Our company claps long and hard at Percy's idea. Buster runs into the front room, his face red with hatred. Hate, it's growing up faster than a stalk of corn inside my boy. Before long, it'll be all people will see when they look at him. They'll say he's just like Maggie. It'll grind every kernel of goodness out of his soul.

♩♫

Janie

"Janie, come here," Uncle Percy yells out. He's sitting on the front porch steps with Rose, motioning for me. Buster wasn't at the fishing hole, so I decided to head back to Ma's house. Uncle Percy moves to sit by Rose on the swing.

"You doing all right?" Rose leans against Uncle Percy and twines her forearm through his. Rose can smile through anything, but she's not trying today.

"I'm all right." But I'm not worried about me. "Where's Buster?" I'm grown-up enough now to get right to the point.

"Janie, a boy can't grow into a man without taking some time by hisself," Uncle Percy says. "He's got to be embarrassed. I sure am. Maggie was plumb drunk and trying hard to ruin Lily's special day. Maggie's jealous, you know."

Rose turns her head toward Uncle Percy. She takes her free hand and runs her index finger along my uncle's shoulder.

"Of Aunt Lily and Nate?"

"Of everybody," Uncle Percy says. "She ain't wanted anything to do with Rose since we got married."

"I know she did wrong today. But the onliest thing I can say about Maggie is that she was my friend when I was in trouble," Rose says.

"Don't take it the wrong way, Rose," Uncle Percy says. "She ain't never had a friend for too long. She's been out to get Bessie back for a long time, still mad over Willard."

"Daddy?" *Daddy?* I want to close my eyes, block this news out, but I can't. I've got to know the truth.

"You ain't heard about that?" Uncle Percy hangs his head.

"Well, maybe." I remember hearing something when I was real little. Trouble is, it scared me so bad I never thought about it again until now. "I told myself it was a joke."

"It ain't no joke," Uncle Percy says. "She knew Willard from an old juke joint. Was real sweet on him."

No wonder Mama's had so much trouble from Aunt Maggie.

"No kidding?" Rose leans over toward me.

"No kidding," my uncle continues. "Willard ain't never had anything to do with drinking, that I knowed of anyway, just there to play the music. Maggie drank a lot, even way back then, and Willard didn't want nothing to do with her. But she told him about how our house needing fixing, and he came out to help. He saw Bessie, and they fell in love. And Willard asked her to marry him just a few weeks later."

"Does Buster know?"

"Girl, Buster's lived here his whole long life. He knows pretty near all there is to know," Uncle Percy tells me. He runs his hands through his thick black hair. "I'll go check on Melody." He gets up and walks into the front room. Rose leans back in the swing and pats the seat next to her. I sit down and lean my head on her shoulder.

"Whatever in the world you feel right now, sweetheart, it's okay," she says.

I want to be grown, but when I finally get to hear things that have been kept secret, I end up throwing my arms around Rose, a papoose needing a dose of milk.

♪♫

Rose

The house gets real quiet with everybody gone. Ma and Dora went to their bedrooms, and Buster still ain't back. The onliest noise is Percy snoring. I lie down next to him on our bed, and he nudges me and winks.

"You were a faking, weren't you?"

"Yeah. I dozed off a couple of minutes. When I heard you coming up the stairs, I thought I'd trick you." He looks at me and winks.

"Well, you did one good job of it." I put my arm around his waist. "You think we should go by Maggie's and check on her?"

"No, it'd make her even madder. Rose, Maggie treated me real good when we were growing up. She was so pretty, landing near about everything she wanted except Willard."

"She ain't never told me about being sweet on him. I'm worried about her, Percy." He looks straight ahead, and I can't figure out what he's thinking. "Are you sure we shouldn't check on her?"

"Naw, honey. It might lead to more trouble." Percy runs his arm under my back, hugging me a little. "Maggie got something she didn't want, Buster. She ain't never treated him like a son, not even like a family member. It's like he's invisible to her. I always felt bad for her boy."

"Percy, do you know who Buster's father is?"

"Sure I know. You mean you don't? Hmm. With all the talk around town and you and Maggie being friends, I figured you knew."

"That's just it, Percy. I've heard a lot of talk, but Maggie ain't never talked about Buster or his daddy. I've heard some people say it's Moody Brown, and I've heard some people say Buster's daddy is a married preacher. I even heard it was a soldier from Camp Blanding. I always wanted to ask Maggie, but I couldn't figure out how in the world to do it without a making her mad."

"You figured right," Percy says.

"I wish she would get saved."

Percy squeezes his eyes shut, and his face goes blank. I brought up something he don't want to hear. I got a good notion he ain't going to tell me more about Maggie any time soon.

Chapter 38

In the Garden

Ma-Ki

Knock. Knock. Knock. A black woodpecker, his head crowned in red, ain't about to stop no matter how hard I wave to shoo him away. He keeps pecking at a little river birch tree. He'll have a hole poked clean through it.

"Aw shaw! I'm trying to sleep!" I holler at the bird.

"Ma?" comes a man's voice not far away.

"Burl?" I call. He stands on the bank of a river, tall, dark, and young and holds his hand out for me. "Don't call me that. I ain't your ma." I grin, so he'll know I'm pure tickled to see him no matter what he calls me.

"Ma! Somebody's at the door," the voice declares. I make my eyes open, but all I see is midnight dark.

"Who's there?"

"Percy. I'm going to answer the door. Okay?" He sounds just like his daddy.

"What time is it?"

"It's near five o'clock in the morning, Ma." I hear his steps walk toward the front room. I sit up, reach for the chalk lamp sitting on my night table. My eyes squint from its soft light. Tarnation. Who's at the door this time of the morning? Gotta be Maggie out there.

"Come on in, Sheriff," I hear Percy say. Sheriff? I must be dreaming this.

"Is your mama here, Percy?" an older man's voice booms.

"Have a seat, if you will. Ma's getting up."

No, I ain't. When somebody comes to this house before daybreak, it ain't good news. I'll stay right here.

"Percy, we don't have any time to waste." *Time. Waste.* It's Sheriff Grainger Tannen's voice.

"I'll get her," Percy says. His footsteps pound the wood floor.

"Ma!" He knocks on my door again. I draw my knees up to me and hug them. More footsteps.

"Ma-Ki?" Grainger calls. He's right outside my door. Somebody's coming down the steps, too. I pull the quilt over me, put my fingers in my ears.

"Ma!" Percy hollers, opening my bedroom door. My fingers ain't doing a bit of good.

Percy and Dora walk into my room. Percy's frowning, running his hands through his hair and chewing on his jaw.

"Ma-Ki," Grainger says, stepping over the threshold of my door. He's done gone back a lot of years now, calling me by my first name. "I'm sorry to bring you bad news. The highway patrol called me. Maggie's had a car wreck down in Alachua County. I want to take you to her." He runs the back of his hand along his forehead.

"Is she dead, Grainger?"

"No, but brace yourself, Ma-Ki. She will be soon."

Dora's eyes roll way back before she lands on the floor beside my bed. I ain't able to move. Percy opens his mouth wide, letting out the cry of a wounded warrior.

♫

Buster

The sun leaves pink streaks through the pale blue sky. Ma's up front with the sheriff in his police car. Dora and I sit in the back. Percy and Rose are on the road behind us. Their headlights have been shining like two penlights in the dark, pointing the way to where Maggie is dying. All I feel is relief.

"Hold yourself together for Ma," Rose told me earlier, when she woke me up. "Maggie may not be living still by the time we get there."

"It's not far now," the sheriff says.

Ma's hair is down around her shoulders instead of piled onto the back of her head. She hasn't said a word to me, barely looked at any of us. She sits stiff. Dora sits next to me, shifting around, moaning, and crying. Up ahead, car lights shine from the side of the road, and the sheriff brakes hard.

"This is it," he says, nodding toward Ma's car window. "She went down a ravine." He pulls off the side of the road, behind a highway patrol car and stops. Ma opens her door.

"Buster, come with me," she whispers. But I can't.

I can't because I'm afraid this is going to kill Ma, and I don't want to see her hurt. I wish I could hurt, too, but I don't care what happens to Maggie. I think I've heard about my real mother, the *whore,* too many times. Get me free of the woman who brought me into this world! I'm ready for her to go far away, where her madness can't touch me. Where her shame can't smother me.

"You've got to, Buster," Dora says, still sitting on the seat next to me. I shake my head.

"Somebody needs to stay with your grandson, Ma-Ki," the sheriff says.

"Rose'll stay. She's got that baby," Ma says, tugging on her quilt wrapped around her.

"All right. Let's head on down," he says. Ma and Dora follow him. Percy's car pulls up behind us, and he runs down the ravine, too.

The sun is shining a little brighter now, casting its pink hue over the brush. The golden raintrees, the Bradford pears, and the maples reflect the sunlight. Maggie picked a pretty place to die. I get out of the car to walk a little.

"Buster!" Rose calls from Percy's car. I go over to her car door. "Why don't you get in here with Melody and me?"

I shake my head and turn on my heel to look at Florida's jungle. I don't want to see the look on Rose's face when I say no. Percy runs up from the gully, waving his arms in the air.

"Buster, Maggie wants you, quick, boy! You too, Rose!" he hollers. Percy goes to Rose's side and lifts Melody into his arms.

"Buster, Buster!" somebody screams.

"We don't have much time," the state trooper says to Rose. "I'll take you on down, ma'am."

Rose

I follow the lawman on down the slope. It's steep, and I have to go slow. "Do you know how it happened? The wreck?"

"It was raining, and she was drunk. A truck driver heard a horn honking from down below and radioed us."

"Why ain't you a getting her to the hospital?" My foot catches on a vine, and he grabs my elbow to steady me.

"You all right, ma'am?"

I nod at him, and he gives me a wee smile. "Her car went down the embankment. It made a path here. See?" He points ahead to some mowed-down palmettos, circled by a bunch of pine trees. Way down yonder is a stream and a sandhill. We get started through the trail made by Maggie's Buick. "She's trapped inside. We can't get her out. The car rolled over a few times, and it's pretty near crushed."

I ain't even all the way down there yet, and I can picture Ma a standing at Maggie's car door, watching her daughter die. Ma's heart must be chopped down the middle. I slide down the hill a wee bit more. The patrolman puts his arm around my shoulder, a cupping it.

"I'm not trying to get fresh, ma'am. Want to keep you steady."

I ain't worried about him getting fresh, just worried about my family and how Maggie's a going to look when I get down this slope. "Is Maggie bloody?"

"Not too much, ma'am. She's got a few cuts, but most of her injuries are internal. But she's twisted up inside the car, and it's mighty frightening."

Through the bramble, I spot Ma's quilt, but I don't see Maggie's car. My guts start to shake, a knowing I'm about to see something that'll change this family forever. "What was she doing out this way?"

"When I found her, she told me she had been looking for some land, used to be a Seminole village."

I look back over my shoulder, a hoping Buster is behind us, but he ain't. Getting closer, there's Maggie's Buick. It's sitting on all four tires, crushed until the roof ain't no higher than my chin. The windshield is mostly busted out, with a few pieces of glass hanging onto its rim. Ma leans into the opening on the driver's side. Dora reaches out her hand for me, a putting her arm around me when I get close enough.

"I'm going back for the boy," the trooper calls.

Ma moves to the left, a letting me see Maggie stuck behind the twisted steering wheel. She's bent over it, and the speedometer and dash jut into her chest. Her head lays on its right side, her eyes half open and bloodshot. But I ain't able to see her hips or legs anywhere. The smell of rotten apples, the same whiskey Percy used to drink, rises up and tries to gag me. "Maggie," I say.

"Rose, get Buster. I got to tell him I love him." She closes her eyes and moans. Her face goes gray.

"Maggie," Ma says. "Anything you got to say, do it right now." She reaches in and puts her hand on the side of Maggie's neck.

"Tell Buster I love him," Maggie whispers. "I didn't want to love him. But I do. You hear me? I love him. It's me I hate. Me. And I'm going now, Ma."

Dora's sobs bellow through the air. She grabs ahold of her stomach. "No!" she yells. "Not my sister. Not now!"

"Ma, I always knew who it was," Maggie says. Her breath gets weaker, and she looks into Ma's eyes.

"The bad man, Maggie? Is that what you mean?" Ma's voice is as soft as a feather. Her hand, now on Maggie's shoulder, starts trembling.

"Yep. I wanted to kill him," Maggie says. Her voice is quiet, so I lean in closer to hear. "Rose?"

"Uh huh?" I reach out and cover Ma's hand with mine, bawling when I want to be strong.

"Pray," Maggie gasps.

I gulp air. *I ain't good with words. Please, Father God, not like this.*

"Maggie, say these words after me. Dear Jesus."

"Dear Jesus," Maggie drones. And then a rattle hits her chest and throat, a sounding like an electric mixer, its beaters clanging up against a big metal spoon. Her shoulders shake, and her head jerks in every direction. When it stops, Maggie slumps backwards and lets out a little gasp as she goes still.

"Maggie!" I holler. "No, God! Don't take her yet!" Somewhere between a split second and eternity, I hear the angel band. I look above the treetops, but the band ain't up there. It ain't up slant of the ravine, either. I close my eyes, hoping to catch a peek of them angels, but I see Maggie's face instead. I hear her singing:

Oh, come, angel band,

Come and around me stand . . .

I wish I could show everybody what I see. Maggie's eyes turn a deeper shade of violet, and her face starts to glow.

Oh, bear me away on your snowy wings

To my eternal home.

The angels hush, and so do the birds, the hoot owl, and the breeze. I take a deep breath. My legs teeter, my arms flail, and my mouth clamps shut.

"She's gone," Ma says, turning toward me. Her face don't show her feelings, but all of a sudden she looks real old. Her cheeks hollow out and her eyes dull, Ma takes the quilt from around her. She turns back to the car, lifts up Maggie's chin, and tucks the blanket under it. She spreads the rest of it around Maggie's shoulders.

"Dora, Rose, you two go back up the bank. This girl and me, we need to be alone."

"Yes, ma'am," Dora sniffles. She puts her arm around my waist, and I hug her back. Me and her start up the hill, arm in arm.

"Buster! Buster?" Ma hollers.

I jerk away from Dora, a running back down to Ma, but Dora reaches out, trying to grab me. I fall into the brush, hands and arms first. Dora helps me stand up, and I hear something moving through the trees and bushes.

"I hope it ain't no wild panther," Dora says. "Buster!" she screams, seeing his head through the briars.

Buster don't pay her no mind, running, his head low, his arms by his sides. He don't look at me and Dora, just straight down to Maggie's ruined car. He jumps the last ten feet or so, landing at Ma's feet. They wrap their arms around each other, and I hear Ma yell again.

"*Hisakitamisi! Hisakitamisi!*"

"Maggie's dead, ain't she?" Percy says. I turn to see my husband standing behind me.

"Yep!" Dora says. Tears slosh down her face.

"Oh, God, no. Please, no," Percy says. He bends over and pulls me up next to him.

"Percy, I ain't heard you coming," I say. "Who's got Melody?"

"The sheriff's up there holding her," he says. "We got to go back down there. Come on, Dora." He lifts her up from behind, the same way he did me. We start slow down the ravine, Percy in the middle and a holding me and Dora's hands. The bottom of my legs are a bleeding from cuts. Dora's ankles are a bleeding, too. It ain't much farther now, and I can hear Ma's and Buster's voices.

Face-to-face, Ma stands with both her hands cupped over Buster's shoulders. He's doing the same thing with her, like they're in a stand-off. Ma jerks her head over in the direction of Maggie's car window, but Buster shakes his head.

"Ma!" Percy shouts. He lets go of my hand and Dora's, too, and starts a leaping to Ma's side. Dora and I follow, watching Percy stick his head in Maggie's window.

"Maggie!" He reaches in and puts his hands on the sides of her face. "Maggie, Buster's here. We got him for you!" Percy holds his face up to the sky and starts to yowl. Dora grabs me by the shoulder and moves me fast over to Percy's side. I wrap my arm around his waist, and he takes my hand in his.

"Ma, what else did she say? Before she died?" Percy gulps and chortles like a clogged-up sink.

Ma reaches for her quilt that's a covering Maggie. "Buster," Ma says. "This ain't gonna be easy." She looks at me. "Rose, you and Dora make sure I get this right."

"Buster," Dora says. "Maggie said it weren't you she hated. It was herself." She stares into Buster's eyes.

"Dora's right," Ma says. "Talked about how much she always loved you."

"She sure didn't show it," Buster says. He covers his face with his hands.

"Son, she talked about who we always called the 'bad man.' Says she always knew who it was. I reckon it ate away at Maggie real bad, all her life." Ma fans her face.

"Buster," Percy says. "Sometimes people can't love someone else because they hate themselves so much. But Maggie loved you. I always knew it."

"Percy's surefire telling the truth. She told us just now about hating herself, but she was a loving you till the minute she stopped breathing."

Buster turns toward the car, leans his forehead on it, and crosses his arms above his head.

"Ma," Percy pleads, "what were Maggie's last words?"

Ma closes her eyes. Her chin quivers, and her lips starts to crumble. She holds one finger up and shakes her head. "You tell him, Rose," she says.

"Buster, Maggie wanted me to pray with her. Her last words were, 'Dear Jesus.' She died before she could pray anything else."

Buster slides to his knees and then lays himself face-first onto the ground. His whole body shakes, but he don't make a sound. He reaches out his hand and holds onto my ankle with it. I stoop down, a trying to get close enough to see what he wants.

"Rose, I've got to finish the prayer for Maggie."

What is Buster thinking? That if he prays, it will bring Maggie back? I stand still, not knowing what in the world to do.

"Rosie," he says, rolling onto his back. "I've got to finish it. I've got to make sure she goes to Heaven. Rose, help me pray. All my life . . . I've been tormented. It's time to pray now, Rose." He closes his eyes. "Dear Jesus . . ."

When Buster starts praying, my spirit sparks with lightning. I bend down on one knee and grab Buster's hand.

"Dear Jesus," I pray, "Buster comes to you this day with a heavy heart."

"*I come to you with a heavy heart*," Buster says, too.

"But you came here, Lord, to heal the lonely, the sad, and the lost . . ."

"*Heal my heart, Lord*."

"I ask You to come into my heart, Jesus . . ."

"*I ask You to come into my heart, Jesus*." Buster leaps to his feet, bangs on the left side of his chest with the palm of his hand, looks up to the sky, and hollers out. "Set me free!" Buster lifts his arms to the sky, closes his eyes, and stays still just a wee minute. He laughs like a soft chord on a piano.

"I'm free. I'm free." He rushes over to the window of Maggie's broken car. "Maggie, I always loved you. Always. And I'm sorry for anything I did to hurt you." He reaches in and strokes her hair. It ain't possible to know what he says next, his words drowned by a march of his tears.

We run to Buster and wrap ourselves around him. *Dear God, please tie a cord around this family. Don't let us fall apart.*

♩♫

Janie

Flowers fill Ma's living room, making it hard to find a seat. Purple, pink, red, yellow white, peach, and orange. Against the wall and by the door is an old upright piano that Uncle Percy bought for Rose. I sit down on the bench, plunking out a few notes. Rose and Uncle Percy walk out the door, followed by my other aunts and uncles. They walk single file, silent like kids who are on their way to the school library. Mama and Daddy go along, too. Then Ma walks out, a buckskin knapsack thrown over her shoulder.

"Janie," Mama says, wiping the tears on her cheek with her fingertips, "we're gonna head down to the fishing hole for a while. See about helping Sister Daisy in the kitchen. Your daddy will take care of them brothers of yours."

I want to ask Ma why she goes by the water every time somebody dies, but no, sir. I know this isn't the time. "Yes, ma'am."

"How you doing, honey?" Rose puts her arm around my shoulder.

"Mama's real torn up. Daddy, too."

"Percy's real tore up and can't stop a bawling. Me, either." Rose sits on the bench next to me, and I scoot over to give her more room.

"Rose, I never knew Aunt Maggie too good, but I'll miss her. I'm more worried about Buster than anything."

"Don't worry about him," Rose says. "It's been one rough day, but he gave his heart to the Lord. He's at peace."

At peace? That's what everybody says about dead people. I try to imagine Buster shouting "hallelujah" or singing "Bringing in the Sheaves," but I can't. I get tickled, just thinking about it, here in the middle of all these flowers.

"It looks like a garden in here. Doesn't it, Rose?" I put my head on her shoulder, as I have done a few times before.

"Surefire does."

"Where did all these flowers come from? I didn't know Aunt Maggie had so many friends."

"She didn't. Moody Brown sent nearly all of them. He owns the flower shop. I imagine he sent every last petal they had over here."

"You mean my old school teacher?"

"Yep, him." Rose nods her head and stares at the piano keys.

"I guess he owns near about everything." I plunk one of the ivories. "These flowers remind me of that song Sister Daisy sings, 'In the Garden.' Can you play it, Rose?"

She nods her head and begins to sing.

I come to the garden alone
While the dew is still on the roses.

"Now you, Janie."

And the voice I hear falling on my ear.

A knock on the wood part of the screen door makes me and Rose jump a little. A man wearing a police uniform with grass, blood, and dirt stains on it stands on the porch.

"Sheriff," Rose says. "Seeing you twice in one day makes me nervous. Come on in."

"Thank you, Mrs. Ebbing, but I've got to get home, cleaned up and back over here," he says, taking his hat off.

"Over here?" I butt in.

"Yes, young lady, at the request of your grandmother. Is she here?" The sheriff takes out his handkerchief and wipes his brow.

"She went down to the fishing hole," Rose says. "She'll be back before long."

"Buster down there with them?" the sheriff wants to know.

"Yes," Rose says. "Is there something I can help you with?"

"Yes, ma'am. I got word about Maggie to Buster's father, and he'll be here tomorrow night."

"Buster's daddy?" I yell out. Great day in Green Cove. Buster's daddy! The sheriff jumped a little when I yelled out. I can feel my cheeks turning red, acting like a little kid.

"Yes, sir. I will," Rose says.

The sheriff rushes across the porch and down the steps. Rose walks back over and sits with me.

"You know anything about this, Rose?" I run my finger along the keyboard.

"I ain't got the slightest notion," she says, shaking her head.

"Wow! I can't wait to tell Buster. I'm going on down to the fishing hole." I jump up from the piano bench, but Rose motions for me to sit back down.

"Honey, I think we should let Ma tell Buster about this. How about if I tell Ma so she can give Buster the news?"

"I reckon." Shoot. I could already see Buster's eyes bugging out and some freckles falling from his face when I tell him.

"All right, Janie," Rose says. She nods her head once. "That's how we'll do it. Hey, how about we sing the chorus together?"

And He walks with me.
And He talks with me.

Rose and I harmonize better than ever. Real gentle, I take my elbow and knock her side with it. A smile spreads across her face.

And the joy we share as we tarry there,
No other has ever known.

Like we're being led by a conductor and his wand, Rose and I hold our notes for exactly the same amount of time. I bring my hand up, my index finger and thumb pressed together and forming a circle. I hold it up high.

Chapter 39

Bochonkom: Touching

Ma-Ki

Ain't a flower in this here house near as pretty as Maggie, even on her worst days. She had a lot of them worst days, drinking, giving birth, brawling, and dying. I snap a yellow mum from one of the arrangements, running its tiny, pointed leaves through my thumb and index finger. Pretending it's Maggie's hair, that I can touch her if I want to.

Bochonkom. Touch. Let me back up a few hours, scoop her out of her car, warm her body in my blanket, and tell her I done wrong. Tell her how sorry I am for the secrets. Tell her none of this family's hurts been her fault. It's mine.

How I want to go back to the ravine and tell her I'm fixing to take my family to face the bad man. *Bad man.* It's what we called him, back when my young'uns talked about what happened. But I told them to forget it all. I knew Bessie was old enough to recollect it good, so I made her swear she'd never tell. The secret about the bad man's been the ruin of us, but I ain't letting ruin turn to rot.

"Young'uns!" I holler. Footsteps come from every part of the house.

"What is it, Ma?" Bessie got here first.

"Get every last one of us ready."

"What's going on, Ma?" Percy got here second.

"Later tonight, we're gonna sing Maggie's favorite songs. But right now, we're fixing to drive over to the bad man's house. First we got to tell the sheriff. We ain't heading out there without a witness."

Bessie looks at me, her chin crumbling like soft clay that's getting pelted by raindrops. I wrap my arm around her shoulder and look into her eyes.

"You're Seminole strong, Bessie. Hardy."

"I ain't sure I can do this, Ma."

"Ain't you got Jesus with you?"

Bessie's sobs take hold. She puts both her arms around me. I feel life coursing through her.

Chapter 40
The Widow's Walk

Janie

The ride to the bad man's house is real long, and my heart's been about to choke the last hour. There are four cars in front of us, led by the sheriff. Others trail us, too, like an old-fashioned wagon train. We come to a stop, and Uncle Percy turns off his car's ignition. I don't see nary a house anywhere, but Mama motions for me to get out.

"You going with us, Buster?" I can hear my own voice shake, worried about Mama and Ma. Ever since I can remember, I've wanted to know what happened to them way back when. Buster opens the car door and takes my hand. My wobbly feet hit the grass.

"Come on," Buster says, guiding me to Mama's side. "Hey, ain't that Mr. Moody Brown's car way down there?"

"It sure enough is," Percy says, coming up right behind us.

Buster's face turns ashen, like a ghost who's just figured out he's dead. Ma, Dora, and Lily stand in a circle around Mama.

"Bessie and me," Ma says, "we're walking to the front door with the sheriff. You follow."

Ma starts walking up a path surrounded by tall grass and weeds. Mama and Sheriff Tannen walk side by side behind her. Daddy and Aunt Dora are next and then Aunt Lily and Uncle Nate. Uncle Percy and Rose go behind them, with me and Buster next. Brother and Sister Little follow after us. I wonder if Ma knows about the Pied Piper and how we follow her like people followed him.

The path bends a few times, taking us up to a two-story colonial house, so big and beautiful it could be in a movie. We learned about historical styles like this in school. The front entrance is a portico, with four white colonial columns. The walls are red brick. A widow's walk, rectangular with white rails around it, sits like a crown on top of the roof.

I think about the stories behind those widows' walks, women who lost their husbands to the sea. Trying to catch sight of their men coming home from the ship, ladies went up to the tops of their houses and walked around, hoping to see their loved ones' homecomings. Sometimes the men didn't make it back. But the ladies didn't give up, even when most everybody understood that the sailor had died. Those women kept going upstairs to look for their lost loves. They paced around those rooftops, wailing.

I picture Ma up there, young and pretty, dressed in full-blood Seminole clothes, waiting for her husband to come in from the fields. Supper is cooked, and the smell of fried chicken, roasted corn, and biscuits float up to the rooftop. And the later Burl Ebbing gets, the more Ma cries, wrings her hands, and yells out to the Master of Breath. *Hica! Let me see the father of my children!* She points her finger at the sky. *Hakla! Hear my plea, Master of Breath!*

The sound of the sheriff pounding on the big brass knocker shuts down my daydreaming. The front door of the house opens, and Mr. Moody Brown stands inside. I hear a gasp come from Buster's lips. He squeezes my shoulder hard, and I lean toward him, to hear his whispering.

"How could he do it, Janie? Mr. Brown ain't old enough to have killed my grandaddy." Ma hears him, turns around, and points her finger at him. I shrug my shoulders, hoping if Ma gets mad, it won't be at me. But I wonder, too, how Mr. Moody Brown could've killed Burl Ebbing.

"Moody, how are you this evening?" the sheriff asks, removing his hat.

"We're fairly well, Grainger. You and those folks have some business here?" Mr. Brown's face is a little red, even without a bowtie to strangle his neck.

"It's your father we're looking for. Is he up and around today?" the sheriff touches the star-badge pinned to the left side of his uniform shirt.

"Daddy's ill. You know that, Grainger. He is not able to receive visitors."

"Moody," the sheriff says. Real slow, he lunges forward with one knee, putting it inside the doorway. "I can come back with a warrant, or you can bring your father to this door."

"A warrant? For my infirmed, elderly father? Has he broken the law?" Mr. Moody Brown purses his lips and stays put. So does the sheriff.

Ma turns around and locks arms with Mama. "You can do this, Bessie." They step up to the open door, next to the sheriff. Daddy centers himself around right behind Mama. Mr. Moody Brown goes back into the house but leaves the door wide open.

"Yes, sister. You can," says Dora. The back of her hair falls from its silver comb, and she reaches up with trembling hands to tuck some of the stray locks into place.

Both front doors creak as they open wide. Mr. Moody Brown stands behind his old father, who sits in a wheelchair. "What business do you have with my father?" Moody Brown asks. He looks from the left to the right at Ma, Mama, and the sheriff. "Take a look at him. He is near death."

"He looks near half-dead, but that means he is half-alive. We got business with him," Mama says. She steps up, crossing the threshold of the house. Ma and the sheriff stay where they are.

"Watch out, Mrs. DelChamp. This is private property. Grainger? What is your plan? Are you low enough to arrest a dying old man?" I can just see him at the chalkboard, diagramming those questions. But he gets my attention again when his lips poke way out, and he shoves the wheelchair towards Mama a little bit. Mama and Ma take a tiny step closer, hip to hip, like dancers who have practiced a whole lot.

"Let's get right to the point," Ma says. She gets her face closer to Old Man Brown's. "When you done shot and killed my husband, you shoulda been scalped good. It ain't a quick death. Suffering, begging, and hollering for somebody to finish them off, that's what you deserve."

"Hush!" Mr. Moody Brown yells out. With his right hand balled into a fist, he thrusts it and his whole arm toward Ma. "If you're here to threaten and intimidate my father, Ma-Ki Ebbing, I will have Grainger arrest you."

"Comes a time when everybody pays for their evil doings," Ma says.

Sheriff Tannen stands still, one foot still planted inside the house. Mr. Moody Brown stands still. Old Man Brown hangs his head, drool spilling from his lips onto the chambray shirt that barely covers his big, hairy white belly.

"My father has never killed anyone," says Mr. Moody Brown.

"We both know better than that, Moody," the sheriff says. "It's why he came out here to live in obscurity, to keep his head low in exchange for not being prosecuted. It was a deal his cousin made for him up in Tallahassee. But your cousin's been dead a while, and you don't have anybody left in the state senate to cover up for you."

"But my father is too old to go to jail," Mr. Moody Brown says, his face even redder than the carpet covering Scarlet O'Hara's stairs. "It is time to call our lawyer."

"Before you do that, Moody, you may want to hear Bessie out," the lawman says. He nods at Mama.

I didn't notice until now, but Mama is carrying a Bible. She puts it on her chest and crisscrosses her arms over it and takes two steps closer to the Brown men.

"Old Man Brown, why did you pretend to be a man of God," Mama shouts, "so you could do something as evil as plundering the private parts of me and my sisters? We were just little girls. Maggie was right around six when it happened."

Nobody moves. There's no wind or air. No sound, nothing.

"Maggie?" Mr. Moody Brown's mouth hangs open.

"Yes, Maggie. As she was dying, she talked about the man who molested us when we were young'uns."

"She never got over it," Dora yells out. "None of us have! You harmed this sister, too. She points to her chest." One tear runs down her right cheek.

Rusty-looking snuff juice pours down the side of Old Man Brown's mouth. He cocks his head up straight, opens his mouth full wide and grins. Now it's like mud, ground tobacco falling over his lips and down his chin. "You half-breeds are trash," he says.

"You came to us talking about Christian charity," Dora yells out. "All my life I hated anything and everything called Christian. Didn't even know why. But it was because of you, you hypocrite!"

Mr. Moody Brown holds on tight to the top of the wheelchair, his hands going white, and his eyeballs rolling backwards. Great day in Green Cove. Maybe he's figuring out his daddy for sure took advantage of his sweetheart Maggie and her sisters.

"Murderer." Uncle Percy says it soft and high, almost a yodel carrying his voice through the breeze.

"Child molester!" Dora hollers.

That's when pretty near everybody starts yelling something out. Trouble is, it's hard to tell who's saying what. "Dirty old man! You're gonna rot in hell! Why'd you do it? Admit your sins!"

Somehow Mr. Moody Brown pulls a Humpty Dumpty, pretty near falling down at the back of the wheelchair, putting himself back together, and getting back up. He stands in front of his father's wheelchair and thumps on the old man's chest.

"Moody!" shouts the sheriff. But Mr. Moody Brown doesn't pay him nary a bit of mind and jumps onto the wheelchair, straddling his legs over his father's. It's getting real hard to see what's going on inside, but I get a peek of him grabbing the old man by the collar.

"It's the reason she never wanted to marry me! Right, Daddy?" Mr. Moody Brown yells out. "You ruined Maggie! You ruined me, too!"

"She was never good enough for you," sputters Old Man Brown. "From a family of Seminoles. Ready for the spoiling."

Mr. Moody Brown rocks the chair back and forth, causing it and his father to topple over onto the floor. He stands over his daddy, with his right foot on top of one of the wheels, like a soldier claiming victory over a fallen enemy.

"Maggie was the only woman I ever loved," yells out the man who taught my English class. "No wonder she couldn't stand to be around you! Why didn't I see it?" He bashes his fist against the wall and yelps like a puppy that's stepped into a big ant bed. "I'll kill you!"

The sheriff and Daddy grab Mr. Moody Brown by his forearms, pulling him off the old man. Sheriff Tannen kneels down, takes out his handcuffs, and locks Old Man Brown's hands with them.

"Alopecious Brown, you are under arrest for the murder of Burl Ebbing," the sheriff says. He looks at Ma and Mama. "That one charge ought to be enough, ladies? You can keep your dignity this way."

"Yes, sir," Mama says. Her eyes sparkle, and she smiles real faint, the way I do when I know I'll get in trouble if I laugh. Ma must be feeling tickled, too, because she's covered her mouth with the back of her hand.

"Just let me kill him, put him out of his misery," Mr. Moody Brown yells out.

"You know I can't allow nothing like that, Moody. I'm taking your father on in now. I think everybody ought to go on back home now." The sheriff tilts the wheelchair upright and gently pushes it out the front door and toward the patrol car.

"Moody Brown *loved* Maggie?" Buster yells out. Until now, I forgot he was standing next to me.

"I reckon he did, Buster." I elbow my cousin like I did when we were kids but real gentle this time.

Here we stand, our family's secrets out in the open. We know who killed Ma's husband and what's made Mama, Maggie, and Dora sad all these years. Up ahead, Ma, Mama, and Aunt Dora, walk down the path back towards the car. Sometimes they stop, bend over, point, or look back to the house and shake their fists. I turn to look back at the house, too, wondering if I'll ever own a mansion like this. Up on the widow's walk is a young, beautiful Ma. She's not crying or wringing her hands. She's waltzing with a man I've seen only in old pictures. It's Burl Ebbing, laughing loud with his Seminole wife, their love floating down like notes from a musical, magical pipe.

Chapter 41

The Sheriff

Grainger

Today, as sheriff, I did something I wanted to do more than twenty years ago. I arrested Alopecious Brown.

At the time, I was a young lawman who was trusted to deliver some terrible news. I stood at Ma-Ki Ebbing's screen door with an awareness that part of me had died when she married my best friend, Burl Ebbing, several years ago. I remember pondering the possible spiritual implications of delivering the body of a dead man, one whose heart had been shot completely out of his body, home to his Seminole Indian wife.

I looked upward, asking God to give me a sign about how I should approach this situation. But I saw nothing but an early evening sun, radiating its fever and brushing sultry orange feathers against a deep blue sky. I wished for the black of night, a way to hide my regret, my sorrow, and most of all, my love.

Rapping on the Ebbing's screen door, I surveyed the cornfield surrounding the modest farmhouse, nestled deep in Bradford County's agricultural land. It lay miles from the progress and the bustle of the new Highway 301, which provided a path to northern states or on down to Miami.

"Grainger. I been expecting you." Her soft voice awakened memories of our history.

Although I yearned to see Ma-Ki, the circumstances of this visit made me want to run from this county. I had gone north twice, once a mere sixty miles to Jacksonville with Burl Ebbing. It's where we met Ma-Ki, who cooked and served at the boarding house where we took our meals. More than an allurement, the young woman's skill with food, fabric, and finery embodied the Proverbs Thirty-One woman my parents had urged me to find. Neither Burl nor I were bothered by the young beauty being half-Seminole or having a young child to rear, a girl born out of wedlock.

"It's good to see your face, Ma-Ki."

In my youth, I had secretly thought of her as Cleopatra. Every moment I had spent gazing at Ma-Ki's golden skin, tiny but curvaceous body, and into her amber eyes, threatened to steal a moment of eternity from my soul. But even as a young man, I already had enough self-insight to know I wouldn't buck my parents' wishes by marrying someone far beneath their social station, a woman with a questionable heritage and a soiled past.

"You got the old man down at the jail?" Ma-Ki inquired.

With no church or social position to claim, Burl Ebbing's parents had no objections to Ma-Ki or her daughter Bessie. But I was suspended between duty and lament and returned to Bradford County. I began to serve as a deputy under the supervision of my father, who had been the sheriff for more than ten years.

A few years after Ma-Ki and Burl married, the wiles of the Great Depression halted Jacksonville's economic growth. Burl, Ma-Ki, and the girl Burl claimed as his own, also returned. Burl stepped in to help run the family's dry goods store. The locals showed their disapproval of the young man's marriage, refusing to acknowledge Ma-Ki and Bessie and travelling extra miles to purchase their almanacs, shoes, and parts for their broken Victrolas. The store's business began to suffer even more.

Their presence in Bradford County wounded me, too. I took a train to Chicago to live with my uncle and to work in his slaughterhouse.

"Ma-Ki, could I come in?"

She opened the door for me, wiping her hands on her apron. I stepped into her parlor. I saw her supple body stiffen, and I realized she had noticed my harrowed expression.

"How are the children, Ma-Ki?"

"They ain't doing so good. Burl didn't kill the old man, did he?"

"Ma-Ki . . ."

"That hypocrite has done gotten away with plundering my young'uns private parts. Ain't he, Grainger?"

I silently questioned how the perpetrator's family could govern a county without holding office, oppressing its citizens with inequity. Confounded by residents who were willing to live in a place where progress moved backward instead of forward, I reminded myself that I, too, lived among them.

"I got proof, Grainger, at least proof about Bessie. Her clothes still got her blood on them."

Still wondering how I should respond to Ma-Ki's question, I remembered how a telegram of my own father's death brought me back to Bradford County from Illinois. After returning, it wasn't terribly long before I held the same office as sheriff. Now, standing at the Ebbings' home and having my childhood friend's body in the back of my pickup truck, I questioned my decision to depart from Chicago's stockyards.

Earlier today, a deputy had advised me about the blood on little Bessie's clothes and the attack on her and her sisters. But I have to focus on the news I am now here to give Ma-Ki. *Dear God.*

"Ma-Ki. I'm so sorry. Another deputy said it was bad, but I didn't know it got so out of hand. Would it be all right if I talked to her?"

"Yep. She's in there, Grainger." Ma-Ki pointed to the bedroom she shared with her husband. I stepped in the room quickly, seeing nothing but a bed, a knotty pine night table, and a cypress chifforobe. In the farthest corner, I heard a sigh. A couple of more steps and I saw Burl's children. They huddled together on the pine floor, the one in the middle causing me to rock backwards on my heels. On another day, I would have laughed when I saw a brown burlap sack covering the head of one of the girls. But on this day, I was startled by Bessie's attempt to hide her face. She held two of her siblings close.

"Bessie?" I asked as softly and gently as possible.

The child didn't respond.

"Bessie, how are you?"

I had no doubt about Alopecious being guilty of the accusations Ma-Ki's girls made against him. Arresting the reprobate would be futile. The old man's relatives, who had been appointed to positions in the state's capitol, would have him freed within a couple of days.

"She's cut herself some holes in that there bag for her eyes and nose," Ma-Ki said. "She went and turned it backwards when you knocked on the door." She edged toward her children. "Bessie, you got to breathe. Turn that burlap around, girl."

The child raised her hands to the sack, turning it until I could see her eyes and nose. But I was concerned when I realized Bessie had not made an opening for her mouth.

"Looks like Bessie isn't ready to talk, Ma-Ki. I'll leave her alone for now." I took a breath so deep it caused pain to sear my ribs. "I'm afraid I've got more bad news for you."

My mind wandered once more, stalling for time. Maybe I would leave this place again, return to the North and do my best to assume its Yankee ways. I wanted to forget Bradford County and its unwillingness to embrace progress. Even before the crash, when the stock market had pumped its way to record highs, North Florida seemed to resist growth.

"Grainger, what could be worse? My little girls done been attacked by a savage. One who calls himself Christian."

"I am afraid there *is* something." I heard my voice falter and wondered if she heard it, too.

"Well, tell me."

I hesitated. Again.

"Grainger, get done with holding back the truth!" she said, stomping her tiny foot.

"Burl's been shot, Ma-Ki."

"What?" She took an audible breath and held her stomach with both hands. "How bad is it?"

I knew she deserved the details, but I didn't have the courage to provide them. I would have to tell her another time how Burl had no chance to talk with the degenerate, let alone time to raise his rifle in defense.

"It killed him, Ma-Ki." I wanted to offer words of comfort, but I knew they would crumble my self-control.

Ma-Ki's eyes danced upwards in their sockets. Her mouth fell open, exposing a couple of missing back teeth. Her knees melted, and I rushed to catch her. For the first and only time, I held the woman I loved in my arms.

Chapter 42

Porch Music

Buster

The worst thing about Maggie dying is now I ain't got a chance to tell her about how Bessie and Ma confronted Old Man Brown and how he got arrested for murdering Grandaddy. She'd want to know. All my life, people around here have talked bad about her and her wild ways. I've been ashamed of her since I can remember, but now I get the picture about why she was so mad. She had a right to be.

I stretch out on my bed, my belly plumb full from food brought over here by church folks. Pistol lies beside my bed. Ma didn't say a word today when I let him follow us into the house. I pat the bed, and he jumps up, his eyes big and his tongue hanging out of his mouth.

"Yeah, boy. I don't know how long we'll get away with you being in here, but we'll make it fun while we can." I run my hand along the top of his head, and he settles down by my side. "You done know something is different, don't you? Well, you're right." Now he sits up and stares down at me. I weave my hands together underneath my head. "It's Jesus. Now don't ask me to go explaining it, but somehow it feels so good. A whole lotta hurt got washed away."

"Buster?" Percy calls from the hallway. "Ma wants you."

Bitin' bass. She's going to tell me to get Pistol out of the house. "Wait here," I tell my dog. I stand up and stretch, bracing myself in case I have to run through Mowgli's jungle.

Except for the trip to Old Man Brown's house, Ma's barely left her room since Maggie died. I walk down the stairs to her door and gently knock.

"Come on in." I open the door, and Ma sits on her bed. Her chifforobe doors are wide open, and boxes that are usually in the attic are at her feet. "Son, there's another secret coming to an end."

"Yes, ma'am." What now?

"I done wondered how I might tell you this, Buster. I think you ought to sit down." She points to an old pine rocking chair, and I take a seat. "Only way I can figure is getting to the point." Her hands shake. "Buster, comes a time when a boy turns into a man whether he's ready or not. I sent word about Maggie to your father. He'll be here sometime this evening."

"What? My father! Here? Who is he, Ma?" My head feels like it's about to explode, like all Three Stooges have slapped my face at the same time. But Ma sits there nice and quiet, her eyes holding onto the secret.

"Buster, I'm wore out," she says, before letting out a loud sigh. "You'll have a lot of questions, and it's his job to answer them. If he leaves here and you ain't satisfied, I'll be obliged to tell you then."

I lean over, cross my hands over my chest and hold onto my shoulders with them. I close my eyes. Things are changing way too fast. *I just lost a mother I never had.* And now a father I've never known is fixing to show up. I feel the muscles above my knees jerking up and down, and my calves twitch like a fox is biting at them. I slide out of the rocker, onto my knees and bury my face in the seat.

"Dear God," I whisper, so Ma won't hear. "Please help me. I don't know how much more shock I can survive."

A jolt barrels through my body. With my eyes closed, I picture something shooting through the night sky, somersaulting around the stars like a Viking rocket performing stunts. It stops in midair, turns toward me, and stops. Another whammy hits my gut, fueling me with energy more powerful than a firebolt. At the speed of light, Maggie's face flies up in front of mine. Without any words, she tells me she's forgotten about the troubles that haunted her back on earth.

Rose

A casket with Maggie's body, right in Ma's front room, spooks me real bad. Ma wouldn't hear of nothing else, though. People talk about how good Maggie looks, and I think about how the sheriff said her injuries were internal. I'm a wondering why in the world it's the things we can't see that hurt the most, the things hidden deep down inside.

Thelma Green and Sister Daisy take charge of women from the church who are doing the cooking and cleaning. It's too crowded to stay in the kitchen with them, so I walk back to the front room, where Percy stands at the casket, shoulder to shoulder with Leona Bailey, the music teacher.

I walk to his other side, remembering that Maggie and Leona played music together sometimes. Leona's dressed real fine, a black suit with a white lace collar, fancy black heels with a white flower near the toe of them, and black stockings. She turns to look at me, a smiling, a string of pearls around her neck and pearls on her ears, too. I get a whiff of something.

"Rosie, you remember Leona, don't you?" Percy looks a little gray, worse than he has since Maggie died. I lean closer to him, sniffing Shalimar and forgetting I'm a standing in front of Maggie's dead body.

"Leona Bailey, you ain't welcome here. Leave *my home* right now." I hold my chin up high.

"Pardon me?" Leona looks down real slow, at my brown cotton shirtwaist dress and worn-out flats. But it don't matter what she thinks of me and my clothes. Percy's *my* husband. And I just may take a notion and toss this floozy out of here.

"Leona," I say, waiting for her to look me in the eyes. But she don't. "Leona, I know you sung with Maggie now and then, but you ain't got no right goin' with my husband, a sending him home wearing your lipstick and perfume. Especially when he was about to become a daddy." Her and Percy look like they've froze. Finally, Percy clears his throat.

"Leona," Percy says, "Maggie'd appreciate you coming over, but Rose done asked you to leave. And she's right. It ain't fit for you to be here."

Leona Bailey dabs at her eyes with Percy's handkerchief. I stick my hand out for the hanky, and she puts it in my palm. Tossing her beauty parlor hair, she squares her shoulders and walks out of the living room. I hear people on the front porch just a calling her name and asking her to stay a little while longer, but there ain't a trace of her left when I walk to the edge of the porch and look out. I turn back around and notice Percy's followed me. He's slumping over pretty bad.

"Percy, look at me."

He puts his hands in his pockets and looks me in the eyes. I put my hands on my hips, a holding on to his handkerchief.

"You got your lighter?"

"Rosie, I'm sorry. I didn't know she was coming here. I didn't want you to find out who it was." He hands me his Zippo. I take his hand, and we walk back through the kitchen, all the women a looking at us as we pass through. When we step out onto the back porch, I give him his handkerchief.

"Hold it up, Percy." He holds it up by the corner. I flick the lighter and hold it to the bottom of the cloth.

"Have you gone slap dab crazy?" Percy yells. He throws the kerchief into the yard, races down the steps, and stomps out the fire.

"Don't touch that woman again," I holler. "And don't let her touch you or nothing belonging to you again." I wonder if he compares me to that smart woman. She's got an education, a fancy hairdo, and nice clothes. The whole county thinks she's special, but she ain't. She's a married woman who was sleeping with a married man. And right now, I got a good notion to tell everybody.

I walk down the steps and notice a few cars parked in the backyard, but it's dark, and I ain't able to tell if anybody's in them or not. I stop right in front of my husband and look him in the eyes.

"Percy Ebbing, don't you go a messing with me. I've got angels watching over me. You understand? They'll make war, if that's what it takes, to protect me!"

"War?" Percy scratches the top part of his chest. "Angels make war?"

"Yes, they do. Seminoles ain't the onliest ones been warring all these years." I reach out for his forearms and shove him a little, but he stays surefooted. My husband holds his arms out wide.

"Come on, Rosie. Angels, war . . . it don't matter. I don't want Leona Bailey or nobody else. You're the one I love, honey. Just you."

From somebody's car radio, Slim Whitman sings "Indian Love Call." My mind's a picturing it, the young Indian man calling to his sweetheart. My heart dances to the song, and I feel it up and down, inside and out. I walk into Percy's Seminole arms, remembering a Bible verse saying, 'Two shall become one."

♩♪

Janie

Kenny and Benny follow me and Buster everywhere we go. I wish I could get away from them for a while, so Buster could tell me what he knows about his daddy coming. Something is different about him. He walks lighter, taller, and his shoulders seem broader. But I'm not crazy enough to talk in front of the twins, who repeat everything they hear. No sir. We settle into Buster's room, where he takes out his Sorry! game and lays it on his bed.

"I wanna play!" Kenny says.

"Me, too. I'm gonna win." Benny brags all the time lately.

"No, you don't!" Kenny yells out.

"I always help you two play. Hey, Buster. How about if you help Benny, and I help Kenny? It'll be more fair that way."

"Sure thing," Buster says. He picks the blue game pieces for himself and the red ones for me.

"Moody!" Uncle Percy yells out from the front porch.

I look at Buster and wonder if he's thinking the same thing I am. Mr. Moody Brown is downstairs, the first time ever. Even with all the porch music, I haven't seen him here at Ma's nary a time. Buster folds up the board and puts the game away.

"Come on, boys. Let's go downstairs," my cousin says.

♪♩

"Singing is not something I do well," Mr. Moody Brown says. "But I would like to honor Maggie tonight by singing her favorite song, 'Nobody's Darlin but Mine.'"

Great day in Green Cove, he wasn't lying about not being able to sing. Worst of all, when he gets to the chorus, Old Man Tucker's new young widow, Luella, who used to promenade around Junior's Dance Hall, sits on the porch swing next to him. They sound even worse together. I hope Pistol can hold himself back from howling.

While they're crooning about being honest, faithful, and kind, I try to figure out if it's her singing that killed Old Man Tucker or if it's what everybody says: a young bride will love an old man to death before he has a chance to draw up a will. She's got a mighty big diamond flashing in the light, so I have a feeling she got his last nickel.

Buster nudges me with his elbow, and I lean over, thinking he must have a secret to tell me.

"Janie, will you sing a song with me?"

"Sure, what you want to sing?"

"I feel like 'I'll Fly Away.'"

"Buster, what about Hank Williams' song about the Indian? 'Kaw-Liga.'"

"Naw, Janie. I want to sing about Heaven. Some of y'all may not know this, but when Maggie died, she was praying to Jesus. I've given my heart to Him, too. And Janie's gonna sing this one with me."

He gave his heart to the Lord? I get up from the wicker chair to stand beside Buster, and Kenny and Benny follow me.

Some glad morning, when this life is o'er . . .

The twins know some of the words and start clapping their hands. Everybody else joins in. When we finish, Buster races from the porch and back up to his room. I run up as fast as I can, shooing the boys back with my hand. When I get to Buster's room, I shut the door behind me.

"Janie, you're my best friend. I've been missing you." He jabs me with his elbow, and I kick him in the back of his knee.

♫♪

Ma-Ki

I ain't been fishing but a short spell when something tugs my line. There's some good catches here on the St. Johns. My people call it the River of the Sun. I pull my line in, but there ain't a single thing on it, not even the worm. Hook's gone, too.

Down the river, somebody's singing "Nobody's Darling but Mine." I start humming to it, then recollect why I'm here. My young'uns and me got to have something to eat. On a sunny day like this, my mind is pure apt to wander. I look at the river, hoping to see a sign of a big catch. Through the bushes, a canoe heads toward me. Maggie rows at the oars pretty hard. Her hair is long, how she wore it as a girl. And she's wearing a Seminole patchwork dress.

"Maggie!" I holler. She looks around, and I wave.

"Ma!" Her winsome smile makes my old heart flutter. I grin back at her, and she steers in my direction.

"I thought you was lost."

"No, Ma. You just couldn't see me."

She works the oars harder and harder, but they don't bring her to the bank. Tarnation. She gets close enough for me to see Bettie in the canoe with her. How about that, the Seminole doll I made for Maggie. I ain't seen Bettie since Maggie was near about ten. I thought my girl would never stop crying when it turned up missing. I wanted to make her another one, but Maggie said if it ain't Bettie, she didn't want no doll. Period.

The sky goes dark, a storm coming up faster than I ever seen. I got to help Maggie get to land. I run into the river, but rain's done started to pour. Every bit of me is wet, but not even a drop's touched Maggie.

"It'll be trouble if you don't get out of this storm," I holler.

She smiles again. "Don't worry about me, Ma, but you get on out of this rain."

In a pea's snap, the sun comes out, even stronger. I look at the sky, trying to figure out this weather, then back at Maggie. She's already gone, but I can hear her calling to me.

"Ma, I've got a river of peace running right through me."

"Maggie!" There's the sound of clapping and more clapping, but I ain't able to see who's making such a commotion. I turn over, feeling my featherbed beneath me. *My girl is really gone.* I been dreaming about her while somebody's out there trying to sing her favorite song. I sit up and turn on the lamp.

Something at the foot of my bed don't seem right. I lean up toward it and see Bettie, dressed spotless in her sawtooth top and skirt. I pick the doll up and hold it to my breast. My tears kiss its cheek. I ain't letting go.

All right, Mr. Jesus. My girl's happy being with You. She's done found what she lost.

Thank you so much for reading *Porch Music*. If you've enjoyed the book, we would be grateful if you would post a review on the bookseller's website. Just a few words is all it takes!

The University of Florida Museum offers a rich display of the Seminole culture

(L) Kathy's great-grandmother, Lavida Dyal with her children; (R) Kathy's great-great grandmother is seated. Lavida is standing on the far left with her mother and siblings.

Acknowledgements

Porch Music shows a time when the Sunshine State had uncrowded beaches, dirt roads, and colossal oak trees. I miss "Old Florida."

My daughter, Kelli Paugh, offered a world of support as I hammered out rough drafts and rewrites. Thank you, Kelli, for allowing me to love you and for loving me in return. Without you, I don't know that Ma-Ki could love Rose so thoroughly.

Proofing my manuscript with finesse and precision that only a seasoned English teacher can offer, Mary Shepard provided me with grammar rules I had forgotten and caught my slips of the "pen." Mary, your assistance is a priceless pearl. Dr. Patty Hendrix, my friend and favorite ophthalmologist, thank you for your feedback, your questions, and your encouragement.

Betty Surrency, your fact-checking was instrumental in achieving historical accuracy. Thanks for loving me and *Porch Music* as only a mother can. Granny Elsie, my Seminole queen, I hope you have an opportunity to read this story in Heaven.

Shelly Perkins, you believed in me from the start, coined a pivotal phrase, and volunteered as a beta reader. Thank you, Shelly, for serving as my muse. For providing an authentic dialect for my characters, I thank my aunts and uncles. Maybe you think I wasn't listening to your advice, but I was. Judy, you are the onliest one of us who used this word, and I did my best to capture your voice.

To the TouchPoint Press team, thank you for embracing this story. You've been fabulous to work with. I have received wonderful encouragement from fellow authors Shanessa Gluhm and Rob Samborn: you two rock.

Connie May Fowler, thank you for giving this story its wings. Thank you, Kelly Esparza, my editor. You possess wisdom beyond your years.

Keith, without your loving support, *Porch Music* wouldn't have crossed the finish line. Thank you.

Most of all, I am thankful for God's blessings. He heard me knock, time after time, asking for *Porch Music* to be published. How wonderful it is to be a child of the great I AM.

About Kathy Maresca

A native Floridian, Kathy Maresca grew up with a grandmother of Seminole heritage. Kathy served in the Air Force, at the Academy cadet chapel and then at a special operations command. She edited for the University of Florida and taught English, journalism, and drama. Kathy later earned a master's degree and became credentialed as a rehabilitation counselor, helping people who have cranial nerve disorders. Kathy has been a Guardian ad Litem and a volunteer for a prison fellowship ministry. She lives in North Carolina with her husband, Keith. They enjoy traveling and spending time with their dogs.